And the Blood Ran Black

And the Blood Ran Black

Written by
Nathan E. Harvey

Harvey Brothers Publishing ™ 2015

ISBN 978-0-692-59409-4

For Mom

- *One* -

"Life is pleasant. Death is peaceful. It's the transition that's troublesome." -Isaac Asimov

John Chow struggled to regain his balance despite the dozens of hands stinging his back as they struck him. He winced at the sharp pain that raced out from each swollen mark on his skin. He wondered if those at fault even understood the pain they were inflicting on him. Was their intent to cause him pain? He pictured the unseen owners of the hands. Any one of them individually would be little cause for concern for a trained soldier such as himself. Together, though, they were a formidable force.

The irrelevant thoughts were quickly pounded from his mind by the onslaught still raining down on him from the primary attacker who stood before him. One particularly forceful blow forced John even deeper into the crowd behind him, and John tried to gather himself by grasping for the loose, rope barrier that served as the ring's perimeter. A man from the rabid crowd shoved him forward violently, and John found himself once again lying face first in the moist sand.

An impressive mob had packed the bar's appropriately named "Pit" well beyond its intended capacity. Though walking paths and a perimeter around the ring were usually established, tonight there was an uncontrollable horde spilling over into the usual buffers. Their collective body heat lingered in the stagnant, tight quarters. The hot, humid air was so thick that one could almost sense its weight pressing down on them. As if the heat and the pain pulsing with each heartbeat weren't enough, the deafening cheers were now condensed into a constant moaning from the multitude that had assembled. The dull roar augmented the throbbing of John's head, making it hard for him to focus on the task at hand. His own muffled groans sounded to John as if his head was submerged under water, and everything slowed to a dreamlike state, except for the pain. The pain was immediate and real.

John raised his hand to his face and felt that the warmth of the damp sand was from his own blood, which was now flowing freely from his mangled nose as well as the deep laceration above his right eye. John exhaled violently, in the way that a horse would snort, and sent a spray of blood to the floor and across his bare chest as he steadied himself back to his feet. The sweat and blood mingled as it spider legged through each crevice in his toned

1

frame. John blinked rapidly, trying to disperse the involuntary tears that blurred his vision, finally bringing his opponent back into focus.

John's anger and overall presence appeared to visibly swell as he grimaced and dropped his fists to his side, rotating each shoulder. His adversary's back was still turned as the man continued to celebrate and play to the crowd. John walked to the edge of the ring and snatched a beer out of a spectator's hand. He kicked his head back as he tilted the bottle's bottom to the ceiling and forcefully downed the brew as quickly as its neck would allow.

John had learned early on to never end a fight too quickly. The gamblers didn't come just to lose their money; it was more about the show than the result. Any longtime gambler, if you could find one honest enough, would acknowledge that it's more about the rush than the money. Because any gambler worth his salt is well aware of the fact that eventually, the house always wins. They pay for the adrenaline, and there is no rush quite like that of riding a comeback into a big payout. That brief moment of ecstasy he'd give to those who had already counted tonight's bet as lost would make him their hero. To the others, he would undoubtedly become infamous. It really didn't matter to him if he was loved or hated. It mattered only that he was remembered.

John would normally stumble around in an awkward American style of boxing, letting the opponent grow overly confident. The locals loved watching their quicker, more agile fighter run laps around the big, slow American. John gained a lot of satisfaction out of letting the little guys grow arrogant and play to the crowd before he would strike down their hopes with a speed and ferocity that The Pit never witnessed in other fights. He enjoyed the game of toying with them, like a cat with its prey, letting them think they stood a chance. One way or another, though, the ending was always the same. Having seen it all before, many spectators who attended the fights with any kind of regularity had come to embrace the American, and many would continue to attend solely to watch John fight.

Though dominating, John usually let his bouts remain relatively tame compared to some of the other beatings that went on in The Pit due to the anything-goes nature of the establishment.

2

But tonight's opposition had cheated in a place where almost nothing was considered cheating.

Early in the fight, while John had been sandbagging his efforts, the opponent had landed a lucky blow straight to his nose. Once Corporal Chow's eyes had begun watering, the man had open season as John swiped blindly at the attacker. John wasn't unaccustomed to losing some blood for the good of the show, but this time was different. The young fighter was below average at best, but had found a way to severely bloody John's face. The bleeding was so significant that it was impairing his vision considerably.

As the anticipation of the crowd palpably grew, his opponent sensed the change in atmosphere and turned back to face John. With both of his fists slowly descending from their celebrative position above his head, the under-matched opponent had almost no time to react to the fact that John was not only back on his feet, but rapidly approaching. A barrage of flying fists to the mid-section from Chow had the Asian man hunched over and bug-eyed in shock with his facial complexion quickly flooding to a sickly greenish tint. The kid blindly swung in desperation and wound up swinging straight over the top of John's ducked head and connecting with his own face in a tremendous whiff. Sensing the impending loss, the large crowd of John's antagonists re-directed the hurling of insults and threats toward their own fighter for his idiocy.

John sensed the brief window of opportunity as the young man's center of gravity had rocked back to his heels, and John caught him with a forceful leg sweep, strategically lifting the man's feet out from under him. The gambit proved a decisive one as he followed through with his attack for just a few extra inches than most fighters would've, lifting the man's legs up so high that the first thing to make contact with the ground was the back of the man's skull. Even the sand could provide little cushion to the violent fall, as the blow to the cerebellum sent all of the man's muscles into a spastic, convulsive state. His arms quickly pulled to his chest like those of a cerebral palsy patient, and the crowd couldn't decide whether to cheer or gasp at the sudden brutality.

The crowd stood with jaws gaping as John's upward momentum from the perfectly executed leg sweep had carried him off the ground and into a twisting motion until the length of his body was parallel to the ground and positioned directly above the fallen foe. Everyone that was in attendance had their next breath stolen for the brief moment that it took for John to fall back to the sand with the full force of his weight striking through his right elbow into the over-matched opponent's chest. The fluidity of the dance-like agility that was being displayed was abruptly broken by the gruesome, echoing thud that only a chest cavity can produce when its framework has been struck with a debilitating force. Then, with his left hand grasping the man's throat, John proceeded to batter the barely conscious man mercilessly. The opponent's efforts to protect himself grew less and less inspired, until he finally lay motionless, leaving the blood-thirsty crowd standing in awe.

Chow stood, breathing heavily as he straddled the man, and glared down at him. After a long, silent pause, the solemn crowd began to slowly react with favor to the ominous force before them. The shouts of praise started in the back as John was already exiting the ring, and grew into an uproar of appreciation as John tried to navigate his way through the massive crowd.

There were more congratulatory slaps to his bare back as John pressed to get through all of the people pushing and shoving to get as close to him as possible. The hand slaps now felt much different than those during the fight--fearfully respectful if you could describe a slap in such a way. John kept his chin to his chest and his eyes down as the adulation of the crowd reached levels that no one in the arena had ever seen before or would likely ever see again.

John had initially intended to collect his winnings and make a quick escape as the next fighters entered the ring, but all of the attention remained tightly concentrated on him. He would just have to leave and hope that his manager could collect his share of the money.

His half-brother, Moto, more often intoxicated than not, stumbled to catch up to John as he fought his way toward the exit.

"John, man, let me take a look at your nose. Just because you haven't had any excitement since the cease-fire doesn't mean you have to stand around with your hands down and give the other guy free blows."

John blew another stream of blood from his nostrils with no regard for the spray splattering across Moto's pants.

"I didn't let him hit me," John grumbled. "The kid blinded me with a jack shit little jab before we ever even really got going. He must've snuck a razor blade in the padding of his glove. I didn't mean to go off like that, but that cheap shit pisses me off to the point of just..."

"You don't have to justify it to me, big guy. No one would've blamed you if you'd have killed the kid," Moto laughed.

John let his shoulders sag, and let out a displeased grunt as he shoved open the exit door, avoiding eye contact. "I swear they let that stuff slip into the ring against you if you start winning too often. I'm done with this."

"You might just be. I don't know if there's anyone stupid enough to go toe to toe with you after the show you just put on! I've never seen anything like it!" Moto said cheerfully as he slung John's shirt over his blood spattered shoulder. "C'mon, John, I'd be floating three inches off the ground right now if I were you. At least crack a smile. I've never seen you this solemn after a fight! You must've won yourself a month's salary in there tonight, and I'm pretty sure you're never gonna have to buy yourself another drink in that hole. Speaking of which, hold up for a second, I need to return this beer I rented."

Moto staggered over to the outside corner of the bar to relieve himself and leaned up against a propaganda littered telephone pole as he yelled over his shoulder, "Every fighter knows the risk of stepping into that ring, man. And you said it yourself, the punk had it coming. You think he didn't have some ill intent when he snuck that razor in?"

John purposely changed the subject and asked, "Where'd Marty get off to anyways? He usually comes to find me right after the fight."

"I don't know; he was with me until the fight was just about over. An Asian and a local looking guy came and got him about the time you had the dude on his back. I didn't think anything of it in the moment, but looking back it was kinda weird."

John looked up, attempting to ignore the disgusted, judgmental glares from some of the exiting locals. When he wasn't in uniform and carrying his rifle, John found it much easier to decipher which of the Puerto Ricans was an ally and which had given in to the growing Chinese influence. John expected the hate from the Chinese, and even understood it. Everything about John was what they were taught to hate. The disloyal Puerto Ricans were the ones that kept him up at night. It was impossible for the visiting U.S. troops to truly ever know who they could trust on the island, and their intentions were anything but obvious.

One Asian man muttered something about a turncoat as he made brief eye contact with John before spitting at the ground near his feet. Since several months had passed with no real violent exchanges with the Americans, this sort of behavior had become more than common. John had grown accustomed at an early age to the bigotry of others when it came to his mixed race. The dramatic rise in Chinese aggression and the resulting change in people's opinion of him while he was still only in grade school had fueled John's mental and physical transformation. As he often did, John chose to say nothing in return to the passing men, answering the foolishness with nothing but an unwavering confident eye until the previously confident man was forced to look away.

John turned impatiently, "What's the holdup over there, do you need me to aim it for you?"

"Stop changing the subject," Moto's loud voice shook as he drunkenly battled his zipper, beginning to worry that he was going to lose the battle against time. "What I want to know is why are you acting so remorseful over some little Ho Chi Minh that was just taunting you back there?"

"Idiot, Ho Chi Minh was Vietnamese," John whispered in hopes that it would cue Moto to talk more softly. "Being my brother, I would really expect that you would know the difference. Puerto Rico may not have officially fallen, but that doesn't change the fact that we're surrounded by Chinese."

6

"Whatever, man, I don't see the point in learning all the pre-World War 3 stuff. Besides, growing up with your Chinese ass is probably the reason I assume every Asian *is* Chinese."

John always got defensive when Moto brought up his ethnicity. He couldn't help but imagine how much easier his life might've been if he'd been born a full-blooded American--if such a thing even existed. But still, he'd lay awake some nights, imagining a life where his father might've been a white man. Anything would've been a welcome change from the soldier that took advantage of his mother all those years ago. Even Moto's biological father wasn't much of a step up in the dad department, but John would've taken him in a heartbeat.

"First off, never call me Chinese. We were raised by the same people. The way you talk, it's like I had to choose which side I was gonna fight for."

Moto sighed, finally winning the battle with his zipper, and leaned into the wall with his one free hand. "Explain to me how a tough guy like you is so sensitive? Why is being PC everybody's first priority now. Call me Miguel con Queso for all I care. It don't change nothin'."

"...and second, it's not smart to piss somebody off when you're *pissing*," John said with emphasis as he punched Moto hard on the shoulder.

John pretended not to give it much oomph, but he hit him hard. Moto reacted quickly by pretending to lose his balance and spin around, peeing on John's shoes. John jumped back a moment too late and motioned his hand in a crude gesture. He stopped short of his planned comment after realizing that they'd drawn the attention of several local men who were slowing and staring as they passed. Without further conversation, the brothers began their long walk back from the bar.

Moto realized that he had overstepped his bounds with his racially insensitive comments and, in doing so, had lost the privilege of speaking with John. He was relieved when two of their squad members, Andrew and Garrett, caught up to them and relieved some of the tension.

"Why the hell did you guys take off so fast?" Andrew asked.

7

"Yeah, man. We've gotta celebrate! I'll even cover your tab," Garrett said with as much enthusiasm as John had ever heard him speak. "I knew that guy was doneski the second I saw him climb into the ring. You won me almost a grand in there."

"You hear the man?" Moto asked. "Let him buy us a few!"

"Well, I'm glad I could be a cheap date for you," John said, slapping Garrett on the back. "If it's really gonna bug you, I guess I'll just have to let you owe me."

"Man, you two are getting' old on me," Andrew said. "You can't even stay up for one drink anymore?"

"Whoa. Whoa," Moto said with a hand pressed up to Andrew's chest. "Weren't you watching the fight? John already had his first drink in the ring; that was my favorite part."

"I completely forgot about that!" Garrett laughed as they crested the last hill before their bunkhouse. "Totally disrespected that fool. Easily the best fight I've ever seen."

The men returned to their bunk and found that none of the other squad members had yet returned.

"Maybe we really are getting old," Moto said as he plopped onto his bunk and attempted to untie his shoes.

"Nah, don't listen to Andrew," Garrett said as he walked by. "He just gets antsy when there's no women around."

"Ah, don't be like that!" Andrew said as the two walked to their end of the large tent. "Who needs women when I've got you guys?"

The Chow brothers laughed as Andrew snuck up behind Garrett and went in for a hug. Garrett instinctively ducked under the outstretched arms, and shoved Andrew away. He hated nothing more than being hugged and almost everybody knew it.

John halfheartedly wiped at the blood spatter from his face and chest before climbing up to his bunk above Moto's. He climbed across the mattress as he did in the exact same fashion each night, but tonight he did it with muddy boots and all. By the time he recalled the reason for their muddiness, the damage to his sheets had already been done.

When Moto's drunken fingers had finally won their battle with his shoelaces, he flopped onto his back with a thud. Moto couldn't ignore the feeling that something was still wrong, and decided to interrupt the silence.

"Dude, it's ok. No one would have blamed you even if you'd kept wailing on that guy until he really was doneski. It happens. Playing to the crowd like that, not to mention cheating... someone else would've taught him a lesson eventually if you hadn't done it."

John rolled over onto his side as if showing his back to his brother as well as positioning himself into the bed's perfect depression.

"Night, bro," John said coldly.

Moto could tell there was no use pressing him any further, and began to rustle around uncomfortably in his bed, shaking the top bunk noticeably.

"What the hell are you doing down there?" John barked.

"It's hot, dude," Moto grinned to himself. "I'm goin' sans pants."

The familiar blaring of reveille jolted John and Moto back into consciousness. John stuffed his face into the mattress and pulled the pillow over his head, convincing himself that he had enough time to rest a bit longer.

Moto released a long groan of displeasure and mumbled in a raspy voice, "When I go AWOL, I swear it's going to be because that stupid trumpet finally broke me." The cold, morning air quickly made him regret his decision to sleep in the nude. "Why do they have to wake us up at the butt crack of dawn when there's not even anything for us to do?" he whined.

John noticed that several of their squad members had still not returned from the previous night out. Many of them would come running up the hill several minutes late, still buckling their belts with shoelaces flying free. John had almost fallen back into slumber when Andrew came flying into the bunkhouse from his early morning jog. John forced himself awake and glanced down at the remaining blood streaks on his stomach. He realized that he couldn't enjoy the luxury of stalling until the last possible moment as he and Garrett usually did; waiting until the absolute last minute to emerge from their bunks. He climbed out to begin his morning routine, but John didn't intend to suffer alone. After his feet had clumsily found their way to the bottom of the ladder, John yanked the covers from Moto's bed so hard that they flew to the tent's opposite wall.

The culture of the overseas U.S. military had changed drastically as more and more time lapsed with the U.S. troops being stationed abroad. Unlike previous wars, World War 3 had America and its allies at a heavy numerical disadvantage, leaving any and all able-bodied young men stuck overseas for unreasonable stints of service.

Though there had been numerous early warning signs, no country intervened as China cultivated the most dominant military force in modern history. Rumors about the inhumane tactics that the Chinese had adopted to grow their forces were a common topic of conversation in coffee shops across the states. China's previous policies on limiting the number of children per household, coupled with technological advances allowing parents to choose the gender of their children, had resulted in a significant imbalance between sexes. Females in China made up an estimated 20% of the overall population, with the majority of them now being over the age of 40.

In the years leading up to the war, the anti-bullying sentiment of the West evolved into an all-out anti-violence movement which Americans had accepted as an obvious step in leading the way to a better world. That way of thinking eventually grew into an overwhelming anti-military sentiment, resulting in a popular trend of decreased funding for all militaristic endeavors. Politicians gave in to tremendous pressure to not only halt all advancements in technology that could in some way result in massive losses of life, but also to do away with almost all such technology which had already been created. Politicians with more than a shred of ambition quickly adopted the policy as one of their main platforms after polls consistently reflected what an easy sell it would be to the self-proclaimed civilized nations. A promise of decreased spending and a balanced national budget, even while lowering taxes, seemed almost too good to be true. The show of good faith toward the rest of the world meant more money in a voter's pocket while still being able to feel as if they'd contributed to the greater good. The U.S. withheld much of its arsenal for a time but eventually matched the sacrifices of other world powers as they joined the cause.

During that same span, it was rumored that China had mandated the comparatively few remaining young women into conceiving at least once every three years. The political cartoons that depicted the Chinese women as militarized cattle were found to be little more than slightly humorous in the States, and raised no concerns. Though many of the rumors were a gross exaggeration, there were well-documented incentives for the Chinese women to conceive. Many of the young women didn't oppose the policies at all, and commonly embraced the opportunity. Most considered their sacrifice to be a service to their country and willingly prostituted their bodies beginning at a young age.

The Chinese didn't initially intend to take advantage of the world's collective attempt at peace. Apologists would later argue that they had little other choice. With a significant decrease in their spending toward military research and development, China *had* been on board for a better world. It didn't take long, though, for Chinese leadership to realize that sacrificing many of the jobs in the industry of which they'd become pioneers was going to result in a lasting blow to their economy.

China didn't quickly give up on the cause, but the world power eventually slid into near insignificance, even as its population swelled beyond measure. The end result, after some ill-advised decisions by some opportunistic neighboring countries, was an overnight resurgence in the Chinese economy.

The obvious solution for having too many young men eventually became apparent. There had been plenty of examples throughout history showing a struggling China how to rapidly grow their economy and return their factories to capacity production. Soon, the plethora of men would be put to good use. The derelict factories were utilized to their fullest potential again as workers began mass production of rifles, Jeeps, and all the other goods that the rest of the world had cumulatively cut spending toward. By the time anyone took notice of what was occurring, it was China's own de-Hollywoodized version of the clone wars.

The numbers for the Chinese military were historic and images of their soldiers training in formation terrorized the free world. The pictures and videos that had leaked into the media were claimed as fakes at first. Seas of people executed precise drills in near perfect unison. The only perceivable flaw was in the wave caused by the slight delay it took for the sounds to reach those who were farthest from the speakers. Each stomp of a boot and slap against a rifle sent ripples of fear throughout the peace-loving world.

It was an uphill battle for everyone in opposition to the world's largest military force. Decade-old technologies and boots to dirt with rifles in hands was all it took for the neighboring countries to be quickly absorbed into the new China. The first to go was Mongolia. The actual fighting was brief and, though the sudden attack was more than a blip on the worldwide radar, most of the world's reaction was to simply begin talks of diplomacy. The aversion and avoidance of needless killings and violence that the Chinese demonstrated during their advance was largely applauded, and many considered it a victory that the world had avoided the use of outdated tactics and hellacious devastation as its first option.

Soon after, though, the borders of China began to creep south through Laos, Thailand, Cambodia, and Vietnam. Despite repeated promises of peace by the President of the People's Republic of China, the newly infamous war hero known as Hung Ju-long grew in both power and title as he expertly swept through country after country. Rumors began to swirl that the Chinese president had become nothing more than a figurehead. The world's concern grew as the Chinese territory continued to swell, but with the U.N. no longer in place, the opposition of each singular victim was all the antagonistic country had to overcome. With each passing victory, the next country in line would face even more insurmountable odds. Hung Ju-long drew heavily from the tactics of Nazi Germany and found much success in the methods. It wasn't until the country's expansion reached the 38th parallel that the free world's voters began to take full notice.

Upon crossing the South Korean border, the Chinese army was surprised to encounter a largely American opposition. The U.S. troops stationed at the border were originally intended to help intimidate North Korea into participating in the world's peace movement. After the successful Chinese aggressions, South Korean officials were nervous that North Korea may follow a similar model and strike while South Korea's own military had willingly weakened. The United States answered their plea, and doubled the American presence in an attempt to deter any threat. It wasn't until the Chinese had plowed through the thousands of American citizens with seemingly little effort that the threat began to demand the world's attention.

Months of mass recruitment and propaganda littering the landscapes had gone unanswered until the plea for volunteers transitioned into an all-out draft after the massacre. Families were being pulled into the war in a more immediate and intimate way than they had ever feared.

Almost overnight, news channels began to cover the secretive practices of China who, over recent years, had slowly cut off almost all outside trade. Other countries no longer held power in the form of threats to cut off fuel, food, or any other Chinese imports. China had grown strategically self-sufficient, and it was now obvious why.

Despite the sudden, overwhelming media interest, China was still able to enshroud their practices from the public's eye. No one knew what they were capable of or how far they were planning to go. Any troops that the Chinese lost in battle were more than replaced by the absorbance of the survivors from the overtaken countries. As it was in Nazi Germany, the new recruits were only able to protect their loved ones by holding firm to the ideals of the new authority and by ratting out any neighbor who was unwilling to do so.

Though they were met with more opposition at the obvious borders, the Chinese attacks did not slow. When resistance swelled against them in Russia, a sudden influx of Chinese troops would instead arrive in Cuba. When attention was diverted to Northeast Africa, Hung Ju-long would instead infiltrate the borders of South America.

Soon, the world began to take necessary steps to stop China's seemingly infinite army. The rest of the world had not yet forgotten how fortunate they'd been to survive the Nazis of World War II, and countries were quick to ally in opposition of the growing Chinese threat. For the first time, in fact, there was no neutral country. As more and more countries jumped on board and began drafting men into service, the few remaining holdouts were guilted into action. No one wanted to be burdened with the albatross that they would undoubtedly carry throughout history if they were to try and spare their own young men.

Those who had just recently unified in peace were now joined together to defend that same cause by a willingness to engage in tremendous violence. The Chinese forces were so transcendent that the rest of the world could not afford to have anyone sit idly by. Never before had such a power been achieved, and never before had a line been so perfectly drawn across the globe, dividing its adversaries.

Many historians had been teaching for decades that there was an inevitable war, plague, or starvation looming that the world would soon have to endure. More people were currently living in the world than had ever lived and died before them. The sustainability of the earth's resources had long ago been surpassed. The question of when and how the earth's population would be brought back down was seemingly very close to being answered.

And so, once the entire world had been prepped for battle, the talks of diplomacy grew more effective. No one wanted to witness the greatest loss of life in the history of the world, but all were prepared for it. Both sides knew that, if the negotiations soured, the unavoidable consequences would echo throughout history. And so, they waited.

After months of fruitless mediation, officers struggled to keep morale up for their troops who found themselves stationed indefinitely on the other side of the world. The former teachers and students were stuck waiting--waiting and knowing that their fate lay in the hands of the rich men who spent their days behind a desk and slept comfortably in their own beds each night.

At this point, commanding officers didn't even enforce the usual protocol. Soldiers were free to wander aimlessly, and pass the time in whatever manner they chose, so long as they showed up to the few remaining head counts. As the living conditions and available food diminished, so too did the frequency of inspections and visits from supervisors. Service, though involuntary, was considered by many to be an easy paycheck for simply keeping one's nose out of trouble. Everyone knew how stagnant the negotiation talks had become but also knew that neither side wanted to fire the shot that signified the end of the world. As a result, the cultures at the front lines across the globe were slowly blurred, and the world that had been in utter turmoil sat in comfortable disarray.

It was now a common occurrence for the opposing sides to cross paths at popular night spots and commiserate. The undercurrents of hatred and racism would oftentimes boil over at the local bars, and the resulting brawls were eventually organized into a profitable, underground business.

John and Moto had quickly discovered the ripe opportunity in their new Puerto Rican home and had gained a stronghold on the untapped market to multiply their checks with the help of their former accountant friend, Marty.

After the morning's assembly, the brothers spent this morning the way they spent almost every morning following a successful fight. The two had hung hammocks tucked a couple of hills away from their encampment, a perfect spot for recovering from the previous night. They had established a nice little bricolage of forgotten logs far enough from the garrison to avoid getting volunteered into some tedious chore a superior had dreamed up.

"This is actually kind of a sweet deal, John, living off Uncle Sam's dime, chilling every day, drinking and fighting every night. It's like college, but free."

"Yeah, I guess it could be worse," John said as he rubbed his swollen knuckles. "I'll be sure and remind you tomorrow morning when you start bitching about the bugle again. I'm just glad we didn't get stuck in the Middle East."

"Yeah, yeah. Oh, hey, I almost forgot, I've got a good one for you!" Moto said.

"Oh please no," John sighed. "We were having such a good morning."

"Trust me, you'll be repeating this to one to everybody," Moto spun around upside down with the edges of the hammock clung tightly to his chest so that he wouldn't fall out as he faced the ground. He groaned as he concentrated on maintaining his balance while lowering his zipper to relieve himself, and he began. "Okay. If quizzes are quizzical, then imagine how my testicles feel."

"One day soon, you're gonna belly flop into your own piss if you won't just stand up and pee like a normal guy; and you slaughtered that joke, by the way," John said as he waved over his acting agent, Marty.

Marty's shoulders sagged heavily as he ducked tree branches while navigating down the heavily-traveled path.

"No, no. Wait I've got it. If tests are testicle, then what about my balls?" Moto laughed.

"You're done," John said. "You've really got to start thinking these through before you open your mouth."

17

Moto zipped up his pants and turned his hammock right-side up before silently mouthing the beginning of his joke with a puzzled countenance.

"Your pockets look a little light, Marty," John started. "Just turn around and come back after you've got it."

"Listen..." Marty started before being interrupted.

"No good sentence ever starts with 'Listen'. If I've ever earned an honest day's pay, my nose is telling me it was last night. The only thing that will make this crooked schnoz of mine feel any better is to catch a stiff whiff of my cut of the cash. So how about you go and do what I pay you to do?"

Marty avoided eye contact as he worked his way over to John's hammock. "John, they're not paying. Apparently, the guy you buried in the sand last night has friends in high places, and he still hasn't come to. They said to tell you that they're using your winnings to pay for his hospital expenses."

John was no longer kicked back in his hammock, soaking up the sun. "Are you serious? If they don't want their guys being hospitalized, maybe they should find a fighter that's on my level. It's insulting, some of the kids they put me up against out there."

"So what are you going to do?" Marty asked.

"Well, I guess I'm gonna have to do your job. I'm gonna find whichever ass has my money, and do whatever I hafta do to get it."

John cussed under his breath while he fought to balance in his hammock and lace up his boots. Moto, anticipating his brother's need for backup, quickly followed suit and began to throw on his gear.

"Where are you going, John? What could you possibly accomplish right now by doing this? You know no one goes over there in the middle of the day," Marty called out. "I'm pretty sure whoever is in charge is not gonna be an Ally."

It was too late. John was already upright and navigating the narrow forest trail as he set off with Moto straggling behind.

"The Pit" was little more than the basement of a large, dilapidated wooden building that had been rejuvenated with the sudden rise in the local male population carrying wads of cash that burned at their pockets. The building appeared to have been built ages ago, and it was apparent that the original function of the structure was something very different from what it had recently become.

Posted all over the exterior of the building were Chinese propaganda posters, hinting at the already obvious fact that this region wasn't exactly friendly territory to the American ideals. John and Moto always knew that they were entering enemy territory when they made the trek over for a night out, but today was their first time to visit prior to sundown. That fact and the glaring absence of other Americans made the establishment seem significantly less welcoming on this day. The posters included text in Chinese as well as Spanish for the local population, but it added no understanding for the Chow brothers. The familiar face of Hung Ju-long was being depicted as the savior of a needy people. The fact that his face was the one being plastered across the globe indicated that there might be some truth behind the rumors that he'd usurped the president's power, though he had allowed the president to keep the official title.

The ground floor of the building that served solely as a bar had become affectionately known as "Beer Here." None of the Allies knew the place's actual name, but as that was the only English sign outside, the name stuck. Apparently, a single sign reading "beer here" was enough of a welcome to Americans for them to overlook the barrage of propaganda glorifying their enemy.

The building's location--in the middle of the forest between the opposing encampments--was its only redeeming quality. The walk reminded Moto of his days driving to back country liquor stores scattered across the county line. The comparison was lost on his friends that weren't raised in the dry counties of the South.

The most unique feature of Beer Here was its glaring lack of females. Most all Puerto Rican women were aware of the reputation the bar had quickly gained and elected to steer clear. Moto often blamed the behavior of the Chinese men who weren't used to having so many women to choose from, but, in truth, the behavior of the Americans, including Moto, was not much better. The Chinese men had perfected the art of mitigating their sexual lust as the number of potential mates in their home country dwindled, but it took some getting used to for the Americans in the recently evacuated region. Currently, bloodlust and alcohol were their substitutes of choice. As it was, most men on both sides of the line had given up on their expectations to make it back home, and Beer Here was the perfect place for a man to blow through his accumulating wealth, as well as quench the demands of his ever accumulating testosterone. For how unappealing the place was aesthetically, John knew that a great deal of wealth must pass through the doors, and he had every intention of getting his earned share.

As they entered, the muscular bartender glanced up from his hunched-over position as he continued adding water to the half empty liquor bottles behind the bar.

"Hey, uh, we were hoping to..." the speech John had practiced in his head wasn't coming out as confidently as he'd hoped. He was glad when the large man pointed them with his funnel toward the stairs behind the bar.

A voice rang out from behind the closed door at the end of the brief hallway upstairs, "Wait there for just a second, and we'll get this thing over with."

There was a hint of an accent, but the Chinaman's English was surprisingly smooth. The brothers could partially hear his conversation but could only understand the voice coming from the man in the next room.

"We don't need to explain why. Just let them know it will work out for both of us in the long run. He doesn't get a say in the matter," the man's voice commanded with authority. "There's no time for slow playing this any longer than we already have. The estimates are well over seven billion, and if we want some say in how that decreases fourteen fold, we'd better get started," the man spoke into a wireless phone as he nudged the door opened with his foot. He motioned over his shoulder for the brothers to enter.

The two walked into the room as the source of the voice had already turned his back and now walked behind his desk and began rustling through maps and diagrams with an annoyed look on his face. A face that, from the new angle, the brothers could see was grotesquely scarred. There was a small circular scar on the right side of the man's head which appeared to be a gunshot wound. In the area where you would normally expect to find an ear, there was nothing more than a hairless crater of unnatural, wrinkled skin. The brothers found themselves looking at any inanimate object in the room that could be used to avoid eye contact with the monstrous man as he spoke into the phone. "It shouldn't be a hard sell. Just explain that most are a peaceful people, and that this union will only ensure peace for future generations. Listen, I've got company, we'll have to finish this later."

The man hung up the phone without waiting for a response and sat behind his large, cedar desk in an impressive leather chair. It was centered in front of a wide window with the curtains drawn. The gaudy furniture didn't at all match the rest of the room's décor, much less the rest of the building. Water stains littered the white ceiling, and carpet had been had been carelessly cut to cover the original rickety, wooden floors. Atop the immaculate desk set a laptop, and several ancient-looking books. John recognized a bible, the Quran, the Torah, and a few others he couldn't distinguish. The book that sat atop the pile was an impressive, leather bound book with golden, unfamiliar text and an owl insignia on the spine, marked 5778. He looked up and realized that the man was waiting for him to refocus so that he could begin.

"I'm not actually here very often," the disfigured man began. "You're lucky you caught me. I understand that you expect you have some money coming to you."

John and Moto exchanged an uncomfortable glance, but remained silent. The man was well-informed.

"Take a seat, gentlemen. You'll have to forgive my behavior, but I knew that the best way to get an American's attention was through his finances, and since that theory proved true for you, then what I have to say should really capture your full consideration."

The two brothers sat uncomfortably on the front edges of the two chairs facing the man's desk.

"Listen man, I just want my money," John feebly offered as he shifted his weight to lean his elbow against the narrow, wooden armrest.

The Asian grinned, "Oh, I can do you one better. Why settle for a small percentage of each fight's winnings when you're the one that has to wake up the next morning with the broken nose?"

John realized he had been rubbing his index finger across the swollen crest of his nose. Trying to look casual, he stiffly lowered his elbows to the awkwardly arranged arm rests and cupped each of his palms over his kneecaps.

The man grinned and continued. "I propose that you fight for me, and I can assure you that the increase in compensation will be considerable. You will fight who I say, when I say, and most importantly, how I say."

John raised his eyebrows in response. "I'm guessing the guy I fought last night was one of yours?"

The Asian leaned back in his chair and offered only a brief exhale to serve as his laugh. "As far as you're concerned, every man in this building who's worth a damn is one of mine."

"Listen man, I'm not trying to step on any toes or anything, I just wanted to come get what I've already earned. I appreciate the offer, but I think you're confused as to which side I'm on."

The gruesomely scarred man stood and walked over to his personal, un-diluted bar. All John could see was the man's back, but he could hear the clinking of ice cubes falling into a glass.

"This Russian stuff is fantastic," the man commented. "Though, nothing compares to the stuff those Cambodians drink. You boys ever had that? I suppose you haven't had much reason to go over that way. I spent some important days out there a few years ago. Ended up leaving with a little keepsake," he said as he turned and indicated the gruesome scars. "It worked out, though. I also acquired my Owl of Athena book you were admiring. Anyways, as I was saying, out there they drink the venom sacs of a viper with a glass of cognac. It beats the hell out of those tequila worms you guys are probably more accustomed to." He held out another glass, rattling the ice as a question.

"No thank you, I'm still feeling last night," John replied.

Moto stood and nodded to take him up on his offer and, after catching a scolding look from John, asked, "What? Hair of the dog that bit ya."

John also stood, but in protest. "Look, sir. Nothing against what you've got going on here, but I'm not interested in winding up like your other fighter from last night. There's always someone bigger and stronger... and when it comes to fighting, I don't take orders. That's it. If you could just give me my share, we'll be out of your hair, and in all likelihood, be right back tonight to spend the money in this fine little establishment you've got here."

The man's body language stiffened as he stared down the much larger American. "Believe me when I tell you that the little establishment I've got *going here* is just a drop in the bucket. Son, I hate to be the one to let you know, but you've ignored one of the most important rules of war and *grossly* underestimated me." He took a gulp of his drink, and continued in a raspy voice, "Understand that the sole reason *my* face is not the one plastered on all of these walls is the lacking marketability of my profile."

"I'm sorry if I've insulted you. I can see that you're a religious man," John said, acknowledging the bible on the desk.

"This Bible? This is for research, not your feel good stories. I'm not a pawn like you. We have nothing in common. These aren't my rules to live by. They're my guides for shepherding," the disfigured man scoffed. "You pawns. You like to preach on the teachings that make you feel warm inside. You ignore the prophecies where a third of your people perish from pestilence and with famine, and another third fall by the sword, leaving the rest to scatter into the winds only to be pursued by the sword. Your emotions are tossed around with every ebb and flow that your leaders dream up. You don't know what you believe. They tell you what you believe."

The grotesque man's watch beeped.

The man signaled with a dismissive wave of his hand. He muttered something as he waved, but John only recognized one word. "Adhan" was a word his childhood friend had used, but John couldn't recall its meaning. The brothers turned to check the exit when they heard the squeak of a floor board behind them. The most imposing soldiers that they had yet seen were entering the room.

"You were right. There is *almost* always someone bigger and stronger. But you are wrong when it comes to following orders. What I say goes. Soon enough, even the people that have been leading you around by the nose will be eating out of my hand." He re-directed his attention to the soldiers behind them. "They're not willing to do this the easy way."

The two brothers turned back again and saw the largest of the soldiers approaching with shotgun in hand. The glanced at each other and raised their hands in surrender, each carrying a baffled expression for what had unfolded.

John pleaded, "Whoa, man. This isn't gonna gain you anything. What do you think this is gonna accomplish? If this is my other option, I'll happily fight for you."

The disfigured man walked over behind his chair, glass of New Stolichnaya in hand. "The time for talk has come and gone. I appreciate the offer, but rest assured that I'll get what I need from you. Unfortunately, I may have not been entirely truthful with you earlier about what exactly that is. Please accept my apology."

The man inhaled as he slid a coaster under his glass with his middle finger. He then turned his back to the men and tore open the central window's curtain to reveal a large area at the back of the building and what appeared to be dozens of dog kennels hidden from the outside world by ten foot fences and camouflage netting atop the entire yard. He motioned to the nearest of his men, and the soldier gestured with a jerk of his shotgun barrel for the brothers to head back down the stairs behind a leading guard.

Once out back, John realized that the kennels weren't intended for dogs at all, but people. The faces of those entrapped were alarmingly stoical. The victims were covered in what appeared to be their own blood, and most of them lay completely still, save for the rising of their chests from an occasional breath. Their eyes carried the glazed, emotionless look of a dead fish that sent a chill down John's spine. Once closer, John could see that the pupil of each person was piercingly white. The sight froze John and Moto who could do nothing but stare. The guard shoved the

24

brothers forward, but their shock remained. The unblinking prisoners appeared as if they were strung out on drugs, and only when John walked past a cage too closely did a prisoner begin to show any further sign of life. Instead of the expected acknowledgment of his existence, their dull eyes jolted into awareness with an animalistic look of rage. Those nearest to John began to feed off of each other's anger and excitement, and the group grew more and more vocal and violent. Grunts spread throughout the yard and progressed into moaning and high shrieks of growling displeasure. The voices multiplied and grew into a symphony of animalistic aggression. Some of the imprisoned grinded their faces so forcefully against the bars that their thin, dry flesh began to peel back. Their disregard for their own well-being reminded John of the way a Siamese fighting fish would slam its face into a glass bowl attempting to attack its own reflection, even to the point of death.

The odor lingering in the dirt yard was unbearable, as the prisoners hadn't even a coffee can for their excrement. The distinct odor that only death can produce lingered mercilessly in the breezeless yard. Even the nearest soldier had trouble stomaching the aroma and reached to his back pocket for his handkerchief.

The guards' radios simultaneously erupted in chatter. The soldier that appeared to be in charge pressed the call button and began attempting to speak to someone on the other end, but there was no pause in the broadcast that was now escalating into screams. The unoccupied soldier tried to keep the brothers at gunpoint as he slowly began to lose his composure and gave in to a relentless coughing fit, struggling to cover his mouth and nose to avoid the putrid aroma with each inhalation. The other soldier scolded the younger man and shouted out some unknown orders before rushing back inside the building as he yelled into his radio. John realized that the young, coughing soldier was now the only one watching them. The screams of the other guard's conversation were still ringing out loudly on the young guard's radio. The man finally controlled his breathing and lowered his shotgun to his side as he reached with his free hand to lower his radio's volume.

John had been anticipating that this might occur and that the guard would temporarily have only one hand on the heavy shotgun. For a brief moment, it would be impossible for the man to raise, aim, and fire the weapon with any sort of urgency. Apparently, Moto had the same exact thought and was already in action. Moto's donkey kick backwards into the soldier's right knee sent the man straight to the dirt. The joint was severely hyper extended and completely mangled, his lower leg pointing in an impossible direction.

In a flash, Moto scooped up the shotgun and had it pointed squarely at the young soldier's face.

"No shoot--no shoot!" the man begged repeatedly in his best attempt at English and between his sporadic gasps for air. His attention would wander temporarily to his knee as he rolled around, writhing in pain, before looking back to make desperate eye contact with Moto.

John turned his head, anticipating what would happen next. He knew how hotheaded Moto could be and fully expected a deafening blast from the gun at any moment. Instead, though, he heard just a thud of the stock slamming into the man's head and a slap as his sweaty back clapped against the compacted dirt. Pleasantly surprised, John noted that the upstairs shades were once again drawn on the office windows, and he passed some nearby cages in search of anything that could be useful in tying up the unconscious soldier.

With all of the commotion, the men in cages grew hysterical. One became so worked up that he had actually begun to spew vomit through his cage's bars. John despised vomit. The lingering smells were already enough, but hearing the splatter as a person disgorged was always too much for him, and he instinctively turned back. Looking up, he noticed that Moto was looking past him with concerned bewilderment. Turning again, John noticed that the vomit was very odd looking, almost like spent coffee grounds. Then he saw it. The man who had just vomited was the same man he had fought the previous night. The man's skin had lost its color, and his eyes now carried that same hate-filled, animal look as all of the rest, accentuated by the absence of color in his pupil.

26

"What do you think could have…?" Before John could finish his thought, a blast rang out behind him and echoed across the yard.

John turned in disbelief to find that it was not Moto who had fired. A loud voice rang out from above them, and Moto dropped to a knee as he swung around, taking aim at the balcony above. It was the disfigured man, accompanied by several Chinese soldiers with their guns drawn.

"I had feared that trying to do this the polite way would cause more trouble than you're worth," the man was saying. "A mistake I won't make again. Lock them up for testing."

Moto surrendered his gun to the numerous approaching soldiers and again held his hands up in surrender. A soldier forced each of the brothers to their knees with a forceful kick to the back of the leg. John turned as he heard a brief yelp from his brother, and then everything went black.

John awoke to the chill of a bare, concrete floor underneath him. He was trapped behind bars, and his head throbbed mercilessly. He looked through the bars to see what appeared to be a make-shift lab filled with primitive chemistry equipment in a windowless, cinderblock room. He realized that Moto was already awake and sitting upright on his cot in the separate but adjoining cell. John was used to thinking himself out of predicaments, but the current situation didn't leave him much to work with. All of the room's lab equipment was well out of reach from the two cells which were surrounded on three sides by sturdy walls. The cells held nothing but an aluminum framed cot and a small bucket. He even noticed that the lock on each gate was tamper proof, and there was only one door into and out of the lab.

"What do you think?" John asked, "What do they have planned for us?"

"I don't know, man. The only thing I can come up with is that they're working on super soldiers or something. Why else would they have these cages in here? That could explain those guys in the pens outside, too. They're doing some human testing stuff on prisoners. The poor guys outside probably got the wrong mixture of testosterone and pain-killers, and we're the next crop of guinea pigs."

"That doesn't make sense," John said, shaking his head. "Why would they keep so many failed attempts alive out in the courtyard. Why would they keep the evidence around and have to feed them all? You'd think they'd want to bury as much evidence as possible. If the Allies were to catch wind of this, you can bet they would start dropping bombs."

"Maybe those aren't failed attempts," Moto suggested.

The two fell silent at the sound of the room's lone door opening as a man entered. It was a tall, slender man whose ethnicity wasn't obvious, though he didn't appear to be Chinese. He was wearing a white lab coat and chatting away on his phone as he re-locked the door as quickly as he could with one hand, but not before the brothers saw that the door led back into the outside courtyard. He rushed over to the nearest table top and began writing furiously.

"Okay; yessir; okay."

He stopped writing long enough to set the phone down, and switched it to speaker phone.

"...effects are not showing up where we'd expected, but it still seems to be getting out of hand. Something you've assumed isn't accurate."

The scientist sighed and answered. "The only explanation that makes any sense for what you're describing is that DEWW must..."

The scientist gave a suspicious glance toward the caged brothers and switched off the speaker phone. The rest of his sentence was unintelligible.

After a pause, he responded, "Right, sir, the boxing thing is my best guess. If we're right, the other camp..."

A pause.

"Unfortunately, we can't know for sure until the hosts..."

Another pause.

"Yes sir. I will find out. If the two they sent me are indeed regulars, we should be able to find that out for sure." His voice intensified. "There's no reason to even consider such measures until--or unless--we know it's already gotten that bad! I need you to make sure he will hold off until I can get the results! For God's sake, fine, I'll talk to him." The man slammed the phone down on the table.

The door opened again, and an armed soldier entered the room. They acknowledged each other as the scientist continued to

30

write. The guard was tall and built, with an assault rifle strapped around his back. He looked annoyed that the scientist didn't offer any assistance and struggled to juggle two trays of food on one arm as he locked the door behind him. He shot an annoyed glare at the scientist as he dug for his keys. It was obvious he hadn't been asked to waiter often. Water was dripping to the floor, and he struggled not to slosh what remained in the prisoners' glasses.

"Sir," the scientist spoke into the phone again, "I was hoping you had a second to talk now that everything is under control here. Yes, sir, some of the theories regarding antibodies in the plasma are still holding true. There's still a lot we don't know, but we're well past the point of this just being a guess." After a brief silence, the scientist continued. "They seem to ultimately suffer from fevers that should be fatal. The swelling in the brain causes what effectively becomes a frontal lobotomy, though some areas of the brain tend to become hyperactive instead of dormant, and the cerebrum is largely unaffected. I'm gathering my notes right now if you'd like to see specifics, but there's another reason I called." The scientist gathered his papers and continued his conversation as he moved outside--again, taking care to relock the door.

John remained in his original position lying on the floor, pretending to lay unconscious as the guard came near. Moto backed away as far as he could to the opposite corner of his cell from the door. John inconspicuously noted every move the guard made as he left Moto's tray of food, and struggled to re-lock the cell's door. When the guard came over to his own cell, John did his best to visualize the guard's position and movements by sound alone. Upon hearing the door swing open, and the keys fall to the concrete, John knew this was going to be his best opportunity.

He instinctively pushed off from a sprinter's starting block position full force into the unsuspecting guard. In the split second it took for the guard to shift his focus from the now unimportant food tray, John was on him. John positioned his forearms under the guard's buttocks and lifted until the larger man's feet left the ground, form-tackling him into a table. The guard slammed the food tray down on John's back as he landed hard, but to no avail. The weight of the two men collapsed the lab table, scattering beakers and flasks filled with unknown liquids across the floor.

31

John fought to hold the guard down as he frantically reached for any tool or weapon within his arm's reach that could be used to maintain his advantage. He had discarded the Bunsen burner and crucible and was considering one of the larger shards of glass before realizing that the guard beneath him now lay motionless. As John attempted to salvage the man's gun, he saw that one of the large shards had already lodged itself in the guard's spine. John cautiously wrestled the rifle strap free from the man, though he acknowledged the pointlessness in his care. Even so, John gingerly rested the guard's head back on the floor.

"Let's get out of here," Moto said. "I don't intend to stick around and find out what that lab rat has planned for us."

"Technically, I think we're the lab rats," John said as he stood and strapped the rifle around his shoulder.

He turned to see the key ring still lying on the floor in his cell and used it to release Moto. Without missing a beat, Moto made for the door.

"Hang on, I have an idea," John said.

Moto nodded in agreement as John turned back, stepped over the lifeless guard, and unplugged the tubing to a nearby Bunsen burner, turning the gas up to full blast. Moto decided to ransack what he could of the lab, carelessly knocking over the flasks and jars filled with various chemicals and glancing through the incomprehensible documents as he strewed them about-- many of which had large portions of text blacked out.

As John turned to ask Moto if he had anything to light the papers on fire, he noticed that Moto had abruptly halted his pillaging and was again staring past him with a now familiar, wide-eyed look of terror. John turned and looked over his shoulder to see the guard slipping in his own blood while fighting to get back to his feet. He realized his own jaw was now hanging open as well, and he noted that again his brother's incredulous stare was more than justified. The guard groaned as he gazed around the room with a puzzled look on his emotionless face. His sullen frown was quickly replaced with a look of rage when he saw the brothers scrambling for the door, and he let out a gurgling groan that intensified into a guttural warning. The light colored pupils added an extra sense of terror in the brothers. Moto poetically rattled off a long string of cuss words as he jiggled the doorknob, trying to get the door to open. John handed him the keys, and turned to face the rapidly approaching undead guard. His steps were uncoordinated at best, as he stumbled slowly toward the two brothers.

"None of these keys are working!" Moto said in a panic.

John raised and aimed the rifle that he had retrieved from the guard before thinking better of it. He recalled the whistling Bunsen burner they'd prepared. The guard halted and began vomiting up thick, dark-colored bile. Before the ichor had finished its escape, the guard resumed his rigid stagger across the room. John let the rifle hang from its strap and reached for a nearby fire extinguisher that hung against the wall. He stepped forward and swung, making swift, hard contact with the guard's chin. The impact knocked the guard off balance and sent him clumsily to the concrete. The man's groans turned to muffled gurgles, and his movements became even less fluid and deliberate, though he continued in a futile attempt to return to a standing position. John wailed on the guard's back repeatedly with the heavy extinguisher and every ounce of his strength, but the guard kept fighting.

"Got it!" Moto yelled. "C'mon, c'mon, let's go!"

John made solid contact to the guard's head once more, sending an echoing low-pitched ring through the room. Before exiting, John jabbed the large tank at another of the gas valves, breaking it loose and sending a whistling rush of the flammable gas loose into the room. The guard was upright, and John threw the fire extinguisher at him once more for good measure as he made his way to the door.

Once outside, Moto paused to catch his bearings. The blinding, setting sun was still above the tree line, and the two took a moment to allow their eyes to adjust. A guard from a previously unnoticed guard tower yelled at the men in Chinese. Moto instinctively ducked under the cover of an adjacent building's overhanging roof, with John right behind him, as fountains of loose sand were kicked up all around them from the hail of gunfire. Several more footsteps could be heard upstairs as numerous guards rushed into position.

"Get ready to run!" John yelled as he pointed to the nearest cages that lined the perimeter wall. He leaned out to shoot into the lab's open door but saw that the gore-covered guard was slowly approaching and blocking his shot. John fired off a quick three-round burst into the guard's chest. The sound of three hollow thuds told him he had hit his target, but the guard continued his slow approach.

"He's barely even bleeding!" Moto exclaimed.

John squinted as he lined up his next shot.

"If this works, I'm gonna bolt," John whispered over his shoulder. "You'd better be in my hip pocket if I take off."

With a slow exhale and an almost undetectable squeeze of his trigger finger, John unleashed a perfect shot. The bullet whizzed through the guard's left knee and into the lab behind him where it sparked off of the fire extinguisher that lay forgotten on the floor.

For a brief moment, John feared that his shot had proven fruitless, but the barely audible hissing of escaping gas intensified into a roar. John blindly reached behind him and grabbed Moto's shirt collar as he kicked off into a sprint straight past the hobbled guard and toward the outer row of cages. A fireball blew out a shimmering wall of glass shrapnel as the brothers ducked their heads and ran as quickly as they could in the deep, loose sand. The ground seemed to tremor with the onslaught of blindly fired rounds from the guards above. The leap atop the nearest cage, that would've been an impressive feat any other day, felt effortless as adrenaline coursed through the brothers' veins. The barrage of bullets miraculously missed their intended targets and struck the snarling prisoner in the cage below them as the brothers scaled the high wall.

The air cooled quickly as the setting sun lit up the horizon in a bright, blood red. The brothers ran as quickly as the loose soil would allow with an occasional bullet whistling past them from behind. As their legs weakened, more trees helped to shorten the range of the pursuing guards' bullets until the threat of even an impossibly lucky shot seemed to have diminished entirely. The walk to and from the bar each night that normally seemed somewhat brief stretched on now for what felt like an eternity.

Finally, they found themselves back at the gutted building amidst the darkness where their hammocks still hung lazily. Tucked behind the cover of their sanctuary's logs, John struggled to catch his breath.

"Did you see the way that guard shook those bullets off like it was nothing?" John managed to say between gasps for air. "He just kept walking toward me like nothing happened!"

"You think they're still coming for us?" Moto asked while he sat and situated his back into the opposite corner of the roofless room.

"There's no way," John whispered, "it's almost dark and we're in the middle of a cease fire. They wouldn't chance it just for us."

A mortar whistled as it streaked through the night sky, preceding an explosion that shook the Americans' camp a short distance away. Several more mortars followed, lighting up the terrain as if it was mid-day. The Allies eventually sent up a flare and opened up a hail of returning fire. Hell broke loose around the Chow brothers amidst the confusion of darkness.

The next morning, John awoke to find Moto fast asleep in the opposite corner, drool hanging down from the corner of his mouth in an impressive strand. John thought to himself how stupid Moto had been to plug in his earbuds, and drown out the sounds of battle with his phone's music. The cry of the falling mortar rounds had ceased long before, but a few faint cries from the Allies' camp were still ringing out in the dawn's early light. The continuous gunfire had also deteriorated into sporadic small arms report--all of which seemed to be coming from the Allies' side.

John had kept his right knee bent all night to keep himself wedged into a readied, upright position against the wall. His awkward stance against the corner had caused an unbearable stasis of circulation to everything below his hip, leaving his butt completely numb. John tugged at his pant leg to help dislodge his foot from its hold, and the thousands of resulting pin pricks climbing up and down his leg forced a grimace and sharp inhalation. The sudden sound caused Moto to jerk awake and bang his head against the shelter wall.

"Is it safe to go back?" Moto asked while pulling out his ear buds and rubbing the back of his head.

"I don't know, man. It sounds like it's about as good of a chance as we're gonna get."

As the two neared their camp, the gunshots grew less and less frequent. Several pillars of black smoke became visible as they climbed the last hill, and found that the entire camp lay in ruins. Corpses littered the area. Most, it seemed, had been killed by blasts of shrapnel as well as close-proximity gunshot wounds. If there had been any survivors, it appeared that they'd left. Inside the abandoned tents, the Chow brothers found corpses of some of their friends still lying in their cots, each with a single wound to the head. Many of the wounds were obvious gunshots, but some appeared to have resulted from blows with a blunt weapon.

"It's like they never even woke up," Moto said upon entry to yet another tent filled with the dead.

Once he'd reached their own tent, Moto walked in further to more closely inspect a corpse that lay across a perfectly tucked

37

mattress. John wandered aimlessly as he thought to himself, pausing occasionally to search for ammunition.

"Dammit. Garrett's dead," Moto said after receiving confirmation from the dead man's dog tags. "The hell? Please come explain this to me."

A piece of shrapnel had struck the man and lodged itself deeply into his throat--an obviously fatal wound. In addition, a bullet had been delivered straight through the man's head. The spray of brain matter and skull fragments made it glaringly obvious that the shot had been delivered as the victim lay on his cot--a cot that the man's body remained tethered to.

"Now why would they bring him in here after, I assume, he got the shrapnel outside, only to tie him down and shoot him in the head?" Moto asked, covering his nose with the back of his sleeve. "Trying to get information out of him or something?"

"The guard," John answered while pointing to the small, darkened puddle that had accumulated under the mattress. "Garrett got back up just like the guard did. His blood is the exact same color. Come on, we need to find you a rifle."

The brothers walked solemnly past a handful of men who had become their family over the past several months. Their lives were now nothing more than memories and bodies laid out on the bunks or along the floor.

Moto bent down next to his bottom bunk to see if his rifle or side arm were still stashed under the bed. He caught a glimpse of his now deceased friend Andrew in the bed just a couple of feet over from his own. He could easily recognize him because, unlike Garrett, Andrew hadn't been shot in the head. Moto did his best to not let his eyes linger on his friend's face. He knew that if he looked too closely, then he might not be able to hold back his swelling emotions any longer. Instead, Moto respectfully pulled a sheet over the man's body, unable to avoid noticing the gruesome damage that had been dealt to Andrew's mid-section.

Down on his knees, Moto was glad to find some small ray of hope when he felt the familiar, cold touch of his precious rifle. "We're in business," he called out to John, holding up the gun.

Suddenly, he caught a hint of movement in his peripheral vision. The sheet on Andrew's bed rose almost imperceptibly. At the squeak of the mattress, Moto instinctively leapt up and away from his bunk and into the aisle. Andrew's lungs released a pocket of air and a terrifying groan from his throat as he became aware of the fact that someone was nearby. The man lowered his feet to the floor, allowing the saturated sheets to fall away, and turned his head to focus on the brothers. Moto continued walking backwards toward John while Andrew grunted as he struggled to stand. A large tangle of intestines escaped from his core and splattered to the ground. He took a step forward, straight into his own guts, and slipped down face first onto Moto's bed. Moto raised his gun and released the safety but quickly realized that he could not bring himself to fire.

"Go outside," John said calmly. "I gotcha."

Outside, Moto heard a single gunshot, and it was finished. Seconds later, a pale-faced John emerged and stood silently by his side. After a few brief moments with no one saying anything, the men heard several voices hooting and hollering in apparent celebration. The brothers rushed towards the commotion, realizing that not everyone had left. In a cautious hurry, the brothers crept up and over the nearest hill and silently observed from the safety of the tree line. There, they witnessed a group of deserting Allied soldiers who had assembled in a circle.

The congregation of men backed away excitedly, revealing the reason for their gathering. A Chinese man with paled skin lay before them. The man fought violently from the flat of his back as the group of soldiers dispersed and hopped excitedly into their separate vehicles. As the prisoner had almost returned to his feet, one of the Jeeps pulled forward making it apparent to John and Moto that three of the Chinese man's limbs were restrained, each tied to a separate truck. One line grew taut, and pulled the man's feet out from under him, sending him violently back to the dirt.

"Alright, take it slow guys!" A young soldier in the back of the truck yelled while motioning to progress with a circular motion of his hand.

One of the Jeeps circled around opposite the other two, causing a tangle in the lines. The ropes were able to unknot themselves by violently flipping the tethered man's body around in a blur of force until he was now facing the ground, and all three ropes stiffened. The ropes grew even tighter and pulled the Chinese man's body completely up off the dirt. The man let out a horrible wail that was cut short by a gurgling and forceful vomiting. The scene unfolding before him brought a glower to John's face but seemed to have the opposite effect on the soldiers who were now laughing like giddy school kids and exchanging high fives. Before long, the Jeep that had been tied to an arm lurched forward, towing the severed limb behind it. The other two Jeeps dragged the body several feet before the same instructing soldier had them stop. His demeanor was like that of a driver on the lake after a skiing friend had fallen.

The pale-bodied prisoner jerked around in the sand, the same dark, bile-like substance leaking slowly from the empty shoulder socket. The instigator of the torture hopped down from his Jeep and ran over to the man, whose cries turned to growls at his approach. The determined Chinese man again fought to his feet as the soldier crept forward. The soldier was unaware of just how close he'd come to the prisoner as he walked backwards, facing the men in his truck. He quickly realized his mistake as the captive man swung at him with his single arm, and latched onto the man's shirt. One of the still attached Jeeps alertly jerked forward, pulling the man's leg out from under him, and freeing the young soldier. Another Ally, who didn't appear to be American, laughed hysterically at the wide-eyed shock of the now pale-faced soldier--obviously shaken by his near fatal mistake. Regaining his composure, the soldier retrieved the loose rope, severed limb and all, and re-attached it to the man's remaining arm.

"Alright, round two," the young soldier yelled, trying to regain his nerve. "I was gonna end it quick for ya, you dumb douche," the soldier said while kicking dirt into the face of the helpless man. It was apparent that he was now hesitant to go close enough to actually kick him.

This time, the Jeeps spun their wheels as they all accelerated in opposite directions. An excruciating popping sound echoed from the man's body cavity as two of his remaining limbs gave way. Gore slowly trickled into the sand as the confused man squirmed, trying to stand on his lone, dislocated leg. John was reminded of a pathetic, overturned turtle. The soldiers laughed as they approached, watching the man repeatedly force his face into the dirt as he tried to get upright, apparently unaware of his incapacitating predicament. The depraved soldier kicked the man in the chest a couple of times before bending over to pose for a picture with his victim. The casualty, who lay in literal disarmament, looked up quickly after the camera flashed and then turned his focus to the young soldier at his side. As the young man stood to walk away from his prey, the victim thrust himself forward with his lone leg, latching his teeth into the man's calf. The soldier screamed in a shrill, high-pitched voice as he kicked at the undying man, trying to escape his hold. The other soldiers stood idle, panicked and dumbfounded by the ability of the unyielding enemy to attack. Finally, a solid kick was landed against the side of the ferocious man's head, knocking his teeth loose with flesh and cloth still dangling from his mouth. The AWOL soldiers raced back to the two nearest Jeeps and sped away in a panic.

John nudged his brother and nodded ahead. "They left one of the Jeeps. Let's get the hell outta here."

Upon reaching the truck, Moto fumbled his hand around the ignition area, finding no keys. He reached down under the steering column and tore away a section of paneling that enclosed a bundle of wires. As Moto reached for his knife to strip the insulation, John expectantly pulled down the sun visor--revealing no keys.

"You watch too many movies," Moto laughed.

"Why not check?" John asked. "I leave mine there sometimes when I go running. It's still the last thing anyone assumes."

Moto expertly flicked two wires, sparking the engine to life, and tied the exposed wiring together. He jerked the stick into gear and sped off in a controlled slide, doing his best to catch up to the other soldiers.

"HO, HO!" John yelled, throwing his palm up at Moto.

"What is it, Santa?" Moto yelled in frustration as the Jeep slid to a stop.

John raised the guard's rifle, and fired a single shot into the disfigured man's head, dropping his body instantly into a lifeless heap. Appreciating, but not really understanding John's compassion, Moto floored the gas pedal and released the clutch.

Several miles south of their base, Moto suddenly planted both feet firmly on the brake pedal. He dug the heel of one hand into the steering wheel, expertly turning into each slide before finally swinging the Jeep sideways to a sudden stop. What appeared to be the other men's Jeep lay in a ditch further down the road, consumed by flames. Barely visible to him were several Chinese soldiers lining the sides of the road just before the spot where the Jeep had come to rest. The silhouettes of two men emerged from the burning car, stumbling up and out of the ditch. Their fatigues were still burning, and some of the rounds of ammunition strapped to their person were bursting from the heat of the flames. The Chinese soldiers opened fire as the undead approached them, blasting holes through their chests. One soldier was screaming out orders to the others, and the men began firing off headshots which proved to be much more effective.

John secured his rifle against his shoulder as Moto sped forward, straight into the Chinese soldiers' road block. John narrowed the attention of his fire to whichever men ignored the enflamed soldiers and especially to the few of them who were quick to raise their rifle in the brothers' direction. John systematically eliminated the most immediate threats and prevented any shots from being fired in their direction. As they sped past, one of the American soldiers stumbled backwards into the roadway after he'd fought loose from another man's grasp. He backpedaled to keep some distance between himself and the man who was engulfed with flames. Neither man saw the speeding vehicle as it approached and both stepped out into the road. In order to avoid the live soldier, Moto was forced to slam into the burning man.

Blood smeared across the glass as the windshield wipers swung back and forth. Moto squirted some wiper fluid to help his limited visibility, and inadvertently splashed some over the top of the windshield. John, who was still squatted up on his seat in a firing position, caught a face full of the blood and water.

After it appeared the two were clear of danger, Moto was careful not to laugh. "Sorry, dude."

"Dammit, Moto!" John yelled as he frantically rubbed his sleeve across his face. "You probably just got me infected!"

"Infected? Whoa, you're supposed to be the realist here. I was supposed to tell you that you can't ignore how those guys were getting dropped by nothing but headshots, and you were supposed to make me feel stupid with some logical explanation."

"How about this for logic? If it looks like a duck, walks like a duck, and quacks like a duck..." John trailed off.

"It's a damn zombie," Moto finished, with a contemplative stare down the center of the road. A grin crawled across his mouth and tugged into his cheek.

"I mean, who knows at this point, but it's hard to ignore what we've seen," John said. "I'm racking my brain to piece all this stuff together, but nothing else makes any more sense to me than zombies do."

"Hey look in the back," Moto said. "Did they leave us anything useful?"

John, once appeased by his furious efforts to de-contaminate himself, crawled into the back and fished through the cargo area. In the rear, he found a few mostly filled canteens of water, some ammunition, and perhaps most importantly, a radio. He switched the handheld to life and the sound of desperate, English-speaking voices filled the Jeep. They had already missed much of the conversation, but overheard one of the men reacting to the mention of missiles. The man on the other end of the conversation began sharing the plan of action with the former, in a much more panicked voice. The plan was to head south to the coast. He mentioned rumors that their air bases were already

43

overtaken and burning. The other voice confirmed the fact, but added the importance of avoiding passenger flights, as many areas were now holding Americans captive. The faceless voices agreed that perhaps the best course of action would be to stow away on a random ship and simply bribe whoever could let them aboard. Mid-sentence, once voice went silent. There was a hint of commotion, and then nothing. The other voice didn't call out to ask what had happened but chose instead to speak no more.

"Don't transmit anything," John said. "The Chinese definitely have some of our radios by now, and I can only assume they're listening to all this."

"Well, we're already south of the road block. You want to steal the plan?" Moto asked.

John shrugged. "I really feel like the Chinese probably overheard all that. I don't know, man. I can't think of a better option. If we go for it, we've got to do it fast before they have time to mobilize and do something about it."

Moto nodded and pressed the pedal to the floorboard. Dust kicked up behind the Jeep, and the two felt good to be putting some distance between themselves and the chaos behind them. The good feeling wouldn't last much past dusk, though, when the glow from a missile streaked across the darkening sky. Several more followed behind it--all targeting the coast a few miles ahead.

"Tell me this isn't happening," John said. "Tell me we're not stuck on this damn island."

"At least we were late to the party," Moto sighed. "If we'd been much quicker, we'd have been goners."

"So what now? We know what's waiting for us if we go back," John said.

"I say we go for it," Moto shrugged. "Lightning doesn't strike the same place twice, right? Why would they send another missile strike where they just sent one? Let's just continue on, and we'll figure it out from there."

John agreed, and the two continued south toward the coast as they night air cooled. As they drew nearer to the ocean, the road became impassable from the debris of a decimated convoy. Moto slowed and navigated carefully to avoid any human or inhuman contact and continued to the beach. The visibility soon became limited from the plumes of smoke blowing in off the water. John cautioned Moto to slow down and preserve their only means of transport. Moto began his usual speech that he'd always used whenever his driving abilities were questioned. Moto rattled off examples of his extensive "behind the wheel experience" having driven Motocross for a decade as well as his upbringing as a grease monkey. He assured John that he couldn't be in more capable hands.

Perhaps proving them both right, Moto suddenly slammed his foot onto the brake and guided the truck down an unseen hill. As he steered to avoid the rapidly approaching debris and sharp crevices as they appeared from behind the cover of smoke, the Jeep flirted with but never surpassed its tipping point. The Jeep finally skidded to a stop just before reaching a significant drop off.

"God, you're stubborn," John said as he climbed out and slammed his door.

"What?" Moto smiled as he grabbed his rifle and a canteen from the back. "We made great time."

At the bottom of the slope was a slight beach and then surf. Their only ticket off of the cursed land lapped calmly against the sand. John squinted to look for any light aside from the numerous fires left ignited by the missile strikes. Moto sipped from his

45

canteen and slowly walked down to the water's edge, searching for a boat. In his mind, any boat would do. Truly, anything buoyant would have been a strong option. Seeing nothing, they decided to follow alongside the waterline in the Jeep and see what the headlights would reveal. A few barely audible moans caught the brothers' attention. It was unclear if the sound was coming from the wounded or the dead.

Moto cut the lights and slowed to a stop as they rolled up on an area that had obviously been one of the main targets of the strike. All of the burning ships and piers across the beach made the area visible in spite of the night sky. Human silhouettes would appear and disappear along the beach as they walked past occasional fires. The figures were shuffling awkwardly along the coast, but from a distance it was not obvious whether it was just humans struggling against the deep sand or dozens and dozens of the undead. John nudged Moto and pointed up past the fires. Out on the water, flashlights were visible patrolling the deck of a large freighter. Obviously, the ship had not yet been overrun by zombies. Moto turned to face John and spotted a figure stumbling down the bank next to the Jeep, but still several yards away. He reached for the rifle, but John stopped him.

"We can't attract the rest of 'em," John whispered. "If we can just get to the water by the ship, we're golden! No way those things are coordinated enough to swim. Just get us near that ship!"

The zombie was just steps away from the passenger door as Moto punched the accelerator. Aside from slight adjustments to dodge debris along the beach, the Jeep took a beeline for the ship. The hum of the engine attracted the attention of all the staggering forms within a large radius. Moto hoped that they were indeed all zombies as there were too many for John to shoot, and several began to walk out into his path. He eventually gave up any effort to avoid them. Most of the lost souls were the perfect height for their head to slam against the hood, echoing the unmistakable, resonating sound that the cranium makes when it receives a harsh blow. One of the taller assailants unexpectedly rolled up onto the hood and shattered the windshield before coming to rest in the truck's cargo area. The gangly man had not suffered severe enough damage to keep him down, and he began to creep forward to the front seat. John had fired off the last round of his magazine before realizing that the zombie was in the car with them. He considered the second gun, but turned to realize that the zombie had landed on top of their second rifle, leaving the brothers completely vulnerable. Moto nodded to his brother as he buckled, and John fumbled to latch his belt. The Jeep redlined and the engine whined as they accelerated to an impressive speed considering the drag of the loose sand. Moto's butt lifted out of the chair as he put all of his weight into pinning the gas pedal to the floorboard and bracing himself for impact. The Jeep seemed to skid along the top of the water for a brief moment before hitting an invisible wall and abruptly slamming to a halt in the surf.

The zombie flew out into the sea several feet ahead of the Jeep. Rattled, but aware, the two quickly unstrapped their seatbelts and began their swim toward the ship as the Jeep submerged almost completely from view. Without warning, Moto's swimming motion was violently disrupted as one of his legs jerked him to a stop.

"Hold up!" Moto yelled to John. "I'm stuck on the Jeep or someth..."

His sentence was cut short as he was suddenly lost below the water's surface. He kicked and pulled, before looking back and realizing that it was not the Jeep pulling him under. Illuminated from below the surface by the Jeep's flashing hazard lights were dozens of zombies walking along the seabed. Moto lost what little breath he had in a terrified gasp at the sight of them all. He finally was able to kick loose from the zombie's grip and resurface for a breath of air before being pulled under a second time, this time with more of the decrepit hands grabbing hold. He felt the additional weight pulling him under and looked to see numerous other zombies coming over and clinging onto him, sensing their next meal. The zombies' combined weight was too much for him, and they were easily winning the battle, pulling him closer and closer to their gnashing teeth. As his hopes of escaping were all but gone, Moto felt a tug at his shirt from above as John fought against his own buoyancy and climbed down deeper into the water, pulling himself across Moto's body as he descended. Once low enough, John grabbed a hold of Moto's belt, and began furiously kicking at the underwater zombies. Finally, Moto was able to pull free and swim up for air. After kicking ferociously toward deeper water where the sunken undead couldn't reach them, Moto and John floated on their backs and rested briefly. Each deep exhale sank them enough that the two were forced to paddle slightly.

Before they could fully recuperate, a snarling floater drifted over to them. It was hard to know how many of the moans were carrying across the water from the shore, and how many were floating close by along the surface of the black water, still very active. The nearest floater had severe burns covering its upper body, and a large wave revealed that it had lost almost its entire lower half. The thing's bloated stomach kept it afloat as it drifted nearer the brothers. John and Moto were able to easily swim away from most of the floaters, but were forced to keep moving.

Finally, they neared the large ship and yelled up to the crew for help. Before long, several flashlights were aimed at them, and the crew was frantically searching for a way to pull them aboard. After what seemed like an eternity, a rope was slung over the side of the ship, landing next to the two brothers. Moto knew that he couldn't hold his own weight, as his weary arms could barely tread water any longer. Instead, he tied a looped knot at the bottom of the rope so that he could stand as the survivors pulled him aboard. Waiting his turn, John's arms also began to fatigue as his adrenaline wore off. The moans and splashing of slowly approaching floaters quickly jerked him from his lull, as he anxiously watched for the rope's return. John's concern grew as he heard some commotion up on the deck, but finally the rope was again lowered, and he too was pulled up to safety.

Once aboard there was no time for celebration as he witnessed firsthand what the commotion had been about. One of the men, who appeared to be Russian, was yelling and pointing at Moto's severely scratched legs. John couldn't understand him, but could deduce that this man was convinced Moto had been infected. Several different ethnicities were represented on the ship, and the language barrier caused the confusion to grow exponentially. John pleaded with the English speakers that Moto would be fine; that he had not been bitten. He argued that they were only scratches. He was able to convince a few of the men but for those that mattered, his pleas fell on deaf ears. One of the larger, more outspoken Russians grabbed Moto by the back of his collar and began to drag him away. John jumped to his defense but was held back by some of the other men. For every English speaker that believed John, there were at least three Russians that either didn't understand or didn't care to endanger their own lives for the sake of empathy.

An elderly man, whose version of broken English hinted that he was a local, moved in to defend Moto, and shoved at one of the large Russians as he yelled. Another of the sizeable men, who had been vocal in not letting Moto aboard, moved in and separated the two with extended arms. Unprepared for the shove, the old Puerto Rican man tripped over the foot of someone behind him, and fell head first into the ship's railing. The harder John and the others all fought and pleaded, the more men came to hold them back as Moto was dragged away.

"What are you doing with my brother? Let him go! There is nothing wrong with him! Someone, please stop them!"

One of the Russian men who had previously remained silent spoke up on John's behalf. Whatever he said caused the other men to stop dragging Moto away. He spoke calmly with the other men and, on occasion, would translate for John.

"I tell them you don't think your friend turn evil. I tell them he no bit," the man said.

"Yes, yes!" John said. "Tell them they don't have to kill him. Tell them everything is okay, they're safe."

The man spoke some more in Russian, and it appeared that the other men were considering whatever he'd said. After a brief conversation, the Russians that had been holding John back pushed him forward toward Moto. The two exchanged a brief hug that was cut short as the Russians grabbed each of them and began dragging them both away.

John yelled, as he searched frantically for the translator. "What? What did you say? You've got to believe me! What did you say, you moron? What are you doing?"

John stumbled around in the darkness of the unfamiliar room, fumbling around sacks of flour and scattering canned goods across the floor before finally finding a light switch. Light spilled across the room from a lone, naked bulb. Silently propped against a bare wall sat Moto, gingerly touching the gashes that covered his lower legs. Moto's concern for infection trumped any curiosity one would normally have for their indefinite holding cell. The storage room was small and, for the most part, devoid of any useful items--aside from the extensive canned food supply. There was a vent for air circulation, but John noted that it was much too small to escape through. The lone door had been sealed tightly, though John did notice that the hinges were facing inward. The room was never intended to keep someone in.

"I think I can get us out of here," John said.

"There's no point," Moto responded, still inspecting his wounds. "We're on a ship. What would we do, go hide in another store room? Besides, they wouldn't lock us in here with their food if they thought of us as enemies. They're just holding us here, waiting to see if I turn into a zombie."

"How's your leg?" John asked. "It doesn't look like it's bleeding too bad."

"Nah, nah, I'm good. I can walk fine and everything. I just can't help but wonder if this is the beginning of the end for me."

"Moto, nobody has seen as much of this stuff as we have. These guys are just paranoid. Remember the guard in the lab? He died right in front of us before he turned. He was completely normal up until then."

"I know, I know. But I can't stop thinking that some of those chemicals that spilled are what infected him, and that's why he reanimated when he did. He may have been clean before you tackled him."

"If that's the case, don't you think you would've turned by now?" John asked.

"You're right. Logically, I know that you're right. But... it's just a weird feeling, ya know? You start wondering if you'll be able to feel pain when you become one of them. Wonder if you'll still comprehend what you're doing, but you just can't stop yourself. If there's any chance you could be normal again."

"Tell you what," said John. "The second you start drooling and coming at me all aggressive-like, I will personally put you out of your misery."

"Well, maybe get a little more confirmation before you off me. You pretty much described every morning that you've had to wake me up," Moto said.

"Deal," John said with a slightly crooked smile. "I mean, it's the obvious choice. What else would I do, let you eat me?"

"Whatever," Moto laughed. "You know you'd cry yourself to sleep every night if you ever really had to..."

The door unexpectedly swung open. An American-looking man with closely cropped, brown hair that was beginning to show specks of grey poked his head inside. He smiled uncomfortably and tried to look casual while checking the brothers' hands for weapons before partially shutting the door behind him with one arm, blankets folded neatly under the other.

"I'm Jim," he said softly. "Sorry none of us could really do much more for you guys back there. I'm so glad to see that you're both okay."

"I mean, it would've been nice to know they weren't dragging me to put a bullet through my head and toss me over the side of the ship," Moto grumbled while bracing himself to stand.

"No, you don't have to get up," Jim said before tossing each of the men a blanket. "I didn't come to let you out; they'd throw us all overboard. You just have to understand the guys' paranoia with this whole thing. They roll in to find the docks have all been blown to hell, and there's no one answering the radio. They start spotting these cadaverous things crawling around with no legs. Half of them burned head to toe, others with holes through their chests and eyes hanging out. Before we even realized what was going on, we found ourselves knocking zombies off the deck to try and save the ship. We were just about done cleaning up all the blood and guts when we found you guys. I wasn't even sure we were gonna be able to convince the Russians not to just leave you in the water. Anyhow, they just want to hold you here for the night, make sure everything's cool. I felt bad that I didn't do more for y'all earlier, so I thought I'd at least bring you some stuff to sleep on and let you know where you stand."

"Thank you, Jim. Thanks so much," John said with a handshake.

"Anyhow, we'll catch you guys in the a.m." Jim said while opening the door. "You guys hang tight, and we'll have you back to the States in no time."

The door lock clicked as John processed Jim's last sentence and looked up at Moto who paused his languid effort at arranging his bed. Moto raised his eyebrows with a new, optimistic countenance, and John let slip a full smile.

Moto awoke to the slight tinking sound from a large mosquito bumping into the bare light bulb. John, it appeared, was fast asleep. John had always preferred leaving a light on at night... something he had never even attempted to outgrow. Every time Moto tried to point out how juvenile this was, John would fire back with Moto's desperate need for a fan or music in order to doze off. He had unknowingly become more and more dependent on the white noise in order to slow his racing mind each night. The comforting hum that protected his slumber was so engrained that even basic training couldn't break him from it.

Before he had acquired his handy portable fan, he'd woken up constantly each night to the squeaking of the patrolman's shoes on the pristine floor. This served as a more effective deterrent to his mischievous nature than the actual punishment of cleaning the floors with a toothbrush. The nights following Moto's punishments always produced unbearable squeaks with every step of a rubber-soled boot on the immaculate floor.

Though his phone's case had protected it from the ocean's water, his battery had long since been depleted. Moto squinted into the bright light, and began letting his mind ponder the grotesque nature of mosquitos. It was truly the only one of God's creatures that Moto had never found a purpose for. He began to wonder if even mosquitoes could transmit this new outbreak the way they could other diseases. What if it could extend beyond being just a carrier, and there were undead mosquitos to worry about? Could this plague reach other animals and not just humans? His mind started to run wild with ideas of the fast-spreading epidemic and what could possibly stop it before things got even more out of hand. At the height of his paranoid ponderings, the mosquito floated down next to him. Moto emphatically slammed his hand down on the bare floor, forming a perfect "splat" of potentially infected blood on both his hand and the concrete.

"Bastard!" Moto said and quickly wiped his hand across his chest.

He looked up to see that John was now awake and looking at him curiously.

"Were you able to sleep at all last night?" John asked as he extended his legs with a yawn.

"Not really," Moto answered. "My phone is dead, so I could hear everything that went on. It seemed like every time I was almost out, something would jolt me back awake. I'm surprised you were able to sleep through it. The way they were banging around, it sounded like they were rebuilding the ship out there."

John's stomach growled violently. He rubbed one hand against it and pushed off the ground to stand. He raised his arms up into an action figure pose and twisted at the hip to pop his back. Looking at his watch, he noticed that it was already past noon.

"Hm, that's odd. They should've come for us before now. I can't remember the last time I slept 'til noon. Surely they didn't leave us here expecting us to gnaw these cans open."

"It's noon?" Moto asked. "No wonder the night dragged on."

"How long has it been since you heard any banging?" John asked as he knocked loudly before pressing his ear to the door.

"I don't know. It's kind of hard to tell when you're in and out of sleep. Maybe a few hours," Moto said as he yawned and ran his fingers through his short hair. He caught a concerned glance from John and realized why he'd asked. "You don't think...?"

John walked over to an opened, wooden crate and wiggled out a loose nail. Grabbing a can to use as his hammer, he walked back over to the door and began work at tapping loose the bottom hinge's pin. Moto grew suddenly concerned by the eerie quiet of the ship and pulled loose a small pole from one of the shelves, gripping it like a baseball bat. John pulled out the first pin and held it up to Moto.

"Even easier than I thought it'd be," John said.

"Are you sure we want to go out there?" Moto asked. "If the guys catch us, they're pissed. If they're zombies, they eat us. Shouldn't we just stay in here with the food?"

"If they're zombies, who's gonna steer the ship?" John responded as he pulled loose the second pin and started working at the third. "Besides, I don't hear any zombies out there."

"It's a big ship, John. I don't see the pressing need to get out of this room."

John pulled loose the last pin and turned to look at Moto. "No offense, but you've got better company in here than I..."

The bottom half of the door collapsed inward, hinging at the doorknob and making John jump backwards. A pustule-covered hand emerged with a grotesquely disfigured face following behind it. Its facial musculature was visibly stretching beneath the few remaining jaundiced strings of skin as the zombie let out a miserable groan. Moto recognized the man as one of the more aggressive, outspoken Russians from the night before. The zombie looked up as it crawled into the storage room and snarled at the sight of Moto and John backing against the opposite wall. It appeared as though the man had received a violent blow to the head. Dried, darkened blood now covered half of his face, and the rest had run down and absorbed into what remained of his shirt. When his weight shifted to crawl, Moto caught a glance underneath his loose hanging shirt. The man had been almost completely disemboweled. The destruction to what remained of his organs made it appear that the man had been made into a meal before rising again.

The more injuries Moto observed, the more amazed he became at the being's ability to function. As the zombie pulled clear of the door and started to stand, Moto stepped forward and swung the hollow piping at the creature's head. The brittle shelving piece snapped on impact, leaving nothing but a short, jagged edge in his hand. He instinctively thrust the pole's sharp

55

end into the zombie's eye socket. The thing slumped lifelessly to the ground without theatrics. The black, gelatinous substance which had replaced the man's blood poured neatly out the other end of the pole. It reminded Moto of the PVC pipe he would use in creeks when hiking in order to capture clean, flowing water into his bottle without stirring up silt. Moto caught himself staring at the even flow that was not gushing with propulsion as it would from a heartbeat, but simply flowing with the pull of gravity. Moto held one boot against the zombie's forehead and dislodged the weapon from the corpse, a small stream of black liquid still dripping from its eye. Moto quickly followed John out under the catawampus door and cautiously ducked outside.

Walking a short distance along the deck revealed a gruesome scene with bodies scattered everywhere. Many members of the deceased crew were still grasping makeshift weapons in their hands, now rigid with rigor mortis. One man's intestines had been spilled from his belly and trailed several feet behind him. A trail of blood marked the path he'd crawled along the deck before succumbing. At the beginning of his trail, it was obvious that the eviscerated man had been able to take some revenge against his attacker. The axe's head was stuck firmly in the wooden deck with a section of arm lying next to it. He went down fighting, John thought to himself. As the trail continued, the blood became noticeably darker before reaching the corpse. The attacker was still slumped lifelessly over the railing, one arm missing from the elbow. The haggard corpse's gray skin was splattered with the familiar black discharge and a knife wound to its temple. Someone else had finished the job, and John assumed used the same knife to lay the eviscerated victim to rest as well-- the knife still lodged in his skull.

Suddenly, the ship swung harshly starboard. Ahead they saw the reason for the sudden redirection. A small island was quickly approaching from dead ahead. It appeared to be too late to avoid the obstacle, and the two brothers dove to grasp onto the nearest bolted down object. The unavoidable impact thrust the ship further starboard, sending the zombie corpse overboard.

Soon after, the ship was motionless, and a loud banging rang out from up above. John raced toward the noise and Moto started to but stopped to first release the lodged axe. He'd need a weapon upgrade before pursuing the source of all the commotion.

At the top of the stairs, John found one of the Russians banging at the captain's latched door. The man turned, and John thrust his feet in front of him to stop his forward momentum. John slipped in a trail of gore the man had left behind and fell flat onto his back. The man's movements weren't yet rigid, but up close the inhuman expression and the dead pupils were obvious giveaways.

John's feet skidded along the metal floor as he struggled to get back upright. The zombie redirected his focus from whatever hid behind the door to John, and bared his blood-stained teeth. Almost upon him, the zombie stopped and let loose an involuntary spray of vomit that streamed seemingly without end. John rolled over onto his stomach and covered his face as best he could to shield himself. Moto reached the top of the stairs and saw the torrent of gore spraying out of the zombie's mouth and nose, soaking John's pant legs. Moto had never seen such projection behind vomit but for movies like *The Exorcist*. Ignoring his gag reflex, Moto started his rotation, and slid both hands to the base of the axe handle, heaving it in a perfect cutting motion and releasing it straight toward the infected Russian. The stereotypical whooshing sound indicated the great force behind the throw as the axe spun, splitting the air for one clean rotation before splitting the zombie's head. The lodged axe's handle clanked against the metal floor as the zombie fell limp at John's feet. Moto helped pull John back up to a standing position with a big grin.

"Dude, did you see that?" Moto asked. "I can't believe I actually got him!"

John nodded, and opened his mouth to speak before succumbing to the unavoidable impulse to hurl.

Whoever was behind the latched door must have been listening attentively, because, soon after the infected had been dispelled, the captain's door swung open. It was Jim.

"I'm so glad to see you guys," he said with red eyes and a relieved voice. He cautiously looked over the two men's shoulders and motioned for them to quickly enter.

"My God, what's happening?" Jim murmured as he sat. His eyes began to tear up, and he buried his face into his blood red hands. When the brothers said nothing, he finally spoke again. "I just froze. I don't know why, but I couldn't make myself help."

Moto inspected every hidden corner and closet, making sure the coast was clear. "We're safe, but there are a couple bodies in the bedroom," he said.

"It's okay now," John said and patted Jim on the shoulder. "What happened?"

"Man, and I feel terrible for not coming to get you guys," Jim said as he stood and began to pace back and forth. "I guess I convinced myself that you were safer in the food closet than any of the rest of us running around out here. At least the others were finally able to let you out."

"You mean there are more that survived?" Moto asked, hopefully.

"Well, I'd assume so," Jim said with a raised eyebrow. "No one let you out?"

"No," Moto answered. "We just broke out."

"Well..." Jim paused. "Didn't you come across anyone else on your way up here?"

Sensing from their body language that they hadn't, Jim fell back into the captain's chair. His eyes gazed forward blankly as he tried to process the realization that his friends were dead--or, even worse, had become one of "them".

"I don't know what happened," he started; his eyes still deadlocked straight ahead. "I wasn't able to fall sleep after everything that had gone on, so I decided to walk a few laps on the deck, you know, get some fresh air. After a while, I came across a couple different trails of blood. Before I'd decided which one to follow, I heard some commotion up here where one of the trails led, so I came to investigate. I was hoping at that point that it was just another overreaction to someone having a new scratch or something. When I walked up, the door was open and there was someone inside screaming like I'd never heard before. It was almost inhuman." Jim motioned toward the room where two corpses lay on the floor. "That guy was just attacking the captain. It was like he was on something. He was just snarling and biting and clawing. I've never seen anything like it."

"We've been seeing a lot of that lately," Moto said. "So what'd you do?"

"For some reason, I couldn't admit to myself what I knew was happening. I just yelled at him to stop. I screamed and threatened him, trying to reason with him, but no matter what I said he wouldn't even acknowledge that I was in the room; not until I threw a stapler at him."

John opened the door to the room to investigate the bodies, making sure there wasn't any chance of reanimation.

"I'll never forget the look on his face when he turned after I hit him with the stapler. I've never seen anything like that. I just froze. It was Manuel. He still seemed normal 'til I saw his eyes."

"I recognize this guy," John said while squatting down next to the man's body. "It's that old man that fell and hit his head."

"Yeah, that's the guy," Jim said. "He'd become a pretty close friend of mine, even though he didn't know much English. He was the only guy on the ship that could hold his own across the chess board from me. I guess seeing him like that, it just screwed me up. I couldn't do a thing. I just stood there and watched them fight."

John stood up from investigating and held up a 1911 .45 caliber pistol.

"I really thought the captain was done for as soon as I came in," Jim continued. "There was already so much blood. By the time I'd grabbed the toilet's tank cover for a weapon, Manuel was on his knees, just holding up the intestines and biting at 'em like a kid with spaghetti. The captain turned his head toward me and asked me to kill him. Finally, that snapped me out of it, so I hit Manuel hard in the head. That's what they were doing to the few that were around before you guys showed up. They said you've gotta hit 'em in the head. It worked, but what I wouldn't have given for that gun you found. I'm not gonna sleep for weeks. I thought killing Manuel would help me build up to hitting the captain, but it didn't get any easier. I was looking for any excuse to not have to do it, but his eyes were just begging me. The vibration in my hands when I finally hit him, that sound; I'll never forget that feeling. Never again will I be able to do that."

Jim sat in silent recollection for a moment, as John and Moto waited patiently for him to continue.

"God, it was awful. At that point, I just wanted to get out of here and go be around some other people who could do the killing for me. When I came and opened the door, though, there was one just waiting outside for me. He'd been there all night and morning, until you guys put the axe through his head. I wondered why no one else had come around yet. I never dreamed that it was because everyone was dead. We had no trouble killing dozens of the things back at the coast. I don't understand how they were able to overtake us like this."

"They're pretty easy to dispose of in small numbers," John acknowledged, "but all it takes is for one to catch you off guard. We're gonna have to sleep in shifts from now on, or find a safer place to hole up."

"You guys seem to have some idea what all this is about," Jim said. "Can you tell me what the hell is going on? I can't shake the feeling that this isn't real, that this can't possibly be happening right now."

"From what we overheard before, it seems like an infection or something has taken off," John said.

"More like an epidemic. Or pandemic?" Moto offered.

"Sure. Anyways, even the Chinese seem to be worried about how far it's already spread," John said.

"Yeah, I don't know what it is, but it seems like people that have been around it don't stay dead. I don't know what it takes to get infected, but if they've got jacked up eyes, bleed and puke thick, black crud, and start walking like a marionette with a shoddy puppeteer," Moto summarized.

"Are you saying what I haven't been able to admit?" Jim asked.

After the silence had lasted long enough, Moto chimed in. "Maybe not the George A. Romero variety, but yeah. I don't know how you could call these things anything other than zombies."

"I read about this, but I just couldn't bring myself to believe it. I mean, they've never been wrong before, but this was just too much," Jim said.

"Wait, the news about this has already leaked?" John asked. "What are they saying about it?"

"Well, last I checked, almost no one online seems to know about it still," Jim answered. "But this hacker friend of mine that runs a conspiracy blog that I've been following for years predicted all of this. He's usually more focused on politics and stuff, but lately he's been really diving into all this. The guy comes across as a complete psycho to most people, but his track record keeps me paying attention... at least, until he started talking about how some guy was picking up the research where the Nazis left off with chemical warfare, time travel, all that fun stuff. He lost me completely when he started throwing around the word "zombie". I guess now I need to read back through all of his stuff."

"Yeah, I'm afraid a lot of that might be more accurate than you'd ever care to know," Moto said.

"That guy sounds like he knows his stuff. Did he post anything recently?" John asked.

"I tried to pull up his blog on my phone last night when I couldn't sleep, and we were still close enough to the coast. I couldn't get the site to work but, it was odd, my emails were still able to come in," Jim said.

"Sounds like censorship to me," Moto said. "So, what do we do now?"

The question was becoming more and more annoying as it seemed that there was never one right answer anymore. Moto had always asked the questions, and depended on John for the solution, no matter the insignificance of the situation. He hated making decisions. Where're we eating? Whose car? Should we eat there, or get it to go? They were well-practiced roles between the two. Moto stood expectantly looking at John--anxiously waiting for the perfect, big brother-like answer he had always been able to produce in the past.

"We go home," John said after some deliberation.

A look of confusion spread across Moto's face. "You don't think we should bunker down on an island and let this all blow over or something? Why don't we go somewhere easy to defend, with our closet full of food and let everyone else fight it out for a while?" he asked.

"No. Home," John said decisively. "Mom made me promise when we left that I'd bring you home if it all hit the fan over here. Besides, we need to warn people."

"I don't think this is exactly what she had in mind when she said that," Moto replied skeptically.

"What do you propose, then, Gilligan?" John asked while fingering through dozens of rolled up maps organized in a wall of pigeonholes. "We go sit on some Corona-commercial-looking island, and lay in hammocks? Sit around aiming our guns at everything that moves? Or better yet, wait to run out of food? It'd just be a matter of time before some boat full of infected drifted ashore, and zombies'd eat us in our sleep. The ship has some food, sure, but they sure as hell weren't able to re-stock at port. Without refrigeration, half of the food will be gone in just a few days. Even if we went to a bigger island that did have some food and water sources, that would just mean there's that much more beach line to patrol. We would never be able to keep it contained. Don't forget those things can just walk around under water. The one thing I'm banking on is that this stuff hasn't hit home yet."

Moto hated when John rambled. It was like disagreeing with you wasn't enough. John had to completely annihilate your idea so that everyone knew that it wasn't worth the effort to disagree with him. He knew that John's mind had been made up, and voicing his opinion any further would be pointless.

"We do have more than enough diesel to get to the states," Jim chimed in. They had forgotten he was now a part of this decision too. "It doesn't sound like a bad plan. We'd have a chance to gather supplies and get ourselves prepared before the outbreak arrives. Heck, the U.S. might even be able to keep the infection from ever reaching their shores."

Moto mumbled loud enough to be heard. "Yeah, they have a great track record for preventing that kind of thing."

"The quicker we can warn everyone about this, the better chance we give them of keeping this thing under control," Jim responded. "We've got to let our government know what we've seen out here so they can take the right action before it's too late."

"You're really naïve enough to think that our government doesn't already know about all of this?" Moto laughed. "Hell, they probably started it. They're sure as hell not gonna give millions of people a reason to load up their guns and start shooting at anything that goes bump in the night. They have no shot at stopping this thing, and they know it."

"The important thing is that we give them every opportunity to," Jim said. "We can't just sit on this information."

"I have no doubt they'd do everything in their power to stop this from reaching their shores," John said as he pulled out the map he had been searching for. "The main focus for me is getting our boots to sand before they close up shop. *Then* we can spread the word and pray they don't lock us all in padded rooms."

"Good point," Jim nodded. "I'm all about keeping an open mind. But even I would never have been convinced of walking, dead bodies if I hadn't seen it for myself."

"If we're gonna do this thing, we've gotta move fast," John said. "I don't want to cruise up to the shoreline a day late and get gunned down after the paranoia has set in. I take it you know how to drive this beast?" John asked Jim hopefully.

"It'll take me a few hours to plot the course. We'd have to be careful not to get ourselves into waters where pirates are known to patrol. Cap never left me with anything too involved, but from there it's just a matter of steering, I suppose," Jim said as he dragged his middle finger across the heavily used map, searching for their current location.

"Point us the right direction, and show me how to drive this thing." John said as he walked over to the captain's chair. "You can plot while I steer. We've gotta assume that our window is already closing."

Jim visibly fought back his discomfort and inhibitions about forgoing the procedure. Deciding that John was right, he nodded and approached the chair. Before long, countries would begin doing whatever they could to keep the plague from their borders, cutting off all international travel and gunning down any and all boats or planes on approach. Allowing even one wrong person into the country could kill millions. Moto wondered if this split-second decision was going to do nothing more than that and allow these three to bring the infection to the States. He decided not to voice his concern. There was no reason to remind Jim about his own questionable circumstances, and start a conversation that could very well end up with him being locked back in the food closet. After Jim had reversed the propeller and unstuck the vessel from the island, Moto decided to instead be productive and turned to go clear the deck of the infected corpses that remained. Though he hadn't entirely agreed with the plan, something about heading home now felt right.

"We're receiving several reports of massive explosions along the coast of Puerto Rico. Some witnesses are even claiming to have seen a mushroom cloud, though nothing has been confirmed at this time. The U.S. is denying any involvement with the sudden attack as there are thousands of United States citizens still on the island. We will keep you updated throughout the day as we learn more."

As their trip back to the states neared its conclusion, John had finally been able to find a satellite radio station that was covering the recent battle. The group listened anxiously and hoped that it might actually shed some light on unknown details and, in some way, aid the survivors. To this point, though, there had only been conjecture as to what had most likely occurred that had resulted in the missile strikes along the Puerto Rican coast. Many guesses conflicted in one way or another and none of them ever seemed entirely plausible when lined up with John and Moto's first-hand experiences. It appeared that the brothers knew as much as, if not more than, any of the talking heads back in the states. The three were unable to find any other survivors aboard the ship but had been able to cleanse the deck of any potentially infectious materials.

"Initial reports claiming that the missile strikes were concentrated on areas occupied by the Allied forces are now believed to be inaccurate. At this time, we are not prepared to release any estimates as to the number of casualties, but we are hearing that the number is "significant". Many nations among the Allied forces are calling for retaliation, though it is unclear who the perpetrator of the attack is. No official statements have been released."

"Nukes?" John reacted. "Are they misreporting what we saw, or is this actually happening now?"

"As far as the states are concerned, they're gonna assume it's nuclear until they hear otherwise. Their finger is on the button, guaranteed," Moto said. "We've got to make landfall before the good guys find out much more about what's going on over there."

"We have just received confirmation from several credible sources that biological warfare tactics have been used overseas. It is not apparent at this time..." Static.

"So much for that idea," John said as he shut off the radio.

"How'd we lose signal?" asked Moto. "Isn't this satellite?"

"Maybe something was about to be said that someone didn't want to get out," John said. "There's no reason we should lose signal when we're only getting closer to the shore."

The glare of the setting sun gave an appropriate aura to their destination as the Carolina coast appeared before them on the horizon.

"Our best chance at getting to shore without being questioned and held as deserters is to take the life boat in after sundown," Moto said. "I say we drop anchor and abandon the ship. I know we've got to get ashore as fast as we possibly can, but not if it means more eyeballs. You've gotta assume they've got everyone on full alert now."

John hadn't dealt much in nautical practices, but Moto's assumptions seemed sound. There was no telling how long before all immigration was terminated, if it hadn't already occurred. The men decided that the fewer things they brought along with them, the less suspicious they would seem. They could always resupply once they had quietly made it ashore. Unsure of their chances at making a successful landfall, the group prepared.

In the time it took the men to gather what supplies they wanted to take along on the raft, the sun had almost completely set. They loaded up and sped off toward the scarcely populated section of North Carolina's shoreline with fishing poles, a spotlight, their ID's and wallets, and Manuel's easily concealed .45 caliber pistol.

-*Two*-

"The greatest trick the devil ever pulled was convincing the world he didn't exist." -Keyser Söze

Once the three men were safely ashore, they scurried inland to a residential neighborhood. They weren't thrilled to find that they were going to have to lay low in an upper middle class neighborhood until realizing that the area was dead silent. It wasn't vacation season for this area. The three approached a home with no parked cars, and only two lights showing. One illuminated the front porch, and the other was strategically left on in a front-facing window. Upon closer surveillance of the seemingly abandoned beach house, it appeared that their intuition had not misled them. It took no time at all to find a window left unlocked and the men were inside. They avoided any discussion or disruption until they were able to complete a quick sweep of the house to make sure that they were truly alone and then the feasting could commence. Avoiding windows and leaving the lights as they were was going to be key in not alerting any perceptive neighbors.

The group had quickly begun to regret not having brought along food or water in the lifeboat once they realized how many hours they had gone without a meal. In all of the excitement, they hadn't slowed enough to realize how famished they'd become. The men anxiously slung open the door to the fridge with the utmost hope of what might be waiting for them. To their displeasure, the fridge had been swept clean of perishables, leaving nothing but baking soda, ketchup, and ranch dressing behind. After finding that the bounty in the pantry was largely the same, Moto frantically checked the freezer, but to no avail. Ultimately, the men were forced to settle for dry food with long shelf life, similar to what they'd had available to them on the ship.

Picking out the foods they found most appealing, they all settled in an inner living room with no windows and took full advantage of the opportunity to just sit, eat, and relax. John found the television's remote control in an end table drawer and brought the big screen to life. He was anxious to see what kind of coverage the news had of everything that had been going on in Puerto Rico and if the cease fire had ended as a result. To his disappointment, the main news channels were discussing a new clean water bill and the overpopulation of animal shelters for the local county. After tearing through his beef jerky and eating what he could

71

handle of the Vienna sausages Moto slipped out of the room. He soon returned with a bottle of wine and three crystal glasses.

"Look what I found! I know we're not wanting to take anything we don't need, but come on; I think we've earned this," Moto said as he set down the glasses and began working at the cork. He paused when Jim awkwardly declined and left the room. "Really? If it's that big of a deal..."

"It's not that; he'll be alright. He's kicking himself for not bringing his cell on the life boat. It's driving him crazy to know what is spreading down there and not being able to warn everyone about it. He's wanting to get word to his sister, but he doesn't know her number. He thinks it would help to alert the media, but I've convinced him to wait until we can go about it the best way."

Jim returned to the room with a laptop in hand. "I think the internet is still working," he announced happily. "But my friend Leuschke's blog is still down. Unless he has it hidden from me, I bet I can find his number or email or something on Facebook."

"You should be able to find your sister's number online too, right?" John asked.

"Exactly," Jim said as he typed effortlessly. "Alright here he is, number and email. Finger crossed."

"Hey toss me that remote," Moto said to Jim. "There's no way nobody is talking about all of this. That's impossible."

After flipping through all of the channels twice, Moto left the TV on one of his favorite childhood movies.

Jim dialed the number into the home's cordless phone and waited anxiously. His eyes lit up, but only for a moment.

"Hey, it's Jim," he said, before furrowing his brow. After a long pause, Jim hung up the phone without speaking.

"It's bad," he explained. "Leuschke warned me not to speak and said that he's almost positive that they're watching him. He hasn't been able to get online or make any outgoing calls. He decided to drive over to a coffee shop and upload some updates on another site he has access to. He walked out to his apartment's parking garage and said there were suspicious-looking guys in a black SUV just staring at him. That's as far as he got. The line just went dead after that."

"Oh my God," Moto said. "FBI? Homeland Security?"

"There's no telling," John said. "But you better believe that they're gonna look into who called him. We need to be smart about what we do from here."

"We've got to get the word out however we can," Jim said as he closed the laptop. "Let's call CNN, email our congressmen, host a live vlog, anything. We just have to get the word out to a few people and it'll spread from there."

"Don't you think that would've already happened from your friend's blogging over all this time if it was going to?" Moto said after finishing off his first glass. "Any attempt that we make at alerting everybody is probably going to end in us being tailed by a black SUV of our own." He stood and walked into the kitchen to peek out the window. "I think we need to lay low for the night and stay off the computers and phones. Tomorrow, we can go start the process with people face to face instead of making it easy for them to track our every move."

"I'm with you," John said. "It's just a few hours until sunup. Then we can go rent a car and start tracking down our loved ones."

"I guess a few hours won't make too much of a difference," Jim agreed.

Moto returned with another bottle of wine. "I don't know about y'all, but there's no chance I fall asleep tonight without some self-medication. I don't want to look back on tonight and regret not enjoying my last normal night on earth as we know it."

"Go easy with the drinks, Moto," John cautioned. "Tomorrow's gonna be a long day. We need to stock up, find a car, and head to get Ma first thing. Jim said his sister is even farther West than that, so it's gonna be a trek. The last thing we need is for you to be hung over if and when this outbreak does reach us."

"I hear ya," Moto said with laughter as he rested his feet up on the coffee table and turned up the volume to the old comedy. "I'm actually at my peak when I've been drinking. I was just thinking that we should hold on to the little cash we have. Let's just put everything on credit cards for now," Moto continued as he sank deeper into the leather couch, tilting the bottle to see how much remained. "I'm pretty sure that's rule one of surviving a zombie apocalypse. Stock up on resources by climbing into debt that you'll probably never have to pay back anyways."

"That's actually a great idea," John said while swirling his red wine nearer and nearer the rim of his glass. "I initially wanted to avoid leaving a paper trail, but when you consider every angle, that's probably the way to go. We're going to have to use our ID's when we rent a car anyways."

"We should be fine. Jim called from the land line. This phone doesn't have any connection to us. Assuming they even know about us, they probably think we're dead and washed up on the shore of that Godforsaken island," Moto said while emptying the bottle into his glass.

Jim set down the laptop with a sigh and announced that he was going to shower. The echoing sounds of Adam Sandler's nasally laugh filled the room.

Early the next morning, John awoke to the throbs of an unforgiving headache and an alarm that he didn't recall setting. He cursed Moto for maintaining a steady supply of wine. He initiated a controlled fall off of the couch and stumbled toward the bathroom. Moto was unfazed with his head hanging off the edge of the love seat and his mouth gaping wide open, his snoring had finally subsided. Jim still lay in the recliner with the laptop propped up next to him. Though he didn't move and his eyes remained closed, John sensed that he too had awoken from the alarm. That is, if he was ever able to sleep at all.

John returned from brushing his teeth carrying a large glass of water that he seriously regretted not having chugged the night before. Moto hadn't moved an inch, but he had resumed his sporadic, deep breathing. Scanning the room, John found that Jim had apparently given up on battling Moto's deviated septum and had moved to a different room. Combating a half burp, half hiccup, John pulled his boots back on and began to search the house for Jim. Lying on the floor near the front door John found a hastily scribbled note. Skimming quickly, John surmised that Jim was gone and had no intention of returning. John swung open the door, but saw no sign of him.

"Moto, start stirring," John called into the next room.

He walked over to the recliner to check the laptop for any sign as to where Jim may have gone. There, he found that the laptop was no longer propped up between the chair and the end table. John tossed a few light coasters toward his brother's gaping mouth as he yelled out a couple of creative threats for what would happen if Moto didn't get moving. He went to check the outlet at the desk where the laptop's charger had previously been plugged, and saw that the charger too was gone. Jim had taken it. John suspected that he planned to go online and spread a warning about the outbreak.

"Get up!" John yelled louder and heaved the only object within his reach toward his brother.

"What the...?" Moto gasped and dodged to the floor. "Really? A freakin' paper weight?" he yelled from the hardwood.

"We've gotta go. Get dressed," John said without apology as he read the note more thoroughly.

"I can't not warn my family. I don't expect you to understand. Don't look for me. Thanks for everything. Good luck." -Jim

John was surprised with how fast Moto recovered and walked up behind him, greeting John with a coaster to the back of his head. Amidst an impressive yawn, Moto managed to ask about Jim's decision to disappear. Before John could finish reading the note aloud, Moto had returned to and flopped back down onto his couch.

"No, get up," John said. "We're still leaving."

"Why?" Moto asked, attempting somewhat successfully to drink from John's glass of water while still lying prone. "We wouldn't even know where to look."

"We're not looking for him," John answered. "But we *are* still leaving."

By the time the fog had lifted from Moto's head, they'd already arrived at the rental place. Moto perked up just in time to start a fight, arguing that they should go the more luxurious route and splurge for a Hummer. John was already breathing in to begin listing off some of the numerous reasons why they shouldn't before he remembered the realistic chance that they would never actually have to return the car. Possibly even more important, there was also a very real chance that they would find themselves in some situations that demanded good ground clearance and 4X4 capability. John was about to oblige before a large diesel truck parked further down the aisle caught his attention. After some brief debate about aesthetics, John easily convinced his car-savvy brother by pointing out that the Hummer's chassis was almost identical to that of a Tahoe. In addition, diesel would help avoid some of the predictable gasoline issues that would undoubtedly arise in the case of a major panic. Diesel would get slightly better mileage for such a heavy vehicle, but more importantly, they could re-fuel at any truck stop while all of the minivans filled with families lined up around the block for the gasoline pumps. The less volatile oil would provide a longer shelf life, and if possible, they could commandeer a large storage tank of diesel that could service both the truck and a large generator.

Not knowing how long they had before the outbreak stirred up a panic in their area, the Chow brothers decided to first check their mother out of the hospital, as this would likely be among the worst possible places to seek shelter for a shit-hit-the-fan scenario. If they were quick enough, the necessary supplies should still be readily available once they had secured their mother.

They knew the area well, having visited this hospital every chance they got in between stints of training that led up to their deployment. It had now been almost five years, though, since either brother had seen their mother. She'd been in and out of the hospital for various health issues for much of their upbringing, but being so far away only intensified the pain of being without her. Regardless of what situation they'd find upon entering the hospital, waiting until the next morning to visit their mother was not going to be an option. John feared that the faces blurring past in the hospital's hallways may no longer be those of the staff that they had come to know so well over the years. Even without the extenuating circumstances that had rewritten the course of their existence, it would take much more than a determined nurse to turn away the two sons.

It was already approaching sundown when John finally pulled into the usually packed parking lot nearest the main building. Clipping the curb with his back tire, John took a ticket from the dispenser to raise the lever arm. Moto had unbuckled and was stretching his neck to look for the best possible parking spot even as John was already turning into the first pair of adjacently vacant spots.

"Really? Why don't we just have mom walk home, then?" Moto asked.

"I'll pull around and pick her up," John answered.

"Look at this," Moto said, observing the truck hanging out into the aisle and blocking two spots. "I can't even tell which spot you were aiming for."

"It'll make getting back outta here that much easier," John said, turning his back as the truck chirped. "Lay off."

"Not as easy as if you'd have just backed into the spot like a normal person," Moto chastised.

"These rows are too narrow for this truck," John argued. "The turning radius makes it feel like I'm driving a school bus."

77

Moto let out a chuckle as he jogged to catch up to John. "You know the turning radius is actually tighter when you're going in reverse in a truck like this?"

"If your strategy is to flap your gums at me until I hand over the keys, then I'll just let you know now that it's never gonna happen," John said. "Besides, mom would never climb into a car with you behind the wheel."

The attendant at the front desk was leaned back in her chair, and barking into her cell phone at someone. From the sound of it, John guessed that this was that familiar argument when her boyfriend should know why she's upset, and not have to ask. The distraction made for an easy duck into the elevator without harassment for their social security numbers and thumbprints or whatever current red tape policy some lawyer had dreamed up. Their mom was in room 217 of the newest wing--a spot that they had fought like hell to secure for her. It was a large upgrade from her first room in the old wing where patients had to share. The televisions in the old wing were huge boxes of plastic instead of the familiar, more common flat screens that you now saw in most places. Moto always remembered looking up at the rickety stands that the TVs rested on, wondering how they'd still not fallen.

Upon entering the hall, though, a familiar plain-faced yet kind nurse approached the two. She was shocked to see the brothers, not just because of the long gap between visits, but because their mother had not been in her building for a long while.

"It's so good to see you two! It's been forever," the nurse greeted them. "Hey, did they not give you nametags at the...?" She cut herself off and dismissed the thought with a wave of her hand.

"Yeah, we had to come by and see mom first thing. How've you been?" John asked.

"I'm good, I'm good," the nurse paused. "Listen, I hate to be the one to tell you, but your mom isn't here anymore. She's actually over in Heldenfels... the cancer wing."

"What? Since when?" Moto asked aggressively.

"I'm not sure, but it's been a good while now. Hey, if you can wait a sec, I can get you a room number for her."

She returned with a slip of paper reading 237.

"Oh, she's still on this level?" Moto asked.

"Not exactly, you'll actually have to go up to level three and walk across the sky bridge to get to Heldenfels. The numbering over there makes no sense, so be sure to follow the signs," she said, giving each man an awkward hug, before they went on their way.

"Damn. Cancer," Moto said as they waited for the elevator. John didn't speak.

As they approached the unremarkable cancer wing in Heldenfelds, John admitted that he'd always assumed their mother would outlive her two sons, especially once they were deployed. The two gathered their composure as they drew closer. Her new room was an upgrade for the brothers in that it was on the near side of the nurse's station, giving them an uninterrupted path.

"Oh my God! What a surprise!" Their mom squealed when John stirred her awake. Moto rushed back and shut the door to the hallway as John muted the television. Family Feud was on. His mom had been addicted to the show for so long that he'd lost count of the number of hosts that had come and gone.

It was obvious by her looks that she wasn't doing well, but she was putting on a good show as if nothing had changed in all their time apart. The flowing locks of hair that their mother had always taken such pride in were now replaced with a bandana patterned rag. After brief stories and catching up, John started in with the real reason they were back.

"Mom, the truth is we're not here on leave. Something terrible has happened down south, and we did everything we could to get back here to you. We've got to get you out of here because we think this problem is gonna make its way back to the states... sooner than later."

Moto noticed the rolling tray table next to his mother's bed which held a picked over dinner with untouched pudding.

"Oh, Lord. You mean to tell me there's a chance I might die?" their mom laughed, shrugging off the news and slapping Moto's hand.

"Mind your manners. That's for Puddin'," she scolded. "I'm just so thankful to see you both again. I've probably written you boys a dozen different letters to explain everything here, but I could never bring myself to send them."

"You mean, that's *my* pudding?" Moto asked giving a sideways glance toward John.

"I know what I said," she replied. "Don't think that I'm any less sharp than I ever was because of a little cancer. It's not in my brain, for Pete's sake."

"Mom, I don't know what to say," Moto started.

81

"You don't have to say a thing, Marvin," she smiled. "Just your being here is an answered prayer. This is the last thing I needed to be able to die in peace; no one could've offered me anything more. Wait, scratch that. I need you boys to do one last thing for me."

"Anything," John offered. "What is it?"

"Well, two things, because you're gonna want to kill me before the cancer can after I admit this. One, no judgments. Two, take care of Puddin'." After a pause in which the brothers weren't even sure what to ask, she continued. "When I sneak out to the parking garage for a smoke, I always see a beautiful stray dog. All that he'll eat from my plate of what they swear to me is food is my pudding. He was so skinny. I just knew he'd die right after me once there was no one else to care for him."

"You're still *smoking*?" John asked.

"Well, seeing as you neglected the first thing for me, John, I guess you're in charge of Puddin'."

John sighed and sat down as he processed everything.

"Fine, but I'll feel guilty forever if I don't admit this one thing to you first," John started. His mother eyed him suspiciously. "There is no way I'm calling a dog Puddin'. I can't bring myself to that... not even for you."

"I would be disappointed if you *didn't* make him your own," his mother smiled. "I knew I could count on you. Just like I knew you'd keep your word for getting Marvin out of there if things got too hairy."

"Wait, you really asked him to do that?" Moto scoffed.

"Don't take it the wrong way," his mother shrugged. "You just get a little bit too excited when there's the opportunity for adrenaline."

"Oh, like you've ever been out there with me when I'm doing anything that involves adrenaline."

"I was with you after your father mentioned in passing that the speed limit sign near our house was silly and that no one could possibly be up to 60 miles an hour after the four-way stop just up the hill from it. You took it as a challenge, God knows why."

"A challenge I won."

"A challenge you won with your mother riding shotgun. Who knows what kind of adventures you dreamed up to keep yourself occupied in Puerto Rico," she said. "Marvin, could you please give your brother and me a second to talk? Just a second."

John's mother patted the edge of her bed as Moto shut the door behind him, gesturing for John to come sit next to her.

"There's a conversation that we've tried to have a few times, but it never plays out like I'd hoped. You've been dodging it your whole life, but this just might be our last chance to talk. You know you're the best thing that ever happened to me, right?" she asked.

"Sure, mom," John answered, avoiding eye contact. "What little girl doesn't dream about finding that special someone that is willing to share his Rohypnol..."

"Stop right there!" she interrupted. "I'm not talking about *him*. I'm talking about you."

"But I *am* him," John whimpered, tearing up. "I can't look into the mirror without wondering about him. How you can see me as anything other than what he did to you. I will never understand why you even kept me."

"John, I wasn't exactly innocent back then either. What do you think I was doing out there as a teenager? No one is denying that you came from a bad situation, but the situation doesn't have to define you! Whatever good things there were in that man, you got them. You sure as hell got all the best parts of me. I never would have made it this long without you, John. You were taking care of me when I was supposed to take care of you, and given the chance, I wouldn't change a single thing about you!"

John was crying.

"Your brother relies on you more than you will ever realize. Anything that I am, anything that he becomes, you did that. You are not that man's son. You're *my* son! For God's sake, you never even carried his name. You were *my* boy, and then you became one of the Chow boys.

"A difficult name to take on in middle school for a kid with my looks," John added.

"Stop changing the subject. You need to forget where the sperm came from. That doesn't mean a thing. If you passed your 'father' on the street, you wouldn't look twice. So don't give him a second thought. Don't put any more effort or time into that douche."

John couldn't help but laugh. He leaned in and hugged her after maneuvering his arms around the maze of IVs. "Now go get your brother."

When Moto returned, he could tell that John had been crying and was thankful to have missed the conversation.

"I know you don't want to call a dog Puddin', but he may not come to y'all without a little effort on your parts. It took me days to gain his trust," their mother said, "And, whatever it is, I don't care one bit about the big news you guys think I need to be informed about. Whatever has happened, whatever is coming, I don't want to know about it. Seeing you two was all I needed on my way out... that and my GSN," she said. "Thank you for remembering your mom and coming all this way, but I would just be more trouble than I'm worth. No regrets and no bitching about it. We had a good run," she said as she unmuted her show just in time to hear a sexually suggestive question.

"Don't worry, we won't try to talk you out of it," Moto sighed, trying to keep his eyes from watering. "You're a grown woman, and you make your own decisions. My money is still on you to outlive both of us, anyhow. John can't drive the big rental for shit."

"Dammit, Marvin, your language!" she slapped his hand.

The next morning, John groggily awoke in the awkwardly shaped chair next to his mother's bed, thankful he had been able to sleep at all.

"Code 44, 308. Code 44, 308," a voice echoed down the hallways.

"That one is heart attack," his mom said matter of factly. "You pick up on these things after so much time on the inside."

Moto was still fast asleep on the couch beneath the window where the sun was now spraying small, blinding dots of light through the blinds.

"You boys planning to stick around until breakfast?" their mother asked. "As much as I'd love to keep you around, I don't know how nice my morning nurse is gonna be if she finds that you stayed the night in here with me."

"Is it not anybody we know?" Moto asked with a stretch and a yawn.

"No, she's not nearly as good as the girls that y'all were accustomed to."

Another voice on the PA echoed down the hall. "Doctor Strong to pathology, Doctor Strong to pathology."

"That's odd," she said trying to sit up. "They usually call Dr. Strong as a code when they need some muscle for an unruly patient. I can't imagine why they'd ever call Dr. Strong to the morgue."

John took a second to process this before rushing Moto into action while trying to remain subtle enough as to not startle his mother. He sternly communicated to Moto that it was time, and the two started their separate, brief goodbyes with their mother. Knowing that no words could ever be sufficient for a situation such as this somehow made it easier to shorten the farewell. Their mom also understood the apparent gravity of the situation, and focused on the fact that her boys made coming to see her their first priority. Considering her condition, the men and their mother were all aware of the fact that this would be a final goodbye, though the words were never spoken. The necessity of an immediate departure was no indication of any lack of love for their mother, and she knew it and gracefully forced her boys out the door. On his way out, John ignored his mom's request to leave the door propped open and instead made sure that it shut securely.

"I think we're out of time," John whispered on their way to the elevator. "I mean, they called for assistance with an unruly patient in the morgue. What else could that mean?"

He pressed the down button, remembering a pathology sign down the hall from the cafeteria on the bottom floor.

"Do we just go take care of it?" Moto asked. "I mean, do we just start crackin' skulls? I can't see that ending any other way than with us being arrested."

"We couldn't realistically go public and do any good before," John started as the elevator doors slid apart, "but we *have* to do something now. If nothing else, there are probably worse places we could end up for all of this than to be safely behind bars."

Moto psyched himself up as the elevator doors closed in front of him, pressing the button for the ground floor.

"Ok. Let's do this."

The doors opened and the brothers stepped out, ready for anything. They glanced along the walls for any weapon they could use, be it a fire axe, a piece of a stretcher, whatever was available. A few steps out, though, John realized they weren't in the basement, but down the hall from the main lobby. After what seemed like several minutes waiting on another car to arrive, the elevator doors finally re-opened, letting off a joyful couple with their young daughter. The dad had flowers under one arm and a crutch under the other as they eased their way past John and Moto. The two hurried onto the elevator, along with two elderly women carrying to-go plates of breakfast. John pressed the Lobby button, and the doors sprang back open without changing levels.

"Where is the cafeteria?" John sounded a bit harsh in his confusion. He knew for a fact that it had been on the bottom floor.

"This is the old wing," one of the ladies responded. "The Heldenfelds tower doesn't access the basement."

The elevator began buzzing, having been held opened for too long.

"You have to go up to three and walk the tunnel back to the new Ornelas building. That elevator will take you down to the cafeteria."

John pressed three and released the elevator doors, allowing them to close, silencing the squeal of the electronic alarm. The elevator rose to the second floor and stopped at the destination of the two ladies. Unaware of the brothers' rush, the ladies held the door open momentarily and wished the men good luck in finding some food. Finally to the third floor, the brothers exited and rushed along the extending hallways, following the signs to Ornelas. Their steps grew faster and faster as their frustration grew, and even faster when they heard another request over the loudspeaker for help to make its way to the morgue, and now the kitchen as well. The time for using codes had passed, and the plea was no longer exclusive to only the hospital personnel.

Finally, they reached the Ornelas elevators and pressed the down button to call on a car. While they were waiting, Moto noticed that a large group of people had gathered around a television showing the news. Taking a few steps over, he could tell by the caption that a local policeman had shot an aggressive young child. He could overhear different people in the group that had gathered arguing about self-defense and police brutality. Turning back around, he was surprised to see that the elevator had still not come. Before he had even taken a step, shrieks and gasps erupted from the growing crowd around him. Moto stepped back over to where he could see the screen and observed a bleeding paramedic fending off a crazed police officer who was now completely covered in blood. A few nearby policemen opened fire on the man just as the news station was able to cut away from the live feed.

A staff member who had joined John in waiting for the elevator gave up and instead shoved open a nearby door into a stairwell. Moto and John quickly followed on behind him. Before they could enter, though, a bleeding man shoved his way out of the stairwell door and into the lobby. As the brothers began their descent, the sounds of panic that echoed up the stairs were drowned out by the squeal of a fire alarm. The steps became virtually impassible as the brothers rounded the lobby level, and faced dozens of people fleeing from the cafeteria. The nurse that they'd followed into the stairwell gave up and joined the crowds in escaping toward the lobby's front door.

The two men resisted the temptation to shove their way down the last flight of stairs, and instead helped those that fell and were in real danger of being trampled. Upon reaching the bottom of the stairs, the brothers saw that most of the cafeteria had been completely evacuated. Rounding a corner, the elevator came into view. A man in a Florida Gators t-shirt laid motionless on the floor with his torso in the elevator, blocking the doors from closing. Every few seconds, the doors would slide up against his body, pause, and re-open. The buzzing of the elevator's alarm was continuous. A zombie knelt next to its meal, tugging apart the man's flesh with its teeth. It appeared that the infected man had worked maintenance, and still wore his uniform neatly tucked into his khaki pants with name badge dangling. As Moto moved to claim a metal fork as his weapon, he saw that the victim was now an unrecognizable corpse with no face. The uniformed zombie bared his teeth at Moto, but it refused to stand and leave its kill. The zombie's slow, un-coordinated movements made for an easy approach, and Moto was able to quickly close the gap and stab the zombie with his utensil.

Backing away, Moto realized that the fork did not penetrate deeply enough, and the zombie rose in pursuit of its attacker. From nowhere, John appeared with a broken, wooden handrail and bludgeoned the undead thing until it lay motionless in the hallway. Content that it was finished, the two turned to investigate the morgue. As they approached, another fire alarm was set off. Flashing lights, sprinkler water, and piercing sirens all flooded the hallways simultaneously. Moto worked to arm himself by breaking loose an arm from a stretcher. Down the hall, a zombie appeared. It was obvious that the man had been a doctor, and his intestines dragged across the floor as he staggered toward them. With each uncoordinated step, his eviscerated bowels would swing in a pendulum-like motion and became entangled under his foot. Eventually, the length of intestines reached its full extent and tugged at his core, causing him to stumble like a child with untied shoelaces. Moto, now armed, quickly worked his way down the hall to dispose of the lone zombie.

"Wait!" John yelled ahead to Moto.

Glancing into the opened rooms on either side of him, John realized that they had all been overrun and now contained numerous zombies sharing their various kills. Alerted by the uncommon panic in John's voice, Moto turned to see more of the undead stumbling out into the hallway from the doors behind him. Moto and John fought to work their way toward one another through the growing mob as the remaining food sources were now becoming depleted and all the attention was turning to them. The movements of the undead were slow and awkward, but the brothers had to take care to avoid each potentially infectious bite. Attacking only those that they had to, the brothers regrouped and eventually fell back to safety near the elevators, plotting their next move.

All planning halted abruptly when the desperate pleas for help arose from a woman somewhere down the hall.

"Please! Stop it! Leave us alone!" the woman screamed as John searched frantically for a better weapon.

"We need a gun!" Moto yelled. "There's too many of 'em."

"No time," John said, his eyes lighting up at the sight of the dead maintenance man's cart.

John instinctively lifted a handled shelf section of the box that contained small screwdrivers and other smaller tools to reveal some larger, heavier weapons hidden beneath. He tugged at a large wrench and then noticed an imposing crowbar on the bottom of the cart. He tossed the wrench over to Moto and kept the crowbar for himself. The brothers made eye contact and exchanged a nod of mutual understanding. Moto ran in first, undercutting zombies in the chin with the heavy tool, sprinkling broken teeth across the floor. John's first swing came in sharp side down, and the crook of his weapon penetrated a muscular doctor's forehead. The doctor's legs buckled instantly, but John's crowbar went down with it, securely lodged in the thing's skull. John bent over and pressed his foot against the large doctor's head to dislodge his weapon.

"Use the blunt end!" Moto yelled while cracking a young nurse in the jaw as she approached John's blind side.

"The brain, not the jaw!" John answered as he pinned a now toothless but still standing zombie to the wall with his free hand. Jerking his lodged tool free of the doctor's skull, he swung the crowbar firmly into the toothless man's throat in one swift motion.

"We're good, we're good," Moto said as he brought the full weight of his wrench down on the pinned zombie's head, caving in its skull and spraying blood across John's arms. Their movements grew more and more connected like a well-choreographed dance as they worked their way down the hallway.

"Hang on lady, we're coming!" Moto yelled between gasps for air.

John reached over his brother's shoulder, grabbing the throat of a zombie that had suddenly emerged from a dark room, only illuminated by the flashing emergency lights. He stiff-armed the woman as best he could with his left hand and, once clear, side-armed the crowbar into her temple forcefully. The slight woman did a full 360° rotation before meeting the hard tile floor, splashing down into the rapidly accumulating sprinkler water. Moto voiced his thanks as John continued to attack each new threat, now just feet away from the women's restroom where the trapped lady called out from. John lifted his weapon, ready to swing, before realizing that the last man between himself and the bathroom was no threat. The man sat lifelessly hunched over in a wheelchair against the wall with no obvious bite marks.

At the restroom door, a heavyset elderly man had worked his arm between the door and its frame. He showed no reaction as the trapped woman repeatedly slammed the door against his upper arm and was concerned only with pushing forward to gain entry into the room. His humerus had been completely shattered, and the door appeared to be closing almost entirely with each slam, just a fraction of an inch from latching. Only strands of flesh and cloth seemed to hold the man's arm together. He never saw the brutal attack coming as Moto laid him to rest from behind with a mighty swing.

"C'mon, c'mon!" Moto yelled to the woman. "There's too many down here. We've gotta go now."

To his surprise, a shocked little girl's face appeared as the door cracked open farther. She was young, and visibly distraught. Above the blonde child stood the source of the earlier screams, an attractive woman who was still protectively holding the child back. Both of the girls' focus was on the mutilated body of the man that was now slowly slumping over against the doorframe. Moto couldn't help but appreciate that the woman had the kind of looks that forced a man to take pause, even despite her running mascara and frizzled hair. He felt the impulse to smile and introduce himself, but was interrupted upon hearing that John had already turned his back to the girls and was ferociously hacking his way back down the hall toward the cafeteria.

"Stay close!" Moto yelled as he waved them along with his gore-covered hand. "You hang onto her!"

The woman looked up from the mangled corpse and nodded, allowing Moto to catch direct eye contact with her for the first time. He stopped himself from gazing into the woman's deep, green eyes that were peeking out from behind her wet, brunette hair and forced himself to instead turn and assist John. Moto felt a hint of disappointment that the woman's face didn't reciprocate the same love at first sight kind of countenance that his own surely held, though he supposed that would probably be asking too much considering their predicament. He was shocked to find that the man his brother had left sitting in the wheelchair was now upright and almost upon him. He quickly disposed of the now mobile attacker and led the girls on their way.

Exiting the hallway proved much easier for the brothers than their battle upon arriving. Most of the approaching zombies were constantly slipping and tripping over the corpses that now littered the floor, allowing the brothers to dispose of them with ease as they progressed. Looking back, though, John saw that the girls had begun to fall behind both him and Moto. They were walking up on a zombie that lay on the ground with a now concave cheekbone, still alive and reaching out toward the little girl. The rapidly rising water which now covered most of the zombie's face and extended arm prevented either girl from seeing that he had not been incapacitated.

"Look out!" John yelled back to them, but the girls instead turned to look behind them. They panicked and were inadvertently now walking straight into the dead creature's grasp. John turned and broke into a short sprint. Seeing that the zombie had only inches before reaching the girl's leg, John resorted back to his childhood days. His baseball slide across the sullied water allowed his boot to reach the zombie's face and his crowbar to simultaneously slash the thing's outstretched arm just before it had captured a hold of the girl. He scooped the girl up by her waist and rose back to his feet to carry her the rest of the way. The woman's eyes were focused down into the water, and she stood motionless, ignoring the damp hair that hung down around her face. Sensing that the mother was in shock, John grabbed her hand and pulled it to his belt under the center of his back.

"Stay with me," he said firmly while making intentional eye contact. "Don't you dare let go."

The woman nodded. John felt the little girl's arms tighten up around his neck, and he patted her on the back with his free hand as he took off down the hallway. By the time the three had caught up, Moto was already dragging the half-eaten corpse out of the path of the elevator doors.

Moto jumped onto the elevator with the others just as the doors began to slide shut. A zombie appeared from nowhere, and poked its head into the doors, causing them to re-open. John bashed the thing squarely in the face with his crowbar, and sent it toppling back over the dead man at its feet. Once the doors had fully closed and they were all safely inside, John coaxed the little girl into releasing her stranglehold on his neck, lowering her to the floor. He stopped just short of setting her feet down when he realized that he'd almost placed her squarely in the middle of the man's eviscerated intestines, and instead set her down in the corner by her mother. Moto slapped the button for the lobby and showed the beautiful young woman in the opposite corner a small grin, which was anything but reciprocated. She instead answered his smile with a confused furrow of her brow as she tucked her wet hair behind an ear, and bent to pick up her little girl.

"What happened to Daddy?" the terrified girl managed between sobs.

"I don't know, sweetheart," the woman said.

"What was he wearing?" John asked in the most comforting voice he could manage.

"His favorite alligator shirt," the girl answered, turning to make eye contact.

Moto shot John a glance to make sure he had come to the same realization. The blood leaving John's face showed that he had. The Florida fan whose body had been blocking the elevator...

"Ok sweetie, we'll watch for him," John forced a smile.

The doors opened into the Ornelas tower's lobby, revealing a full-scale evacuation. It was bedlam. Stretchers and beds had been brought down and left by the staff, though now there were no staffers in sight. John assumed that they must have gone to retrieve more patients. It seemed that this was their planned drill in case of emergency, but John couldn't fathom why they had elected to leave all of these people sitting in the lobby alone given the specifics of the situation. The whole floor was quickly approaching pandemonium, with patients who were unable to fend for themselves screaming out for help or explanation. John motioned for the girls and Moto to follow as he began navigating their way through the maze of patients and toward the front door. As John approached the entrance, he saw that the doors had been barricaded from the outside, and spotted the flashing lights of some emergency vehicles parked just beyond the locked doors.

"C'mon," John said, grabbing the two girls' hands. "There's another way."

John turned to see a television showing a news anchor attempting to report on a riot in an unnamed city's downtown. The words scrolling across the bottom of the screen reported widespread panic nationwide, as dozens of cities were suffering identical fates. Moto called on the elevator while John remained glued to the report. The reporter was speaking about possible motivations for the riot when a speeding minivan careened into a zombie which had been staggering up behind her. The newsfeed was cut to a pale-faced personality behind a desk back in the studio. John recognized the man, but he looked different without makeup. The man apologized for the graphic nature of the content, and announced that they would soon be talking with a local man who had been censored for hours while attempting to warn people about the ongoing rabies-like outbreak. The elevator dinged and the doors slid open as the television screen cut to a live feed of Jim sitting in what appeared to be a coffee shop.

"Wait, they're talking about Jim," John argued momentarily as Moto held the elevator. Instead, the channel cut to commercial, and John conceded.

"I thought we'd have more time," John said, punching the button for the sixth floor.

"What is happening?" the woman asked. It was the first time she had spoken since they'd rescued her.

"There's no way there are enough authorities available to completely shut this place in," John thought aloud. "There are outbreaks going on all over the world. I know of an exit they won't have covered."

"There is a reason no one is using the elevators," Moto argued. "And especially why none of them are going up."

"How about a little trust?" John asked.

The elevator rose, uninterrupted, to the sixth floor. Once to the top, John peered out the window to the parking lot and spotted their rental truck. He was right about the authorities. The firemen, police, and paramedics were scrambling just to cover the main exits. The parking lots were completely un-guarded.

"Remember the Batman action figure from when we were kids?" John asked Moto with a knowing look.

"Wait… what?" After a pause, a look of realization spread across Moto's face. "From the sixth floor, though?" Moto asked.

John started off down the nearest hallway but upon reaching a corner heard the frantic whir of a tiny motor above his head. He and Moto both looked up to see a newly installed security camera aggressively turning left and right before stopping and looking back at the girls. Confused, John rounded the corner to continue on with his plan and again heard the even more frantic whirring of the camera. This time, when he looked up, the camera jerked quickly to the left and slowly spanned back right repeatedly.

"I think someone is trying to tell us something," Moto said. "I think they want us to wrap around to the left instead."

John stuck his head out around the next opening to the right where he had been approaching each time the camera had come alive. There, he spotted a horrific scene of blood and gore spread all over the halls with a large group of zombies standing idle.

"Ok, then," John whispered after he'd ducked back behind the corner. "We go left."

He began down the opposite hall and again heard the camera moving frantically. This time, it moved up and down as if nodding.

John and Moto ran down the bare halls, grabbing full, blue bags from plastic bins with signs that read *soiled linen* on one side and *ropa sucia* on the other. They took one bag after another and tossed them back down the hall toward the girls.

"I don't understand how you're planning to escape from the sixth floor," the brunette said, hiking up the little girl to rest on her hip.

John began entering vacant rooms and returning with armfuls of sheets and blankets to add to their growing pile.

"When we visited mom as kids," Moto explained, "we would always find new ways to entertain ourselves. Our favorite game was for one of us to ride up to the top of the elevator with our batman action figures. The other would go down to the loading dock where the trucks loaded up the dirty laundry."

The woman's jaw dropped and Moto knew that she understood. "You don't mean..." she started and glanced toward the laundry chute just next to John's growing pile of laundry. "You can't be serious."

"I've got plenty here to cushion the landing," John said while unloading another armful. "This is our only chance to get out of here. There is no alternative." He opened the hatch, and began dumping bag after bag down the chute. "Just wrap a couple blankets around your back and one between the wall and your shoes. Then you just push your feet against the wall opposite from your back, and let off a little bit of pressure to start the slide. Think of it like rappelling."

The woman said nothing, but her furrowed brow again betrayed her.

"It could be fun!" Moto said while wrapping a blanket around his shoulders.

John laid a blanket over the edge of the hatch's opening. Working as a spotter, John grabbed Moto's hands as he backed into the hole, butt first. Moto climbed up inside the tunnel, standing on the hatch's edge, and slowly squatted down even with the door's opening.

"Show us how it's done," John said as Moto shifted his feet over onto the blanket which John had previously placed. As he shifted his second foot, Moto sank into the dark hole suddenly, much more rapidly than he'd anticipated. Reacting quickly, Moto

97

pressed more firmly against the wall and slowed his descent before stopping completely.

"Works like a charm!" he yelled up to John and the girls.

The woman sighed, and a relieved look spread across her face. The little girl ran up and peered down into the shaft.

"I wanna try!" she shouted.

"You two want to go down together?" John proposed, holding up a blanket.

"Made it!" Moto's voice echoed up. "All clear."

"I can't believe I'm doing this," the woman said as she entered the chute. Once squatted into position, John handed in the little girl onto her lap, facing and straddling the woman like someone being airlifted to a helicopter by a rescue diver.

The woman pressed her feet to the blanket, and didn't budge an inch.

"Now you're gonna have to let up just a little bit to actually get down," John said.

"I'll do it when I'm ready," she barked. "I'll let you know when we're out of the way."

"I'm not going down the hatch!" John laughed as he shoved something into the woman's hand.

John smiled to the lady as her jaw dropped in objection. Losing her concentration, the woman unexpectedly began her descent. A moment later, the thwoomp of the laundry bags echoed up to him.

"Don't wait on me! I'll meet you at the truck!" John yelled down before shutting the hatch.

The woman paused for a brief moment after her long fall down the chute to give her brain time to process the pain that was surely coming. She was embarrassed to not have immediately been concerned for the little girl's safety, but the girl giggled with excitement. Once the adrenaline had been processed, the woman was able to accept that she too was completely unharmed by the desperate maneuver. Moto helped the two out of the receptacle bin, and waited expectantly for John.

"He's not coming," the woman said. "He said he'll meet us at the truck, and he handed me these keys."

Moto's impulse was to ask a clarifying question, though he already knew that the woman wouldn't have the answer.

"Well, at least we've got the keys if he gets his ass killed," Moto sighed.

Seeing the young girl's eyes grow wide, he realized she was not old enough for his language and quickly tried to deflect.

"Sorry, uh, what's your name, sweetie?" he asked.

"Hillary," she answered in a whimper.

"What a beautiful name!" Moto said while smiling up at the woman. "My name's Moto. And what's mommy's name?"

The little girl responded with a confused frown.

"Oh, no, no," the woman said. "I'm not her mother. I was just here to deliver flowers. I saw this one sitting in the cafeteria, a whole booth to herself, when everything went crazy. The staff all seemed to know her, but no one was there when everyone started to panic, so I just grabbed her and tried to find someplace safe."

Unsure of what a proper response might sound like, Moto said simply, "Well, I'm glad you're both ok."

Surprised when the woman didn't offer her name, or a "Thank you for risking your life to come save us," Moto turned to gain his bearings so he could lead them to the truck. He approached the edge of the loading dock and crouched down behind a stack of Texsun unsweetened pineapple grapefruit juice boxes as he surveyed the area. Miraculously, no soldiers were visible from that side of the tower. To get to the truck, though, they would have to round the front corner of the building and cross near the barricaded front entrance.

99

"Stay low, and follow me," Moto instructed as he darted out from behind the elevated loading dock and took cover behind a parked truck. As the girls ran to join him, Moto began to question whether he should leave them behind and just pick them up once he'd reached the truck. A banging rang out above them, and Moto glanced up to see that the three of them were now exposed to the hospital's upper floor windows. Blood was smeared across two of the patient's windows. In one of them, an elderly woman was clawing at the glass in vain. Moto couldn't tell for sure if she had turned, or was only injured. Just as Moto realized that the woman wasn't the source of the banging, a window from the tower's second floor shattered.

"Hey, stop!" a thundering voice rang out.

"Go, go," Moto instructed, sprinting for the front of the hospital. He glanced back to see a man in a security uniform leap from the second floor window onto the cover above the loading dock. Hillary turned and pulled loose from the woman's hand.

"Daddy!" she screamed, running to meet the guard.

"I was looking everywhere for you! I was so worried when you weren't in the cafeteria," the man said as he swept his daughter up into his arms. The woman and Moto walked to meet the man halfway.

"Thank you for rescuing her!" Hillary's father said while greeting the two with handshakes. "I don't know what I would've done if I'd have lost her."

Moto noticed a bandage on the man's arm, blood already seeping through.

"Of course!" Moto responded. I'm just so glad that you're okay. Hey, I thought you said he was wearing a Gators shirt?" Moto said, re-directing his attention to Hillary.

"Oh, she must've been talking about my Lacoste shirt," the man answered. "That's what I was wearing when I dropped her off in the cafeteria. I was so worried you guys weren't going to figure out my camera thing. I felt so helpless, just watching you on the monitors."

"Oh, that was you!" Moto exclaimed. "That was genius. We might not be here if it wasn't for you."

"No, genius was going down the laundry chute," the father responded. "I was screaming and cussing at you guys from the surveillance room. I had no idea what you were thinking, and you just kept taking Hillary farther and farther from me. When I finally realized what you were doing, man I'm forever indebted to y'all. Speaking of which, where's the other guy?"

"Oh, he's coming," Moto answered. "He's just gonna meet us over there by the truck."

As Moto turned to indicate the direction of the truck, he saw a member of the National Guard approaching with rifle ready.

"Stay just where you are," the man ordered. "We're going to need you all to come back inside."

"What the hell for?" Hillary's father asked.

"We're just going to screen you and treat you if necessary," the guard responded. "We have strict orders to keep you all together so we can contain the infection before it spreads further."

"Treat us?" Moto laughed sarcastically. "We just came from the lobby. We saw what kind of treatment is going on in there. It's a death trap."

Moto pegged the guardsman as a scared kid who had signed on with the National Guard in order to dodge being shipped out overseas where the real danger was. Moto considered taking a risk and going for the man's gun, which had probably never been fired outside of target practice. As if the man had seen it in his eyes, the guardsman turned and aimed his weapon squarely at Moto.

"If you'll all just come with me, we can get this all straightened out."

Over the man's shoulder, Moto spotted John off in the distance setting down a brindle-colored dog into the bed of their F-250.

"You can threaten us all you want!" Moto said just loud enough so that John could hear him. "You're just gonna have to shoot me, 'cause I'm not going back inside!"

The man took a step back and switched off his gun's safety. When no one spoke, he reached for the radio on his shoulder.

101

"No!" the woman yelled. "It's fine. We'll cooperate. Whatever you need."

She stepped closer to Moto and put a hand on his shoulder.

"Please, let's just do what the man says," she said, while Hillary smiled squarely at John as he approached. "I couldn't go on living if anything were to happen to you."

The guard began to lower his gun just as John came into striking distance and pistol-whipped him over the head with the 1911. The guard was out cold before he'd hit the pavement, and Moto quickly retrieved the guard's weapon.

"Where did you go?" the woman asked, shoving John.

"I had to take care of something," John said, holding his palms up innocently. "It worked out, right? I assume this guy is with us?" he asked, extending to shake hands with Hillary's father.

"Yeah, get this," Moto laughed, "He'd been wearing a Lacoste shirt..."

As Moto was gesturing with his hands, John snatched the keys away.

John sped out of the hospital's parking lot through a large grassy area to avoid the traditional exits which had already been blockaded with concrete dividers.

"I never caught your name, not Hillary's mom," Moto said.

"Brooke," she reluctantly answered.

"I love that name," Moto said. "For some reason it always reminds me of an old, rustic boys' camp we'd go to every year when we were little."

"It might have something to do with that brunette at the girls' camp being named Brooke." John muttered.

As Moto reminisced, Brooke turned to talk with Hillary's father. "And what was your name?"

"It's Steve, Brooke," he answered with an extended hand and a smile. "Pleasure to know you."

The roads had more traffic than John had anticipated, but getting around was still not a problem for the 4X4 truck as the entire police force was occupied. The group had decided to stick together for the time being and agreed that it would probably be smartest to head for the nearest store and load up on food and other equipment they found necessary before settling on a place to hole up. They had considered Steve's and Brooke's homes for sanctuary, but both lived in crowded apartment buildings that would not likely withstand a massive, city-wide panic. The group decided to seek out another more secluded shelter and save the apartments as a backup.

John asked, "So, Steve, I have to ask you, why were you upstairs while your daughter was down in the cafeteria? Wow, I'm sorry. That didn't sound so judgmental in my head."

"Don't sweat it, man. I work full time as a security officer for the hospital. Once Hillary's mother passed away, I took on a side job sitting in with patients to try and cover some of the medical bills."

"Dang, man, I'm so sorry," John offered. Moto and Brooke each made a barely audible noise and nodded in agreement.

"The staff all knew me, knew our situation, and offered to keep an eye on Hillary whenever I needed. The cost of a babysitter would've almost cancelled out the pay I got for sitting, so I had no choice but to take them up on it. Usually, she can come up to the patient's room with me, but the lady I sat with today can get kind of violent sometimes. My boss had me leave my sitting duties and get into dress when the first calls were coming out about the violent patients. Anyways, I ran down from the patient's room to the morgue as soon as the fire alarm went off. Then, I decided to go get her from the cafeteria once I saw how bad it was, but I couldn't find her anywhere."

"I had already taken her," Brooke noted. "I was going to lock us in the bathroom, but that plan didn't pan out so well."

"After that, I ran back up to the security office and used the new surveillance room to see about tracking her down. Next thing I know, there's my baby running around upstairs with a couple of dipshits I've never seen in my life," Steve laughed. "Thank you all again, by the way, for sticking your necks out for her. Truth be told, even if I *had* found her first, I don't know that I would've been able to get her out of there the way that y'all were."

Toward the end of his sentence, Steve began fighting back tears. Hillary leaned into him and Steve took his daughter under his bandaged arm. John pulled into a shop's lot and again parked with a vacant spot on either side. Without any planning or discussion, everyone quickly began filing out of the truck. The dog in the back didn't bark but leaned over the side rail of the bed, its tail wagging expectantly. The parking lot didn't seem overly crowded, but there was an uncomfortable vibe from the other customers around the store. Many of the people leaving had purchased bottled water, ammunition, canned goods, and the other usual scare items.

Brooke walked up to the dog and began scratching him behind the ears, causing him to pant uncontrollably.

"You're not going to leave the dog here by herself, are you?" she asked.

When Brooke turned to face John, the dog began licking her ear affectionately.

"It's a he," John noted. "You don't have to spend too much time with him, before it becomes glaringly obvious. And by the looks of it, he already likes you more than me. You want to hang out and keep him company?"

"So I guess that means there's no point in me requesting that we name it, Lyla?" Brooke frowned.

"Don't worry," Moto said, patting the butt of the pistol that protruded from his belt, "I'll stay with you and Mongrel."

"Um, no," Brooke frowned. "This beautiful dog is not going to be called Mongrel. That sounds like a dog with mange."

"You two figure that out. We'll be back in a few," John said.

John, Steve, and Hillary walked through the front door and saw that people had already begun stocking up their carts with as much as they could hold. John was relieved to see that the shelves were still, for the time being, mostly stocked.

"What do you think? Split up?" Steve asked.

"I like the way you think," John said, handing his cart to Steve and pulling out another for himself. "Let's do some damage."

John leaned in close enough to whisper. "Don't be frugal; there's a decent chance we're not gonna have to pay off our cards."

"Nice," Steve said, as he leaned back with a big smile across his face, and tapped a finger against his temple. "I like the way you think too, sir."

John reached back to his days of hiking at the summer camp to try and remember the essentials. If worse came to worse, he knew it would pay off to have one bag of the absolute necessities that was still light enough for carrying by foot. Number one on the list of necessities was always potable water. He had started off using a water filter that used a hand pump, but that took only a few weeks for the filter to become clogged. Later, he had upgraded to iodine tablets that made the water taste terrible. He had later perfected the measurements with Crystal Light packets to concoct his famous iodine wine and conceal the horrible aftertaste. The only problem with this method was just how many of the tablets and additives a person would have to carry for even a small group of people, and for what could turn into weeks or even months on the move.

The latest rage was an LED pen light that used UV light to kill off the single celled organisms. A friend had actually informed him that they didn't kill the original organisms in the water, but altered their DNA to prevent them from reproducing. He had never checked to see if that claim was valid, but from what he'd heard, the method was effective. For him, though, the price tag and necessity of carrying along all the extra weight of spare batteries didn't make it a viable option.

For John, the obvious choice was bleach. An old hiking buddy had taught him to put a few drops into a liter or so of water, and it would be good to go after about half an hour. He was initially nervous at the prospect of drinking bleach water, but he'd used the method for years without incident. He'd also learned to throw in some hydrogen peroxide to keep people from bellyaching about the taste of the bleach. Adding the peroxide after the bleach had time to treat the water would cause a chemical reaction leaving nothing toxic. It was an incredible method, and John was shocked by how few people knew about it.

It only took a few drops for each treatment of water, but John invested in several quarts of the potential life saver. Knowing that he too would've complained about bleach water as a child, he decided to also invest in hydrogen peroxide and several boxes of pink lemonade packets. He also snagged a few large containers of Tony Chachere's creole seasoning, and some smaller, more portable shakers. It was possibly his most multi-purpose purchase. Over the years, John had found that Tony made good on its claim of being good on everything.

John felt that most people now latched onto and complained about anything they didn't understand or that they found inconvenient. Even he himself, though he fought to focus on the positives, would catch himself griping about Congress or a number of other annoyances over which he had no control. He acknowledged that he couldn't prevent every discomfort, but he'd do what he could to at least cushion the blow that was sure to fall upon all of these inside pets if they were to be thrust into the great outdoors.

As he was loading up on some of the more common items, he realized that it may not even take a day for things like antibiotics or inhalers to be completely off the shelves, maybe forever. He met up with Steve near the front of the store. Steve had loaded up on a random assortment of goods. John observed at a glance that many of the items in Steve's cart would have been far down on his own list, but they would still be handy to have around in any case.

"Hey, man," John said as he pulled his cart up next to Steve's, "I say we head for the pharmacy after this and get what we can, while we can. After that maybe the Army Navy store to get some sleeping gear and packs... just in case."

Steve nodded and glanced down at his wound. "Man, I like where your head's at. Plan for the worst, and hope for the best. Were you a scout?"

"For a brief while, actually, but not like you're thinking, no," John laughed. "I actually know what I'm doing."

John considered asking Steve how he had received the wound on his arm, but decided to save the conversation for a more appropriate time and setting. Steve steered into the shortest line, but John elected to go down to the longer tobacco line.

"I didn't realize you were a smoker," Steve said. "I smoked most of my life, until this rug rat came along. I never would've pegged you for one."

"Well, I'm not really. I figure it's a good idea to load up on the addictive stuff before everyone resorts to bartering. I'd guess if things really turn south, it won't be long at all before these things become worth more than their weight in gold."

"I'm starting to think we really lucked out in ending up with you, John Chow. Always three steps ahead. I bet you're a hell of a chess player."

The two unloaded all of their items as Hillary entertained herself with the cart's old, frayed seatbelt that John was sure must be contaminated with salmonella and who knew what else. He watched, and considered that it might be quite a burden to have such a young girl tagging along, especially considering her father's significant injury.

The men paid on credit, as planned, and returned to the truck to find that Brooke hadn't given up on her proposed name.

"Lyla, stop," she laughed. "No one is going to want to pet you if you can't learn to let them without you licking them!"

"Seriously, Lucky, calm down," Moto added.

"No names," John said stoically as he pulled the cart up next to the truck. "I don't want y'all gettin' too attached."

"Whoa, you're the one who saved it, man! Are we just supposed to never talk to or about the thing?" Moto asked.

John knew that Moto was right, but, considering their current circumstances, he couldn't ignore the eventual heartache that would surely come if he allowed himself to care about the helpless animal. At least the mutt would be good for morale. And maybe with some training, the brindle could eventually pull its own weight around camp.

John conceded as he loaded the last of his bags into the truck. "Fine, but nothing too cutesy. Bob or Paul would work just fine. We're gonna head for a pharmacy and stock up on whatever antibiotics and stuff we can get our hands on. Maybe after that we'll go for ammunition and an ABC if we can find one."

Steve looked up with a grin as he unloaded his groceries into the truck's toolbox. "Now that wouldn't have to *all* be saved as currency, would it?"

The growing crowds of people were becoming increasingly panicked, and the traffic reflected as much. It quickly became commonplace to bypass a wreck and for all of the witnesses to continue on with an unnatural indifference. Just before making it to the pharmacy they were forced to dodge a young man in an SUV that had spun his tires and pushed an old woman's Cadillac far enough into the intersection that he could run the light. With all of the cops occupied, more and more drivers didn't feel that waiting for stagnant street lights was the best possible use of their time. As people saw others doing it without repercussion, more and more drivers began to completely ignore all of the traffic laws without a second thought.

Unfortunately, many of the copycats were not as cautious or experienced in driving outside of their usual practices, and for several people their instincts eventually failed them. In a shockingly short amount of time, many roads were becoming almost impassable for the average car. For the time being, the large truck was still able to jump curbs and cut through grassy medians in order to navigate around the ever expanding clusters of abandoned cars. They knew though, that it was only a matter of time before others would also become stuck in the perimeters surrounding the traffic jams, making some areas completely impassable. For the group to be able to gather all of the materials they'd hoped to, it would have to happen quickly, and they all agreed that their best option would be to briefly split up. In a rushed discussion, they agreed to separate into two groups with John and Moto being dropped at the pharmacy as the rest of the group took the truck to buy alcohol and the other items that had not been purchased at their last stop.

John was uncomfortable with postponing the purchase of guns and ammunition until last, but spotting a pharmacy across the street from an ABC was something he couldn't pass up. John and Moto watched from the pharmacy's parking lot to ensure that the truck arrived safely at the liquor store, and rushed inside to begin their frantic search up and down the store's aisles. Moto was noisily knocking anything that could possibly be of use into his basket, as the credit card balance was looking more and more like it would be of no consequence. Moto even collected a few maxi pads feeling that besides the obvious use, they could also come in handy in the event of certain injuries. Peroxide was added again, with a different use intended, as well as p.m. cough syrup, earplugs, and a number of other comfort items.

John thought to himself that everything was out of order, buying sleep aids before sleeping bags to keep warm, and liquor before ammunition. Given more time to plan, he would have done things differently. He wasn't even sure where the group was going to spend this night, much less what their ultimate destination should be for riding out the plague. He was certain that the more obvious spots were going to be overrun and overpopulated, likely becoming some of the worst possible places to go.

"Moto?" John asked, "have you put any thought into where we should go?"

"A little, but I just don't know this area anymore. I guess maybe go up to the top floor of a tall building?" Moto suggested as he eyed some energy drinks.

"What happens when somebody panics on the first floor, and lights the thing up with a Molotov?" John asked as he added a large box of matches to his basket.

"I don't know man, then don't ask me. We'll figure something out."

"I'm gonna go see about some antibiotics," John said. "You and Steve could both use them, just in case."

He made his way to the counter to inquire about what items could now be purchased without a prescription and got in the only opened line behind a man with an empty cart. John overheard that the man was having a similar conversation with the attendant. The old, fragile woman could tell that the man was lying about the reason for the ridiculous quantities he'd requested, and the exchange quickly escalated into shouting. From what John could gather, the man was trying to get his hands on asthma inhalers, antibiotics, insulin, and a number of other items that would prove to be extremely valuable in the near future. John, as a survivalist, had the same thought previously, but seeing the opportunity and pillaging were two very different things in his mind. The man was becoming exceedingly threatening toward the previously sweet old woman behind the counter. John couldn't stop himself from intervening when the man put a foot up on the counter and began to climb over toward the terrified clerk.

John grabbed the instigator from behind with one hand on the back of his collar, and pressed his opposite forearm against the man's calves, leaving him no chance to regain his balance, and allowing John to effortlessly sling the man down to the ground. The man sprawled with a wincing groan, and writhed in pain.

"Are you okay?" John asked the old woman.

After she nodded, John turned his attention back to the man on the floor just as the man tugged a pistol loose from the back of his pants. John instinctively reached for his own gun but remembered that he'd left the pistol in the truck with Steve and the girls. Instead, John was forced to hold up his hands in apology and surrender.

"You! Come over here and join us," the man motioned toward Moto with his gun. "Sit on the ground facing the wall with your hands behind your head."

They followed the man's instructions as he began to stock his cart full of everything that was kept behind the counter.

"This is the new world," John thought to himself.

The thought sickened him. This man and countless others like him who were probably once normal citizens would now be using the kindness and weaknesses of others to their advantage until no kindness or weakness could remain.

"No one try and be a hero!" the man commanded on his way out the door, dropping merchandise from his overloaded buggy along the way.

"Do I call the cops?" the woman asked, visibly shaken. Gunfire erupted just outside the door and the old woman ducked her head under her arms, staying tucked down in her position against the wall.

"I'm afraid they probably won't be able to come," John answered. "Things are starting to get pretty crazy out there. In fact, it might not be the worst idea for you to just lock up the store and go home. You probably don't want to be around for whoever else comes by. People are gonna be desperate."

"I guess you're probably right," the woman answered. Just then, Steve appeared with the thief's overflowing cart.

"Everybody okay in here?" he asked as he approached the counter.

"We're fine," Moto answered. "How'd you get the cart?"

"I was pulling into the parking lot, and almost ran over the guy. He pointed a gun at us, and tried to hijack the car. As soon as Hillary started crying, the dog flew across my lap and out the window straight at the guy. It was like something out of a movie."

"We heard the gunshots," John said with a concerned tone. "Is everyone ok?"

"Oh yeah, we're fine," Steve said.

As if on cue, the girls walked into the store. Mongrel led the way, surveying the room with his hackles still standing on end. Hillary was unshaken and whispered to the dog as she patted his upright hairs, trying to calm him.

"He was trying everything he could to get the dog off of him," Steve said. "The guy finally got loose by popping off a couple of shots into the air, but the dog had already bought me enough time to pull out the pistol you left us. The guy didn't stick around once he looked up and saw the business end of the .45 in his face."

"I'm so glad you're all ok, but I think I'm going to take your advice and lock up," the woman said. "It's just not worth it to stay here. Y'all are welcome to grab whatever you need, no charge of course. I'm just going to call home and give my husband a heads up while y'all get what you want."

"We couldn't do that, ma'am," John said, feeling Moto and Steve jerk their heads toward him.

"Please, take whatever you want," she insisted. "It's the least I can do, and heaven knows I'd prefer folks like you get it. By the time I come open up again, there's a pretty good chance the looters will have already gotten to everything."

"Do you think you can get home safely?" Steve asked, concerned that she was grossly underestimating the carnage outside. "Would you like for us to follow you?"

Moto had already begun rummaging for antibiotics in the thief's cart.

"Oh, it shouldn't be any trouble," the woman responded. "I don't live too far from here. I walk it every day."

Moto looked up from the cart, "You don't have a car here?"

"Well no, but like I said it's just a short walk," she said as she held the phone up to her ear. "Hm, nothing."

"The least we could do is give you a ride," John offered. "It's really starting to get ugly out there, and I'd hate to send you on your way without your husband even knowing to expect you."

"Well I suppose that would be nice," she said. "It is a longer trek nowadays than it used to seem."

The men worked quickly to gather the most important items, and were careful to only take what they needed.

Once they had locked up the store and were all safely in the truck, Hillary now sitting on Steve's lap, John offered that the woman was welcome to travel with them if she and her husband hadn't a better option. He knew that such an offer would not sit well with Moto, but after the conflict in the store John couldn't bring himself to oversimplify every decision into one that was purely motivated by self-preservation. He knew that if he started justifying easy decisions now, it would be a lot harder to go back in the future. Though he did now have to consider the well-being of Hillary and Brooke, he fully expected that the woman would tend more toward bugging in. Fortunately, the woman answered quickly before John could catch Moto's stare and feel the ramifications of such an offer.

"Truth be told," the woman started, "I should probably be offering you all a place for the night. I heard you discussing where you should go, and I imagine there's no safer place around these parts than on the other side of my husband's rocking chair. He and his conspiracy-theory, poker friends have told me all this was going to happen. He's been going on about all of this rigmarole for days now, and stocking up on food and such. He's probably going to be more than a little upset with me for not believing him, now that he was right about something for once. He kept telling me this morning not to go into work, and I promise you he's sitting out on the porch right now, just waiting for me so he can say 'I told you so.'"

Sure enough, just a few minutes down the road, as they pulled into the woman's driveway her husband watched closely from his chair on the front porch. The man sat with a shotgun laid across his lap. As the group approached, the old man lifted the gun and took aim at the unfamiliar truck. John noted that the house was easily big enough for them all, and fairly well secluded. With sundown rapidly approaching, they would be hard-pressed to find a better option for the night.

"Put down that gun, sweetie," the woman called out through the opened window. "We've got guests!"

"Well, I guess seeing how you've got your own food and all, the more the merrier," the old man eventually relented. "But y'all had better keep that little 'un quiet when they come."

"When who comes?" Moto asked.

"Oh, come on," the man scoffed. "You folks haven't been listening to them national news media types like my wife, have you? The zombies, that's who."

"We already know about the zombies," Hillary said proudly. "We killed a whole lot of 'em at the hospital."

"Well if that's so, maybe you'll be worth the trouble after all," the man said. "But why are you asking me 'Who?' if you already know full well who it is I mean?"

"I'm just surprised you're already so informed is all. We didn't expect that other people would know the truth about all that's been going on," Moto said. "I was worried about how we were gonna go about telling you all this without making you think we're crazy and kicking us out of your house."

"Shoot, boy. I've known about all this for a lot longer than any of you kids have," the man said.

"I seriously doubt that," Moto mumbled in John's direction.

"Come again?" the old man said with a grimace.

"Forgive my brother. He hasn't gotten much sleep lately," John said, giving Moto an unsubtle elbow to the ribs.

"Shoot. If you two are brothers, then I'm the heir to the throne," the man scoffed.

"Okay, okay," his wife interrupted. "The weather isn't *that* nice out here. Let's get you all on ahead inside and see about getting you cleaned up."

John just then realized how repulsive they all still looked after having run through the sprinkler water and zombie remains that morning. Moto's scrapes were no longer that noticeable, and it seemed he might make a full recovery. Now, Steve was the big concern, with blood still soaking through his bandages. All of the events that had brought them to this point felt like they'd occurred days ago, though only hours had passed. Every time they were able to escape the insanity surrounding the outbreak for a short while, John would find himself still clinging to the hope that everything was back to normal. Deep down, though, he knew that things were not, and might never again be as they once were.

"You all go ahead," John said. "I think I'll hold down this other rocking chair if you don't mind."

The old man cut his eyes toward John and then glanced at the rocker sitting vacant next to him. He couldn't come up with an excuse to secure his desired solitude quickly enough, so he grudgingly shrugged and agreed.

The man's wife leaned in to him and whispered, "Play nice, Virgil," before leaving him with a pat on the shoulder.

John held open the screen door for the old lady and his growing group of friends before taking a seat. John smiled at the man once they were alone, though the man made every attempt to avoid eye contact. Eventually, after John had been holding his pistol at the ready and sitting silently for a long while, he could've sworn he caught the man let out an almost undetectable grin. Trusting the progress, John stayed quiet and left the man to rock in silence. The man watched over his domain attentively, breaking concentration only occasionally to caress the accumulating condensation on his glass of lemonade or to pet the dog that lay silently at his feet.

While Brooke and the old woman attended to Steve's wound upstairs, John could hear Moto successfully entertaining Hillary in the living room. The voice in John's head was becoming more and more insistent that he not waste a single moment that could be used for planning and preparation for what lay ahead. He resisted, though, and for an excruciating, enjoyable while, John sat in peace.

116

"I can't believe what I'm seeing," the old woman said when she came back outside. "He hasn't kicked you off his porch yet? He never even lets me sit out here with him. Maybe it's me that's the problem after all," she said with a laugh.

"I like this one," the man responded. "He knows how to shut up. It's a rare thing these days."

"I appreciate that," John said. "But do let me know when you're ready to talk. I'd love to pick your brain about all this stuff if you ever get the urge to."

"Well, not yet you don't," the old woman responded. "Dinner is ready, and we're not having any of that talk at my table. Y'all come back on inside and eat something."

"Is Steve gonna be alright, you think?" John asked as he and the old man stood to walk inside.

"There's a pretty good chunk out of his arm--a lot worse than I'm used to ever seeing," the woman said. "We gave him and your brother some of those antibiotics from the store, though. Might end up with a pretty nasty scar, but I don't see too much reason to be concerned."

"Can you tell what happened at all?" John asked. "I don't know that he ever told us the details."

"Oh, he mentioned something about breaking down a door when he was looking for his little one," she responded. "He just must've scraped up against something I reckon."

"And it took a *chunk* out of his arm?" the old man asked.

"Oh, come on. I don't think he'd have any reason to lie. Now, enough with all of this gory talk; everyone is already in the kitchen. Let's enjoy a nice meal with some good company and leave all this nastiness behind for a bit."

"Sorry, ma'am," John said. "That sounds great."

The old man gave John a concerned look but nodded as if to say they would talk about it later on.

The dinner was lacking anything of significance, whether in conversation or in taste. The old woman got sick of everyone referring to her as ma'am and divulged that her name was Marie Jensen. The man, after some prodding from Marie, introduced himself as Uncle Virgil. The big meal that Marie had been going on about all afternoon turned out to be a rather simple lasagna, but was held as a delicacy in the eyes of the Chow brothers, considering their past several meals. Brooke and Hillary picked around at the main course before happily diving into the cheesecake that followed. John's concern for Steve's well-being swelled when he wasn't able to eat much at all from his plate. Even after a shower and fresh clothes, his face was an unnatural pale color. Steve was polite when conversation was directed to him, but he had otherwise grown increasingly subdued.

"Who's up for a game?" Virgil asked, shocking the table.

"He means poker," Marie interjected. "Don't get your hopes up for Monopoly. It's poker or nothing with this one."

Moto and John accepted easily, and Brooke promised to watch, but only after helping out with the dishes. Steve excused himself and asked for Marie to show him and Hillary to a place where they might be able to lie down. John was glad when Brooke spoke up and offered to keep her eye on Hillary if Steve needed to rest. John was beginning to fear the worst for the poor man and didn't like the idea of leaving him alone with the helpless little girl.

The only danger present downstairs was a danger to the brothers' wallets. It quickly became apparent that Uncle Virgil was quite a force at the poker table. He wouldn't even have to adjust his temperament from that which he'd shown during the peak of conversation to that point. John was mostly folding and taking in information for the first several rounds as Moto and Virgil butted heads. The worst hands for Moto were the ones where he thought he'd finally have the old man cornered, only to see that Virgil had been slow-playing his unbeatable cards. The game was a lot different from what the soldiers were accustomed to--during which the other soldiers would try too obviously to throw people off their scent when checking their hole cards for the first time. Uncle Virgil's face was an emotionless structure of skin and bone, and his eyes communicated nothing but boredom.

Finally, John turned over an Ace and a King, but didn't have to work very hard on masking his excitement. The exception was becoming the rule, and he was sure that Virgil would complete an improbable hand to take him for all he was worth. John called. To John's surprise everyone called and Moto revealed the flop, turning over an Ace, a King, and an Ace; a full house. Careful to mask any potential tells that the old man could pick up on, John imagined what two cards could possibly ruin the hand this time. There was only one Ace left in the deck, and, even if Virgil held pocket Kings, John would still come out on top. Outside of a miraculous straight flush, John was finally going to take down the table's bully. Deciding to play it slow, John raised the bet by the five-dollar minimum to help set the hook. To his horror, Virgil and Moto quickly folded their hands. John didn't even attempt to hide his disappointment as Moto congratulated him on finally taking down a hand and pushed the chips his way. John flipped over his two hole cards, showing the table his Ace and King.

"Nice hand, John," Virgil said with a previously unimaginable smirk.

It wasn't exactly the way John had envisioned breaking through the wall of stoical emotionlessness. Though Moto had failed to recognize it, this was quite possibly Virgil's most impressive victory yet.

"Thanks, sir," John responded, "but I can see that we're not going to be much competition for you tonight."

"Ah, you're not that bad," Virgil said.

"Would you mind a little side conversation while we play?" John asked. "I'd really like to pick your brain a little bit if that's alright with you. You could just keep raking chips while we talk."

"That doesn't sound like the worst way to spend my night," Virgil said while shuffling.

"Yeah, how'd you figure you knew about all this stuff before us?" Moto asked.

"What he means to say is, how did you come to get such a head start on preparing for all this?" John corrected. "Were you saying that you knew about this outbreak specifically, or were you just into the doomsday-prepper type stuff for a while? We were scouring the news and the web for updates and couldn't find much of anything before it all came to a head today."

"You just have to know where to look is all, I guess," Virgil said while expertly dealing out hands. "About a year ago, one of my favorite webpage sources was reporting on this doctor from Chicago who had gone and started testing some illegal stuff on people. They say he was trying to use cancer to fix Alzheimer's, or something crazy like that. They went to pick him up and take him to the slammer, but he was already gone. Fled the country's what my site says."

"Wait, is that how all of this got started?" Moto asked.

"Well, I can't say that for sure. But it's starting to sound more and more like that's the case. That same site reported that he wound up in China to keep doing his work--got a lot of funding, too. One guy posted some blurry pictures somebody took of some notes that got leaked out on a camera phone or something. It talked about one of his patients that died while he was trying out the newest stuff, ended up with a really bad fever. Well, they thought he'd died. A little while later, the guy wakes back up but he ain't himself no more, but luckily he was tied down on the table still. They said the guy was really violent and stupid. The fever had messed up the front lobe and some other important brain parts and was only working off of the simpler stuff, like instinct. All that was several months ago." Virgil dragged another stack of chips to his side of the table.

"Wow. It really sounds like that's a strong candidate for the source of all this stuff based off what we've encountered," John said. "Was it intentional? Do they know anything else?"

"There's never any tellin'," Virgil responded. "Not many people took those pictures very serious at the time, and you can't hardly read half of 'em anyways--especially me. Here lately, some people started to connect the dots with what's been going on. It doesn't sound too far-fetched to me either. The last thing the government would do, if something like this ever were to happen would be to tell us about it."

"Do you think it'd be possible for us to see the forum where all this was posted?" John asked. "I'd love to see if there's any more information on there that could benefit us."

"I don't see why not," Virgil said while bending down to take another peek at his hole cards. "After this game, of course."

Moto was glad to hear that they weren't going to stop mid-hand, because he had flopped an Ace high straight. If both John and Virgil were to call his sizeable bet, Moto would have an opportunity to win a large portion of his money back in just one hand. Not sensing too much danger from the cards that were shown on the turn and river, even though the river card had paired one of the cards from the flop, Moto pushed in the remainder of his stack of chips. His chair squeaked as it slid backwards, and Moto stood with a satisfied look on his face and both palms pressed down on the table.

"All-in." Moto said.

John began to count up his remaining chips to see how much remained in his own dwindling stack.

"But I will say that I don't know if you guys should be as worried about all this as you are," Virgil said while John timidly pushed his chips into the pile. "If there's one thing I've learned in all my years, it's that things are never quite as bad as they seem, and they're never quite as good as they seem either," Virgil continued as he flipped his cards, revealing that he'd hit both the turn card and the river to secure a game-winning full house.

Brooke returned from the kitchen with Hillary in tow to see that the poker game had already concluded, and the men were huddled around an aged laptop. Virgil was pulling up his conspiracy-theory webpage with Moto and John watching attentively over his shoulder.

"Yeah, here it is," Virgil said, standing to let John take over.

"Wow, this guy is saying that the zombie's muscles are controlled by the central nervous system after death, and that's why they're so uncoordinated," John said as he browsed through the lengthy posts. "Another guy agreed and said that their blood vessels gel over and react to electric pulses to control the body instead of blood flow. That sounds like a reach to me, but it would explain why you have to destroy the brain and can't just shoot them center mass to bleed them out." John glanced up at Moto before clicking for the next page. "There are a few nuts on here, but I have to say I'm impressed with the consensus they've come to so far. Whoa, what happened? Did your internet go down?"

"Now how am I supposed to know?" Virgil grunted as he slid back into the chair. "You're the one that broke the thing."

"Virgil, it wasn't his fault," Marie yelled out from the next room. "The news lady is saying that they just now shut the whole thing down."

Leaving the laptop, the group joined Marie in the living room to watch their last source for news. The ticker flashed updates that the United States government had shut down the internet temporarily for national security reasons. The rest of the screen showed a local reporter standing in front of a barricade talking about several ongoing, mandatory quarantines in the region. She also reported that a nationwide curfew was set for sundown and would continue to be strictly enforced for the upcoming nights.

Moto saw an opportunity and squeezed himself into the narrow gap that remained on the love seat next to Brooke while pretending to be fully focused on the newscaster. The woman on the television continued, saying that not only had all flights been grounded but that state lines as well as county lines were going to be indefinitely closed to any and all civilian traffic. She reported that, in an overwhelmingly unpopular decision, the White House had allowed for not only the National Guard but also for the rest of the available members of the United States military branches to enforce the new quarantines and curfews on U.S. soil.

"They're taking what little bit of freedom we had left," Virgil muttered just loud enough to hear.

"It's not that bad," Moto said. "We weren't planning to leave here anyways, right?"

"Boy, if you haven't figured it out by now, you never will," Virgil said. "They're not looking out for our best interests. Explain to me how shutting down the internet is going to help them fight this thing?"

"It was a matter of national security," Moto said. "We can't very well question their decisions when we don't have all of the information that they do."

"The day I stop questioning these morons is the day you'll have to carry me out feet first," Virgil scoffed.

Moto glanced to John with a confused look.

John interrupted, "Maybe it would be more beneficial for us to stay calm and just figure out what's best for us and control what we can control. We can waste energy all night talking in circles about this, but we're not going to end up in a better situation because of it."

"That's the kind of attitude that makes them free to do whatever the hell they please," Virgil said, standing up. "But I guess that's a fight that'll have to wait for some other time. It's about bedtime for us two old-timers." He began walking toward the bedroom and motioned to his wife.

"Oh, Brooke, can you show the boys where they're sleeping and where the towels are?" Marie asked as she shut off the TV by habit before following behind Virgil.

"Of course," Brooke answered. "Don't you worry yourself any more about all of us. You've already done so much. I'll make sure these guys get to bed soon."

"See you young'uns in the morning, then," Marie said. "Y'all listen to her and don't go stayin' up too late. I'll have breakfast ready bright and early."

Moto leaned over to John and whispered to him with a grin, "Bright and early, I'll be telling you all about how me and Brooke made out like Bonnie and Clyde."

"I see the joke you're going for," John said, "but Bonnie and Clyde both got pumped full of lead in the end. They didn't really make out so well."

John was startled awake early the next morning to the sound of an apparent struggle in the next room. He jolted up to a seated position and saw that Moto was in the adjacent bed fast asleep. He had not completed his share of the all-night vigil. John rushed into the hallway and hesitated for only a brief moment outside the closed door where the sounds were coming from. As the rhythmic breathing and thudding continued on the other side of the door, John wouldn't allow himself to pause and confirm whether or not something was truly wrong.

About the time Brooke reacted with a startle to his sudden intrusion, John realized that not only was she in no danger, but he was standing in her doorway wearing nothing but boxers. Brooke had apparently been working out to an old cardio DVD she'd found while listening to a low-talent but high energy band. She stood like a deer in the headlights, staring at John expectantly.

"Oh, oh, sorry," he muttered. "It sounded like you might be in trouble. I woke up and saw that Moto fell asleep on the job, and I guess I might have panicked a little bit."

"No, it's fine," she answered. "I just couldn't sleep at all. After talking to him for a while, I figured there was no point in us both staying up, so I took over his shift."

Becoming aware of his eyes' desire to drift down to her form clad with tightly fitting athletic pants, John forced himself to concentrate only on maintaining eye contact with Brooke as she spoke. He struggled to really focus on her words at all with the amount of concentration it took for him to maintain control over his eyes. Only now had things calmed enough for John to finally allow himself to really take pause and fully appreciate her beauty.

"It's pretty understandable to not be able to sleep after a day like yesterday," John said. "I actually question my own mental health after sleeping as well as I did."

"Don't get me wrong, I'm exhausted," Brooke said. "It's just my sister. I can't get her out of my head. I can't help but wonder where she is right now--if she needs my help."

"I'm sorry. I didn't even realize you had any siblings close," John said.

"Yeah, I've been doing my best to avoid thinking about it. I guess that translates into not talking about her. I can't let myself

127

picture her alone back at our place without thinking the worst, you know?"

"Believe me, I do," John said. "I had to leave my own mother to fend for herself back at the hospital. I feel this unbearable weight of guilt now every time I try to stop myself from thinking about her, but it's still nothing compared to what I feel when I do let myself think about what might've happened to her after we left."

John stopped himself from going into it any further after he noticed Brooke's unbearable expression. He was shocked at how natural he had felt in unloading his deepest emotions to the beautiful woman whom he still considered a stranger. John spoke awkwardly and without thinking to cut into the silence before Brooke felt any pressure to respond. "Anyways, maybe it's best if we don't leave it up to your imagination. What's stopping us from going to get her?"

"I don't know. We have responsibilities here now," Brooke said. "She's not exactly a few blocks down the street; it would take all day. What if she's better off where she is?"

"If you truly believe that she is, then fine," John said. "But if it's gonna keep nagging at you, I want you to know that we can make it happen. I'm sure Steve could use the extra day to rest up before we head back out. Virgil sure seems like he's warmed up to having us around, so I'm sure we could talk him into another day of company."

"When I was laying there trying to sleep, I actually thought about why I just left my perfectly good van back in the parking lot at the hospital. My sister really isn't far at all from there; we could go get both and be back before dark."

"The second car would definitely come in handy. We don't really want to leave all of our stuff exposed to the elements, and that's how it's going to be now that we have a full truck," John said.

"First things first I guess," Brooke said. "We need to see how Steve is feeling, and then we can mull it over at breakfast."

"Can we go check on him now?" Hillary asked softly.

For the first time, John realized that their entire exchange had taken place in front of the little girl who was still lying comfortably in Brooke's bed. John smiled at her as he thought back on anything inappropriate he may have said.

While the girls spoke with Steve, John dressed and went downstairs for a drink of water. There, he found Virgil emptying the ice trays into a top dollar cooler, and refilling the trays with water. When John inquired about it, Virgil explained that there was probably a decent chance of the power going down, considering everything that was taking place. To avoid losing all of the contents of their refrigerator, should that happen, Virgil was going to accumulate as much ice as he could. John considered how obvious the idea was, but that he would've never thought to do it. He nodded and asked Virgil if he should fill the bath tubs with potable water, like his mom used to do before hurricanes made landfall. Virgil was a fan of the idea.

At breakfast, no opposition was raised when Brooke mentioned her intentions of returning to the hospital and picking up her sister in the city. John had feared that Virgil would be resistant to any commitment of housing their group indefinitely, but most of the energy around the table was directed at Moto's being late for breakfast. Steve had declined any interest in battling his way down the stairs and elected to have a muffin and some orange juice brought up to him instead. Marie was optimistic about his recovery and reported that he had survived the night without his condition worsening, but John remained skeptical.

After breakfast, John pulled Moto aside to ask if he would be okay staying behind to help Virgil keep watch over the house while he and Brooke took the day trip to retrieve her van and sister. He also stressed the importance of keeping a close eye on Steve's condition. Moto understood John's reasoning and forced himself to come to terms with the fact that he didn't have much of a chance at securing Brooke's heart.

"Fine, spend some quality time with your girl," Moto conceded. "All she'll talk to me about is you, anyways. I was giving her some of my best lines last night, but, no matter what I threw at her, she just kept asking about you. You owe me by the way. God help me I don't know why, but I put in a good word for you, and, just a heads up, you're really into books and poetry if she asks."

"Believe it or not, my first priority right now is not some chick," John said. "I've got a million other things going on, if you haven't noticed, and, even if I was looking, she's not my type."

131

Sensing that Moto knew him too well to buy his bit, John continued. "Fine, what kind of poetry specifically?"

"You'll have to do your own leg work from now on," Moto answered. "I'm actually back to hoping you'll strike out, and she'll come around."

"God, you're hopeless. But I appreciate the good word," John said as he turned to leave.

"But, hey," Moto interrupted. "So, if you're going back to the hospital, are you gonna check on mom?"

"Believe me, she's all I've been able to think about, too. I'll have to play it by ear, with the National Guard and everything. She made it clear that she didn't wanna know what was coming, and that she considered that to be our final goodbye. But given the chance, yeah, I'd like to swing by and see how she's doing and let her know the dog is ok."

"If you do see her, could you just tell her that I'm sorry for everything and just that I love her?" Moto asked with as much sincerity as John had ever heard him speak.

"You've got it man. I'll tell her."

Moto forced a smile when he saw that Hillary had returned from feeding the dog her leftover bacon. She ran up and grabbed his hands, begging for his help in solving an old children's puzzle that Marie had dug out for her.

Once John had packed a survival bag, just in case they should be delayed from returning that night, John and Brooke began their drive back to the hospital. There wasn't much conversation between the two; they were both anxious about what condition they might find their loved ones in. The streets were more navigable than John feared they might be, though it wasn't at all uncommon to drive up on a burned out shell of a car still smoldering on the road. The little bit of traffic that was still out traveled slowly in order to dodge the debris that had scattered across the terrain from burnt houses and ransacked businesses.

Upon reaching the hospital, they were happy to see that the building was still almost as intact as it had been before. Near the front entrance, John quickly spotted Brooke's van wrapped with floral designs but continued up to the front door since there was no sign of danger or the National Guard. As he pulled up under the portico, John noticed that all of the lights were off and a sign had been taped to the glass by the front door. It read that all patients, equipment, and meds had been moved to a new location outside of town that was serving as a camp for those in need of assistance.

"I don't like the sound of that at all," John said. "It doesn't add up. Why would they be better off in some tent outside town than to stay here?"

"I'm sure she's fine," Brooke said. "Maybe they were understaffed at all of the hospitals, so they consolidated everything and everyone. The military probably organized everything. They're trained for all this stuff."

"Yeah, I guess there was bound to be a run on the drugs if they'd kept everything here," John said. "Maybe this is the best possible thing for her right now. I am honestly surprised the building is still standing after the way we left it. I'm a lot more optimistic about her now than I was this morning, I'll say that much."

John dropped Brooke off at her van and followed behind her for the short drive to her parents' old place where her sister now lived. John was relieved when Brooke turned into the parking garage of a building that was in far better condition than many of the others they had been driving past.

His attitude changed quickly, though, when several levels up Brooke suddenly jumped from her van and ran frantically toward one home's open door.

"We're too late!" She yelled.

For a moment, John couldn't figure out what had set Brooke off, but he quickly realized that it wasn't as promising of a scene as he had initially suspected. John pulled forward until he could see that the car in front of Brooke's van had been left with its hatchback still open wide, and what remained of the groceries had been strewn about the concrete. Inside, the door to the apartment was also left ajar, and John calmly pulled out his concealed pistol and chambered a round.

"Go back to the van and stay there," he instructed. "Get your gun, and just wait for me to come back for you. I'll be quick."

Brooke was hurt that John didn't want her help in sweeping the apartment but secretly appreciated not having to witness what kind of scene she now expected was waiting inside. She clutched her gun and watched the numerous doorways and cars in the garage closely. The door to the apartment where her childhood friend had grown up had been sprayed with bullets and appeared as if someone had tried to kick it in. A car just a few spaces down from her van had been ransacked for whatever or whoever had been inside. She leaned her seat back to hide herself from the van's more lightly tinted front windows and watched in the side mirror as a group of three men on foot canvased the area. There was no doubt in Brooke's mind that they had seen her and that their intentions were anything but pure as they slowly approached. Before they had any more time to close the narrowing gap, Brooke swung the door of her van open and sprinted through the garage and into the apartment.

Brooke froze when she rounded a corner to find John pointing his gun directly at her face. After she explained what had startled her, John comforted Brooke and went to lock up the van, and investigate the suspicious group.

After calling out for her sister and getting no response, Brooke realized that her palms had become sweaty and were now making it hard to properly grip the pistol. She wiped her hands on her pants and walked to the nearby guest bathroom to rinse her face and calm herself. In the sink, she found bloodied bandages and scattered medicine bottles. Spurred on by new hope that her sister could be alive after all, Brooke couldn't wait any longer for John to return and instead walked straight to her sister's bedroom.

She was disappointed to see that the bedspread was untouched from being meticulously made one morning. John called out from the kitchen that he hadn't found the men and asked where Brooke had gone.

"I'm in the bedroom," Brooke yelled. "She's not here."

She was about to round the corner into the hallway as she had done hundreds of times before to head to the kitchen. She could effortlessly navigate her way in the pitch black if she had to. Something was off this time, though. Brooke paused and then froze. Standing perfectly upright and still, her mind processed that she had caught an almost undetectable glimpse of her sister's silhouette in her periphery. Brooke dared not move, even to release the breath trapped in her lungs, and slowly cut her eyes to confirm that her sister was standing motionless in the darkened bedroom across the hall.

Brooke couldn't remove her gaze from the large dark area that covered her sister's neck and extended downward across most of her shirt. A loose and ineffective length of bandaging hung down from the blackened wound. Brooke slowly raised her pistol, and her hand shook more and more violently as the gun's barrel pointed to her sister's face. Her sister's head tilted to one side, and, before Brooke could react, the creature was rushing toward her with surprising speed. Brooke froze until her attacker clumsily fell to its face and began crawling at her.

Brooke's gun slid out of her reach, and she began a panicked crab walk backwards into her sister's bedroom, fighting to maintain the slight distance between them. She tried to kick the bedroom door closed, but her pistol had wedged itself between the door and its frame. Just as the creature had begun to push the door back open, Brooke glimpsed the old accordion style, folding closet door that stood partially opened. Resorting to her childhood days of living without a lock on the very same door, Brooke slid the closet door the rest of the way open, causing its handle to wedge behind the knob of the bedroom door, jamming it from opening any further.

Brooke heard the rattling on the bedroom door stop, and a violent struggle ensued out in the hallway. Brooke's eyes clinched shut as she stayed lying on the floor, awaiting the inevitable gunshot. Instead, she heard John call out a short time later.

"It's safe; I locked her in the next room," he called out. "You can go outside if you don't want to be here for this."

Without fear of the suspicious men who had been wandering down the garage only moments before, Brooke collected her pistol and returned to the van. She sat stoically for what felt like several minutes, anticipating the crack of gunfire. When the blast finally did come, Brooke felt nothing except guilt for not crying over the loss of her sister. She sat numbly, waiting in silence for John to return.

Inside, John was tempted to collect anything of use from the place but decided against it after considering the condition Brooke was surely in. He left empty-handed and climbed into the van with Brooke. He made a few gentle but vain attempts at consoling her and getting her to talk. It took several minutes of enduring a one-sided conversation before Brooke eventually told John that she was just ready to leave and get back to the house. John tried to offer that she didn't have to drive the van back to the Jensen home if she wasn't up for it, at which point she reached across and opened John's passenger door before cranking the engine to life.

The two drove back separately along the same route they'd come in on to find that more people were now venturing back out into the streets. It was becoming commonplace for the two to hear the report of a single gunshot as they drove. John spotted a few different groups of undead that were barely visible behind the tree line alongside the major highways and a few that had even wandered up onto the asphalt. Less frequently, they would see survivors who had risked coming out from their shelters. Many of the people would try to flag their cars down, but John and Brooke continued on without hesitation. By the time they neared the house, though, the sun had begun its descent and the character of those who remained outside declined along with it. No one dared risk traveling the streets any longer but for the most desperate of looters. One wild-eyed hitchhiker even fired an errant shot at John's truck after he'd refused to slow down and instead swerved off onto the shoulder to avoid hitting the man.

Virgil was rounding the corner of the house when John and Brooke finally pulled into the driveway. He hobbled over to open the garage door and motioned for the two to safely stow the cars inside and out of public view.

"Things are getting bad," Virgil said as the garage door closed. "Seen some desperate looking folks come out this way. I was starting to worry about you two."

"It was a rough day, but we're ok," John answered with a handshake. "Why are you all sweaty? Is everything okay here?"

"Oh, sure. I was just cutting some more firewood just in case," Virgil said.

Brooke walked by without uttering a word. Her countenance had improved significantly from before, but even Virgil picked up on the fact that it hadn't been a good trip for her. He looked to John for an explanation, and John offered only a frown and a slight shake of his head in response. Virgil's reaction showed his understanding, and he patted John on the back before following him inside. The rest of the group, except for Steve, welcomed them back, and John was thankful that they all had sense enough to not ask about the trip or Brooke's sister. Moto explained that the radio had resorted to playing looping generic messages about staying home and what warning signs to watch for in those who might soon turn violent. After that, Virgil had pulled down his old police scanner. The dispatchers had already given up on sending units out to reports of robbery and looting and were focused only on the violent attacks.

"Everyone's gone completely insane," Marie said. "I never would have thought our neighbors would react like this in a panic situation. I always liked to think we would stick together and be all the stronger for it, but they're out there killing each other over gasoline and a couple days' worth of food."

"It ain't just that," Virgil said. "You wouldn't believe the calls about rape and murder. Stuff they don't even try to blame on the zombies. Just evil, evil people out there."

"Wait, where's Hillary?" Brooke asked.

"She's napping on the couch," Moto said. "She wanted to lay with Steve, but his fever went up. I really didn't want to leave her up there alone with him... just in case."

138

"Do you think…?" John didn't know how to finish.

"I'm not saying we give up on him," Moto answered. "But it'd be pretty stupid to pretend there's nothing going on. I hope it's just an infection, but, until we know for sure, I don't know how we could treat him like normal. I can't imagine a scrape from breaking down a door causing something like this. I confronted him about it and tried to guilt him into being honest, but he swears that he's telling the truth."

"What about the outside world?" John asked. "Has it spread everywhere already?"

"No way *to* know," Moto answered. "All sorts of rumors are floating around and most of 'em conflict with each other. If I had to guess, even the places that haven't been infected have still been affected by the outbreak. At this point, I'm as worried about other people as I am about the zombies--if not more-so. Mix in soldiers all armed to the teeth, and I can't imagine all is well."

"We've learned a little I think, though," Virgil said, pulling out a chair for himself while Moto went back to work covering the windows to conceal their light from the zombies. "From what we put together from the reports and from what Moto has seen, the ones who get hit in the head don't get back up. We also think that it matters where you got bit. Take a bite on the hand, and you're probably gonna be fine for a while. Take one on the neck or something, you won't last very long."

John observed Brooke out of the corner of his eye to see if she'd contribute after what they'd witnessed just hours before, but he she gave no reaction.

"Some people are saying that it's airborne, like the flu or what have you," Virgil continued. "We think they have to get you fair, though. Seems like we'd all be zombies already if that's how this thing was going. And besides, if that's really how it works, there ain't much we can do about it anyhow. This one old boy who really seemed to have it all figured out even caught himself a couple of 'em to test his theories on. He said that their bodies were focusing on keeping the important stuff alive by ignoring the less important stuff like their skin, heart, lungs, and the smart part of the brain."

"Wait, you lost me. The heart and brain aren't important?" Brooke asked.

"The guy said that they aren't important to the zombies, and that actually matches up pretty well with what John and I have seen." Moto said. "They somehow don't have to breathe. I wouldn't believe it from the way they moan and everything, but we saw them firsthand walking around underwater in Puerto Rico. The brain apparently only uses the most primal parts that control things like hunger, sight, smell, stuff like that. He thinks that's why you don't see them planning ahead, or using tools, or communicating with each other. They just walk toward what they think might lead to food and eat what they find."

"Okay, but what about the heart?" Marie asked. "How can you move without flowing blood?"

"You're right. They don't have circulation anymore. It's another crazy way they don't waste energy. Now, obviously this isn't 100%, and the guy is just a step past guessing at this point, but it does match up with a lot of what we've observed too. He thinks that they're so uncoordinated and everything because their movements are caused by electric pulses from the brain that go through that black gel stuff that's in their veins instead of blood. He says that, instead of the muscles flexing with blood to help them move, it's the central nervous system bypassing that part of the brain and bypassing the heart and the need for circulation altogether."

"So, it's like when you pull your hand away after burning yourself," John thought aloud. "Your brain doesn't even register what happened until your hand is already moving. I guess that makes sense. And that's why you can shoot them in the heart, and they just keep coming and barely even bleed."

"Right. The scientist gave examples of a lot of the different instances where he says zombies have already occurred in nature at different levels, like that ant fungus in Thailand and the zombie snail parasite. People are starting to understand how they work, but it's not really adding to what we already know about how to take 'em out."

"None of what y'all learned is necessarily bad news, but it doesn't change the fact that these things are probably going to outnumber us sooner than later."

"What do you mean?" Marie asked. "All you have to do is shoot them in the head, right?"

"Right, but fighting them is like fighting a hydra. You might cut a head off once in a while, only for another two to grow back. For every person that we lose to a bite, the zombies also gain one. It's gonna be like every other contagious disease and spread exponentially, but this one is gonna go until they start running out of victims. Unlike the others, this disease actively hunts us down. We can't just sit around and ride it out in hiding."

"He's right," Moto said. "We saw firsthand how quick it'll all overwhelm you. With the police, doctors, and soldiers here all going AWOL to be with their families, I don't see how the U.S. will fare any better than the island did."

Everyone froze at the sound of gunshots just outside the house. John went to the next room and peeked out from behind the trash bag that Moto had taped over the windows to see a group of young men wandering down the street laughing and vandalizing anything and everything that caught their eye. One of the boys was pushing a shopping cart filled with guns, alcohol, junk food, and an assortment of other goods. A zombie approached them after the loud disturbance, and the boys viciously battered it with their makeshift weapons before continuing their stroll through the darkened neighborhood.

"Just some stupid kids," John turned to say. "They're not coming this way."

Before he could peek back out, a barrage of bullets cut across the front of the house in a random spray of automatic gunfire. After it had stopped, John ran into the next room to check on Hillary and peek out a different window.

"Come here, sweetheart," Brooke said as she picked up the terrified, crying girl and carried her into another room.

Outside, John saw a severely drunk boy laughing so hard that he was now hunched over. One of the other teenagers walked up to him and pulled the Uzi out of his hands before kicking the laughing boy onto his back and shooting him. One of the larger

141

guys snatched away the gun and hung behind while the others dug through their cart, pulling out different bottles and goodies for themselves as they waited. After a moment, the dead boy began to rise up, only to be shot again by the larger man with the Uzi, this time in the head. John couldn't hear the boys' conversations, but he was pretty sure they were keeping count of how many zombies each of them had killed. Soon, the boys were out of sight, and John turned around to see that Moto was standing behind him.

"They're gone," John said loud enough for the people in the kitchen to hear, and then spoke only to Moto. "I don't think you have to be bit to come back as a zombie.

Virgil's preparations proved worthwhile when the electricity went out. They first worried that the teenagers had caused it, but the entire neighborhood had gone dark. Marie appeared with a basket full of candles and used a lit one to observe all the bullet holes littering her walls. John offered to help, as it appeared that the weight of the basket might be enough to pull the fragile, old woman over sideways.

"Thank you, son; we need a couple in every room and to leave a few of these lit in the bathroom overnight," Marie said. "I'm afraid little Hillary wet the bed last night. I think she was scared to leave her room in the dark. Leave a few of those with me, and I'll start lighting things up down here."

While placing candles all around the upstairs, John found that Steve was in a serious state. The sheets were drenched in his sweat, and Steve had begun to bleed badly from his nostrils. John informed everyone but Hillary of what he had discovered. Fortunately, after some medical attention from Brooke, Steve's condition improved noticeably. Once his sweating had stopped, and his fever had improved, the group decided to yield to Moto's persistent requests for a rematch at poker. Seeing that Virgil had already lit a fire, the group sat down around the table and played in the flickering light.

Not far into the game, more gunshots rang out in the street. John decided not to fold back the plastic that covered the window for fear of their indoor candlelight attracting the attention of whoever was in the streets. He pardoned himself and explained that he wanted to go observe what was happening from a good vantage point. He'd found a perfect spot on the roof outside his bedroom window. After some prodding, Brooke took his place in the poker game with Hillary sitting excitedly on her lap.

"How come that clock is still working if the 'lectricity is off?" Hillary asked, pointing to an ornate, wooden cuckoo clock whose pendulum still swung hypnotically.

"Well, it probably runs off of batteries," Brooke politely informed the little girl.

"Actually, it doesn't," Virgil said proudly as he laid down the flop. "I made that clock by hand a long, long time ago. It's completely mechanical. No electricity."

143

"Very impressive!" Brooke said, admiring the craftsmanship of the intricate designs. "Does it have the bird and everything?"

"Of course it does, didn't you hear me say I built it?" Virgil laid out the turn card, and tucked away his hole cards face down as he approached the clock. "You just have to raise this little lever on the side to make all the bells and whistles go."

Knowing what the next question would be, Virgil rotated the minute hand around the clock until it reached the next hour and a colorful bird sprung out from its door and chirped its song along with the cadence of bells. The room was very pleased with the showing, except for Moto who grimaced at his now worthless hand of cards. The table checked their hands, and Virgil revealed an Ace as the final community card. Moto raised, and after the rest of the table had folded, Virgil re-raised Moto's bet. Moto responded by making a big show of confidently standing up and pushing all of his chips to the center of the table. Virgil called without hesitation and flipped over his winning hand that had paired on the river. Moto plopped back into his seat, dejected.

"Use attack to exploit victory, never use attack to rescue defeat." Virgil suggested.

"Why is it that every time you decide to talk, you say something that sounds like it belongs in a book?" Moto asked.

"Are you serious?" John asked as he returned from upstairs. "You never read The Art of War? There's a lot of timeless knowledge in that one."

"I find that the more I learn, the more I discover that some dead guy has already put what I know into words in a way that I can't improve on," Virgil said. "And, to be honest, I don't feel quite so smart after that."

"And that's a good thing?" Moto asked.

"It's the only thing," Virgil answered. "Knowing might not bring you to a place of being giddy or rich. But that's not *why* you learn. You learn to avoid the mistakes of others and to gain an understanding of yourself and the world."

"Laying on the knowledge kind of thick tonight!" Moto laughed.

"Shut up, I want to hear him talk," John said. "Please, enlighten us."

144

"If there's one thing I'll leave you with, it's this. Happiness is a choice."

He paused to think for a moment, and no one interrupted.

"It's hard, 'cause the more shit you've lived through, and the more you learn about the world as it really is, the more you're pressed to get bitter and callous. If that's how it's gonna be for ya, you'd be better off being a giddy bigot that just doesn't know any better. But. And there's always a but. But, if you use that big world knowledge and put your stupid little stress and ego back into perspective, that's gonna be a powerful thing."

"Oh, Lord," Marie said as she re-entered the room. "You've got him going."

"But, that...remember what I said about there always being a but. But, that alone isn't gonna bring you happiness. And if you learn more than anyone ever has and it makes you the least happy person ever, well maybe you're not so smart for learning all that shit, now are ya?"

Brooke wanted to cover Hillary's ears but saw that the girl was paying no attention, just staring glossy-eyed at the cuckoo clock with a small smile.

"Happy is nothing more than a decision," Virgil aimed the purest smile John had yet seen him display toward Marie. "Just because I don't skip around smiling like a fool doesn't mean I'm not happy. The good Lord just didn't put me together like that. But every morning, I wake up, I pray my thanks for everything in my life worth having, which takes a while, mind you, and by the time I'm finished, it's a pretty easy decision that I've come to. I'm not just content. I'm happy."

No one spoke.

"Sorry, I rambled. That's why I don't talk much. You can't get me started. I don't know if I even made any sense there. But take it for what it's worth. Advice is the only thing us old farts are good for anymore."

"And winning a fortune at poker, apparently," Moto added.

Hillary had finally begun nodding off, and the back of her head was coming closer and closer to hitting Brooke in the nose. John re-took control of his stack, what little remained of it, and Brooke took Hillary to bed upstairs. Before long, the game was over, and Virgil had collected his effective nightly rent from the two brothers. More speculation dragged on about frontal lobes, Amygdalae, and, thanks to Moto's knowledge of Adam Sandler classics, the Medulla Oblongata. Occasionally, the conversation would be interrupted by the echoes of gunfire, and, eventually John quit investigating each occurrence. Later, once the wisdom being shared had degraded into ranting, the group decided to all turn in. John again offered to take first watch, and, after the recent occurrences outside, he'd decided to include the roof in his rounds so that he could also survey the condition of the neighborhood.

As Brooke lay in bed and listened to the hypnotically rhythmic breathing from Hillary, she reflected back on the horrors of the day and contemplated how she had come away from such a scene in the way that she had. Not even a week ago, such an event would have crippled her emotionally and left her as more of a liability than the asset she now knew herself to be for this hodgepodge of survivors. She wondered if being thrust into such despair at the hospital that first night had brought about her fight-or-flight instincts and somehow prepared her for the future horrors that were still to come. After some consideration, she decided that it wasn't so much her own doing, though that was certainly a factor. She contemplated how it was that, for each thing she had lost of her old life, she knew that there was even more being gained in the full Jensen home. She admitted to herself that any personal growth that was likely to come from her relationship with her sister paled in comparison to the potential future she had with this new family. Little Hillary. Already, she would die to save Hillary. Mr. and Mrs. Jensen, the grandparents she had never even realized she'd been missing. John... she took pause at the thought of John. Even without having any inclination as to what his thoughts of her truly were, she admitted to herself that he was perhaps the greatest personal gain amidst all of the losses. For the first time, the prince in her daydreams now had a face and a name. Whether or not it would play out was another matter. For now, she believed that maybe she could have a future with someone, and that was enough... for now.

John was finally comfortable and not slipping down across the loose granules of the old shingles during his vigil on the roof.

He had retrieved his backpack and secured one of the hiking straps around the exhaust vent pipe that protruded from the roof to hold him in place as he watched the movements of the night in silence. From out here, the gunfire downtown was even more audible, though distant enough to be of little consequence. He thought about all of the people that were dying in each brief moment that he sat in peace--thought about the other countries and what kinds of unthinkable horrors were being carried out on a global scale. When he was callous and bored of these morbid thoughts, he found himself thinking of happier things--things that were worth fighting for and, more importantly, worth living for. The true soldier fights not because he hates what is in front of him but because he loves what is behind him. He wondered for a moment if that quote was also from Sun Tzu, but those thoughts eventually gave way to images of seductively flowing locks of long, brunette hair, and the paralyzing, seductive batting of infectiously green eyes. And then, the day's weight overtook John, and he slept.

John awoke to darkness and the sound of Hillary crying from inside the house. In a rush, he sprung back inside the second story window to see Moto still sleeping deeply despite the noise and the lights being back on. John went toward Brooke's room where he expected he'd find Hillary. Instead, he found her sobbing on the hallway floor next to the bedroom door. A barely awake Brooke was kneeling next to her and consoling the girl while rubbing her back.

"What is it sweetheart?" Brooke asked.

Hillary calmed herself enough to get the words out. "The 'lectricity woke me up, and I thought it would be a good time to use the restroom, but, when I opened the door, I saw Daddy in there throwing up and bleed was coming out his eyes."

"Oh, honey, don't cry. I'm sure he's okay," John said in his most comforting voice. "I'll go check on him now, and you just go ahead and lay back down with Brooke while I talk with him, okay?"

Without waiting for her response, John shut their door and walked to the now closed bathroom door. Hearing some slight commotion on the other side, John knocked and tried to garner some kind of response from Steve to confirm that he was still in his right mind. Though his voice sounded anything but normal, Steve responded with as much comprehension and logic as John could have hoped for. He claimed that he had eaten too much in a brief moment of feeling well and assured John that he was fine. John asked that Steve remain in the bathroom for the time being while he went downstairs to raid the medicine cabinet for something that might help Steve sleep more comfortably through the rest of the night.

Before entering the kitchen, John jumped back in a startle when he heard movement in the room and saw flickers of light from what he thought to be a flashlight dance across the linoleum floor. John cautiously leaned around the corner before realizing that the vertical blinds covering the sliding glass door which led into the back yard had been blown into one another by the air conditioner. Just as he stood up straight, John felt a presence directly behind him, and spun around to find Marie. She explained between breaths that she had come to investigate all of the commotion going on upstairs when she saw his silhouette slinking around. Realizing that he had scared Marie even more than she had scared him, John apologized and attempted to explain himself. She assured him that it was no big deal and began to pour a glass of milk for herself while John peeked in between the dancing blinds. John saw that the source of the dancing light had been nothing more than the garage's flood light which was pointed at their back porch. John laughed to himself and explained that he had thought that it was a flashlight that was showing in through the blinds and into the kitchen.

He continued to summarize all that had occurred upstairs until Marie interrupted.

"Wait, which light was it shining through the blinds?" She asked.

"Just the flood light over on the corner," John answered.

John didn't understand the horror that spread across Marie's face until she whispered, "John, that's a motion light. It only comes on if something's in the yard."

When John turned to look again past the blinds, he was sure that he had caught just a glimpse of a silhouette out on the back porch. It had only been a small hint of a person between the slats of swinging plastic, but he was sure of what he had seen. Just as John reached for the door's lock, the electricity again went out, sweeping the back yard back into total blackness. John still stepped outside without hesitation and pulled his phone from his pocket to try and light up the unknown intruder. He couldn't hear anything out of the ordinary but for a whippoorwill's call. The phone wasn't bright enough to be of much help, and John twisted his ankle on something hidden by the grass. Bending down to inspect, John saw that he'd stepped on the handle of Virgil's axe and decided to keep it handy while he cleared the rest of the back yard. After a brief, unfruitful search of the porch, a scream rang out from upstairs that John knew must belong to Brooke. He slung the sliding door closed behind him as he hurried through the kitchen and up the stairs toward the sounds of panic, still clutching to the axe.

Moto met him at the top of the stairs.

"You've gotta get Hillary outside," he said. "Steve is doing really bad. He locked himself in the bathroom and he won't answer us."

The dog began barking from his spot on the porch. Before they could react, the crash of shattering glass rang out from downstairs, and Marie cried out for them all to run. Her yelling transitioned into screams of horror that were then overcome by the sounds of gargling. A steady, familiar moan resonated up the stairwell, accompanied by the sounds of ripping flesh.

"Shit!" Moto exclaimed. "They got her. They're in the house."

John rushed over to his bedroom window, and stuck his head out to survey the scene from above and settle on an escape route. Outside, a large horde of zombies was barely visible staggering about in the moonlight. A Jeep loaded with survivors unloaded a barrage of bullets into the horde as they fled.

"Okay, we're gonna have to do something else," John said with a forced, unnatural calmness to his voice. "They're covering the whole neighborhood."

When Steve began to bang at the bathroom door and moan that now familiar moan, John rushed the others into a bedroom and had them barricade the door from the inside. He told Moto that he was going back for Virgil and not to leave the girls no matter what. Downstairs, John saw that more than one zombie had come through the sliding glass door that had not fully latched, and were still chewing at Marie's lifeless body. One tugged with its clenched jaws at a long strand of intestines and pulled its head back like a howling wolf. Ducking his head into each door along the hallway, John finally found Virgil retrieving a gun from underneath his bed, muttering expletives to himself for not being more prepared.

"C'mon, we've gotta go," John urged. "They're surrounding the house. We have to get out now."

Virgil followed as quickly as his old joints would allow, while still loading rounds into the bottom of his 12 gauge. John wedged his axe firmly into the skull of the leading zombie and forced it to fall back into the others with a forceful push of the lodged axe's handle. It wasn't until he was to the stairs that John

151

realized Virgil had been unable to tear his attention away from what remained of his departed wife. Ignoring John's calls, Virgil began unloading rounds into the undead men in the kitchen. After the zombies had ceased with their futile attempts at getting back up, Virgil made his way over to John. As they reached the top of the stairs, though, there stood Steve. Somehow he'd apparently dislodged whatever had wedged the bathroom door closed, and Steve now stood at the top of the stairs facing John and Virgil with demonic, soulless eyes.

Virgil raised the gun and pulled the trigger without hesitation, but instead of a deafening blast, there was only a click. The two men scurried back down the stairs and heard crunching glass as more of the zombies entered the kitchen. From behind, they could hear a series of thumps as the uncoordinated Steve tumbled down the stairs and toward the living room. Without time to think, Virgil shoved John into the entry's closet and joined him inside. The two tried to remain as quiet as possible while Virgil loaded more shells from his pockets into the gun.

"I'll clear you a path," Virgil said. "Wait until it's clear and you get back up them stairs and save those girls."

"What about you?" John asked. "You'll be right behind me, won't you?"

"You just worry about what you hafta do," Virgil whispered.

Without any theatrics, Virgil slid back out of the closet and over toward the kitchen. He first took out the two zombies there with just one shot apiece to the head. Then he swung around and killed the momentum of a lunging Steve with a shot to the chest that blew straight through him and out the window behind. Virgil took careful aim and fired at Steve's head just as another zombie grabbed him from behind. The aim was compromised, but the scatter shot still grazed Steve tearing off a large chunk of his face.

"Get to it!" Virgil yelled as he thrust the butt of his shotgun into the zombie behind him, breaking its grasp.

John sprinted from the closet and past the severely hobbled Steve to the bottom of the stairs where he turned to call for the old man. Loud cheery songs rang out from the bird in the cuckoo clock on the wall just next to Virgil. He grabbed at the pendulum and was eventually able to silence the noise by clutching the pine cone shaped weights, but more zombies were already pouring in through the kitchen and the now shattered living room window between him and the stairs. The gunfire and commotion were attracting dozens of zombies in from the street.

"You can make it," John whispered loudly while kicking away a zombie.

Virgil glanced back at his wife's corpse as it began to move again and, without a word, calmly started loading the last of his shells into the gun. He looked up at John and shook his head slowly with an undaunted demeanor.

"Don't waste this chance," Virgil said. "You make it count."

John admitted to himself that there was no longer any realistic chance of getting out of the house with Virgil alive and forced himself to refocus on just getting the girls and Moto to safety. Once they had unbarricaded the door and let John in, they began bombarding him with questions about a plan and about the conditions of Steve and Virgil. John considered lying but, before even acknowledging the others, he found himself already climbing completely out the window. Seeing that the situation on the street hadn't much improved, John scurried to the crest of the angled roof to search in all directions for their best chance at survival. It didn't take long for him to come to the realization that they were not going to be able to make it anywhere on foot, and John climbed back down into the bedroom.

"I might have an idea, but it's kind of risky," John said.

"Well it's better than what we've been able to come up with," Moto answered. "What did you have in mind?"

"Girls, block this door again as soon as Moto and I leave. I don't know how bad it's gotten down there, but we have to run downstairs and get something."

"Please hurry back," Brooke pleaded. "We can't stay here much longer."

John and Moto paused outside the door while Brooke pushed the furniture back into place, and John explained to Moto that there was an axe in the kitchen that they would need. Luckily, it appeared that Virgil had taken out several more of the zombies before finally being overtaken. John navigated his way to the stuck weapon, and Moto was able to hold the remaining zombies at a safe distance with strategic kicks to their chests. By the time John had retrieved the axe, there were already several more zombies piling in behind them and closely pursuing the two brothers up the stairs. Moto sprinted to the girls' bedroom and began calling out and pounding on the door for them to remove the barricade.

"No, leave it. There's no time!" John yelled.

He pushed his way into the adjacent bedroom, and blocked the door after Moto had made it safely inside. Outside the door, it sounded as if dozens of the undead were accumulating.

"Stand back from the wall!" John yelled with his mouth against the shared bedroom wall. "We're coming in."

In what turned out to be surprisingly quick work, John used the axe to cut through the sheet rock and make a path back into the girls' room. The joy of their reunion was tamed, as no one but John understood how their situation had improved in the slightest.

It wasn't until John had backed them all away from the center of the room and began to hack away at the floor that Moto understood what John had in mind.

"We're right over the garage," Moto said aloud as soon as he realized it. "You're a genius, John."

"We're not out of the woods yet," John said between gasps for air.

As the hole was beginning to take shape, the zombies began to push with enough force to compromise both barricaded doors. Moto began throwing every remaining piece of furniture into piles around the doorways, praying that they would be able to buy enough time for John. The zombies were eventually able to force open the hastily blocked door in the adjacent room and began approaching the wall's opening. Though the hole wasn't as wide as he would've liked, John redirected his swings to the heads of the approaching zombies while Moto lowered the girls down into the bed of the truck.

"My keys to the van are in the kitchen," Brooke yelled up to John once she was safely standing on the garage's concrete floor. "I didn't realize it until now."

John tossed the truck keys down into its bed and yelled for everyone to load up and start the engine as he continued to fend off the intruders. Once the massive 6.4-liter engine had roared to life, John jumped down into the truck's bed and yelled for Moto to drive. The truck plowed through the flimsy garage door just as a zombie flung itself down the hole after John, catching its chin on the top of the tailgate and violently slamming to the concrete. John curled into a fetal position in the corner next to the truck's cab to avoid the flying debris as they sped through the massive mob of undead.

"Wait!" John screamed from the back of the truck as they turned onto the less congested street. Moto slammed on the brakes and turned to look at John--and then in the direction John was watching. Their dog was tugging hard at its leash which was tethered to one of the porch rocking chairs. John called out to encourage the dog and whistled as best he could. The dog lowered its head and pulled harder, dragging the chair behind him until the leash was freed from its leg as the chair tumbled down the steps. The zombies observed the dog as it sprinted and juked around them, but showed little interest in pursuing him. The dog leapt up into John's waiting arms above the lowered tailgate just before the nearest zombie had reached the truck. John strained, slammed the tailgate closed from inside, and thought to himself that perhaps Lucky was an appropriate name for the dog after all.

Unlike their Jeep in Puerto Rico, this truck was high enough to keep the zombies from being launched up and over the windshield. Instead, the larger truck motored effortlessly through and over the bodies with little resistance or damage. John knocked onto the back, sliding window and pushed the large dog into the truck before struggling to maneuver his broad shoulders through the narrow opening and into the back seat. He spread out half on the wide bench seat and half on the carpeted floor while he caught his breath. After the dog had stopped licking his face for a moment, John noticed the hopeful and confused face of Hillary next to him.

"What about Daddy?" She said simply.

John fumbled over his words, trying to reason logically with the little girl that her Dad wasn't going to be able to come with them any longer. After talking in circles for a bit, and abruptly redirecting sentences just before saying things that shouldn't be said to a little girl in such a situation, John silently put his arm around Hillary's shoulder. He pulled her in close to his side and said nothing until Moto came to his rescue from the driver's seat.

"Your Dad isn't sick anymore... he's not in any pain now," Moto said. "He asked us to tell you that he can't come with us, but that he loves you more than anything and that he wanted us to take care of you from now on."

"He's dead, huh?" Hillary said while wiping the back of her hand at her running nose, no longer crying.

John and Moto paused for a moment, unsure what to say.

"I'm sorry sweetie. Yes, he's dead," Brooke answered. "He was a very brave man, and we're all going to miss him very much."

Hillary nodded to herself and stared out her window as they drove.

After some discussion about the best place where the group could find sanctuary, Brooke offered that they return to the city and to her sister's apartment. John felt that it was closer to the high population of the city than he would have preferred but agreed to the plan as a temporary solution. As they drove on toward the apartment, John took inventory of what items had fortunately not been unloaded from the truck. Though they now only had one handgun for the group, there was still a moderate stash of food, booze, and other items left in the truck's cab. John counted what remained in his last pistol magazine and was thankful to see that he had also left an extra round loaded in the chamber. John stowed the small pistol inside his jacket pocket and began to rummage through the rest of their remaining stash until he heard a loud gasp escape from Brooke in the front passenger seat. He looked up to see that, on the side of the road up ahead, the Jeep that had fled just moments before them was now lying on its side, engulfed in flames. Half a dozen zombies picked at a body that had flown through the windshield and lay in a pristine lawn twenty feet from the wreck.

The entire drive was more of the same. The same route that John and Brooke had traveled only hours before was now a maze of bodies, vehicles, and zombies. There were several occasions when Moto was forced to drive up over the curb to avoid pile ups. He would drive just slowly enough to be able to avoid any debris that could puncture a tire, and just fast enough to keep out of reach of the countless undead who pursued. On the highway, the roads had become almost useless. The group agreed to work their way back to the less congested residential roads but still had to travel down the highway's grassy median until another navigable exit presented itself.

"Get out of here," John called from the back seat after hearing mud slinging up into the wheel wells.

"This truck can handle a little mud, can't it?" Moto snapped.

"Get out!" John yelled. "I just saw a sign for the French Broad River. We have to get back up on the road."

Moto took the advice without need for further explanation and cut the wheels toward the now steep embankment. Mud had already caked itself into the tires' tread, and the wheels spun on top of the slick, dewy grass. Moto immediately punched the gas and caused the wheels to dig deeper and deeper into the soft earth.

"You've got to rock it," John advised.

"Shut up, it's fine. We've got 4X4," Moto said and turned a knob on the dash.

The truck gained some traction in the front tires but still only slid along the side of the steep hill, gaining no elevation.

"They're coming," Hillary said softly from the back seat.

Previously unseen zombies began their approach from both sides of the highway above and descended toward the truck's bright lights and roaring engine. Moto realized that they had come upon a horde that had likely been the cause of the impasse on the bridge. He stopped his efforts paralleling the highway, and focused on making it back up to the asphalt. The tires quickly trenched down into the soft mud, and the truck lost momentum.

"Open the back window," John said.

Ignoring his usual need to understand, Moto swallowed his pride and opened the electric sliding window. John twisted his shoulders through and climbed back into the bed of the truck. A loud bang rang out when John dropped the tailgate open and began to jump up and down on its back edge significantly bouncing the truck. At the same time, Moto began to rock the truck up and down the slope at a slight angle by driving forward until he lost traction, and then quickly shifting into reverse and riding the momentum back through his rutted tracks and up the other side of the median.

Moto repeated this method, successfully gaining ground with each approach as the hundreds of nearby zombies were almost upon them. Seeing how near the zombies had already gotten, Moto cut the wheel up the hill to get out of his deepening tracks and gunned the engine in an effort to break loose. When the mud-caked tires again lost traction, Moto threw the shifter into reverse and sped backwards down the hill. At the dead on angle, though, the truck wasn't able to clear the steep hill to its rear. Though John was hanging onto the rails, when the tailgate dug into the dirt he was thrown forcefully back onto the grass and the truck slammed to an abrupt halt. Without hesitating, Moto turned the wheels back toward the descending creek bed and drove over the top of several nearby zombies. John heard the sound of Hillary's crying and the truck's engine creep away to be overtaken by the moans of innumerable zombies directly behind him. John ignored the pain of his hard fall and forced himself back to his feet. Not knowing what else to do, he sprinted as quickly as he could through the deep, loose mud toward the retreating taillights.

Relief flooded over him when he saw the truck's reverse lights illuminate, and the truck began to speed back toward him. The feeling was short lived, though, when the truck's lights revealed the numerous zombies between himself and the rapidly approaching truck. One idea stuck out in John's mind, and with no time to consider if there was a better one available, John took action. He timed his run so that he would reach the zombies who were already at the bottom of the median's ravine at the same time as the speeding truck. He began to question his plan about the time he reached them, but he forced his legs into action though his brain screamed for him not to. John leapt up into the air, and tucked his knees against his chest like a child trying for a record cannon ball. He then rotated his body so that his back would be the area to absorb the impact with the zombies and the truck when they inevitably collided.

The sound of his collision froze John for a moment--sure that he had broken his back or a rib at the very least. After a brief while, still holding his knees to his chest, John was shocked at the realization that he felt almost no pain. Hearing that the truck was still speeding backwards, John released his legs and reached for the opened back window. Before he had stood, though, a large zombie below him gathered its bearings and grasped at John. The thing tugged at his shirt collar while John fought to get an arm or leg between the two of them so that he could pry it away from him. Before he had made any progress, several loud thuds sounded from where the tailgate had previously been. Two more zombies were flung up into the truck bed, and John began kicking ferociously at the newcomers while fighting in vain to fend off the powerful zombie that ground its teeth only inches from his face.

He glanced up at his escape window to see Hillary there, dangling his pistol between her thumb and index finger. In a flash,

John released the zombie with one hand and thrust himself toward the gun with arm extended. The muscular zombie began overpowering his one arm as John grabbed the gun and tried to position it correctly in his hand. The zombie's warm, wretched breath assaulted John's senses as it moaned and pulled him in closer. Unable to buy any more time or find the butt of his pistol, John pressed the gun up under the thing's chin to delay its bite for the extra second that he needed to find the trigger. Finally, grasping it with his pinky, John rotated the gun in what he thought to be the right direction, and made a fist. The blinding muzzle flash and deafening report answered John's prayers, and the thing fell lifelessly beside him. The truck's momentum slowed rapidly, and without correcting his hold on the gun, John grabbed at the opened window with his free hand and fired four rounds into the beasts at his feet with the other. John didn't wait to confirm that the bullets had hit their target, but leapt back in through the opened window as soon as his legs were let free.

"Holy shit, you made it!" Moto exclaimed. "I can't believe that actually worked!"

"Really? That was how you envisioned it playing out in your head?" John said in an exacerbated tone. "What were you thinking, driving off without me like that?"

No one said anything for a moment while Moto navigated his way back onto the road and down to the previous exit. When they had reached the smaller, quiet streets Brooke reached into the back seat and patted John on the knee.

"I'm just glad you're ok, man," Moto said. "I didn't realize we'd lost you. I don't know what we'd have done without you."

"Well, you were pretty close to finding out," John sighed.

"Did I do good?" Hillary asked, looking up hopefully at John with her large expectant eyes.

"I'd say so," John smiled to her. "I think I owe you my life."

The deeper they drove into the city, the more destruction they found. On multiple occasions, Moto was forced to return down the path he'd already driven and search for a different route. They were still driving aimlessly around on the small, two lane roads when the sun began to crest over the eastern horizon. The light of the sun came as a blessing, but only at first. Though it illuminated the ever growing number of undead before the truck had to come within several feet of them, it also meant that more survivors were willing to risk some time outside of their shelters. At first, it served as a source of comfort to see other people still endeavoring to persevere. After witnessing the reasons some of the other survivors had ventured out, though, the change was anything but comforting. Bodies that had previously remained ambiguously unrecognizable in the dark cover of night could now be seen as obvious victims of crimes committed by those that were still among the living. Between houses, they could sometimes catch glimpses of grotesque groups of men chasing after frantic, fleeing women. Brooke was upset by how quickly she herself became callous to the sights. She was disappointed at how little time it took for humanity to devolve once no one was appointed to police them. At least, it appeared that there was no one left to police them.

After being forced into a detour through the slums, the crime became a common sight. They knew they needed to get off of the streets and find a place to take shelter, but they couldn't bring themselves to stay in an area where every other house had been broken into and gunshots echoed with telling regularity. Moto drove cautiously between the sea of abandoned vehicles until one of the more organized groups of misfits finally got the best of them.

After crossing through one natural-looking gap between several trees and cars, two men with high-powered rifles stepped out from their hiding spots at the next bottleneck. Moto threw the shifter into reverse, and looked back to see that a truck had already appeared from behind to block them in the narrow gap.

"Now I wouldn't try that if I's you!" One fat, bearded man yelled. "Y'all go ahead and step on outta that truck."

161

Having lost most of their guns at the Jensen house, the group had no choice but to comply. Brooke held Hillary close to her chest, though Hillary didn't seem to understand the gravity of their circumstance. Two of the armed men tied the dog to the truck's trailer hitch and began digging through the truck's cab while another two men shoved them all up against a nearby house's wall.

"Listen, you can take everything you want," Moto started.

"Well thanks for the permission there, kid," the skinnier, dumb-looking man laughed. "Since you say so, I think we're gonna go ahead and take everything, including that mutt and these fine bitches you've been draggin' around witcha."

A handful of zombies that had been tailing the truck wandered up from behind the abandoned cars. The skinny man spotted them, and chastised the fatter after he unnecessarily fired his gun at them.

"Just go poke 'em with somethin'," the skinny man instructed. "Enough with all the damn racket; and you're blowing through more rounds than we'n steal."

"Listen, you don't have to do this," Moto said after the fat one had walked off toward the zombies.

The skinny man showed his blackened, decaying teeth with his widest, repulsive grin and turned to look over his shoulder at the men who were busy emptying the truck. "You hear that, boys? We don't have to do this!"

The other men chuckled at that, and the skinny man turned back, no longer grinning, to see that he was staring into the barrel of John's last remaining gun. He opened his mouth to speak, and John fired--blasting apart the back of the man's skull. Though they weren't close, John quickly fired off two more rounds at the men next to the truck. He struck one in the chest before both ducked for cover behind the truck's engine. Brooke dragged Hillary and lunged for cover around the corner of the house while Moto and John stood behind a large tree as the uninjured men opened fire.

"Help me, idiot," the shot man pleaded from behind the front of the truck.

"Shut up, he's still shooting at us," the other man growled as he fired blindly over the hood.

162

The fat man finished disposing of the zombies, and began firing rounds into the tree trunk which concealed John and Moto.

"Do something," the injured man pleaded again. "I don't wanna die."

A single gunshot echoed from behind the truck, and the man's screaming fell silent. John fired blindly around the side of the tree toward the fat man as he returned, attempting to flank the two brothers.

"If my count is right, I believe you're empty," the fat man said as he closed in on the Chow brothers, waving for his one remaining friend to come out from behind the truck. "All you dipshits are dead," he taunted as he drew closer, ignoring the dog's rabid barking.

John peeked out from the edge of the tree and fired a round into the large man's chest before he could even begin to react.

"One in the chamber, dipshit," John called out.

Though John was truly without ammunition now, the last remaining carjacker ducked back behind cover. Moto and John stayed hidden and whispered about what they could do to take out the last of the men. John contemplated running after the rifle beside the nearest man's body, but the distance was still too great. The cowering man finally worked up enough courage to step out from hiding and began to cautiously approach the brothers, calling out threats to them in his thick New Orleans accent.

"First, I'm gonna gut shot each of y'all so I can leave ya here to bleed out until the zombies come to munch on ya. In fact, while you're laying here bleedin' out, I'm gonna take *your* girls, put 'em in the back of *your* truck and we'll all watch together while the zombies pick at your guts like a bitch sampling her Valentine's Day candy. I wonder who'll squeal louder, you two or the biatches."

A shotgun blast made everyone flinch--followed by a deep, intimidating voice calling out while the threatening man squawked in pain on the ground.

"Let us hear *you* scream, ya low-brow, slack-jawed, sumbitch."

An imposing, muscular black man in a police uniform revealed himself and walked over with shotgun in hand. He calmly approached the bloody man and watched as he writhed in pain on

163

the ground. The officer stepped heavily on the man's hand which had been reaching for his gun and raised his own large shotgun with one arm, pointing it squarely at the man's head. The policeman watched as blood pooled around the desperate man. The victim continued to hurl his threats until he began to cough up blood--mercifully drawing his last breath. The cop stooped to pick up the man's rifle and stood to see Brooke and Hillary step out from cover, shortly followed by John and Moto.

"You all ok?" he asked.

"Thanks to you," Brooke answered.

"Sorry it took me so long. Friends call me Sprite."

"So you're telling me that a guy your size, what, 6'6" and with the last name Sansom pinned to his chest got nicknamed Sprite?" Moto asked. "Your co-workers really dropped the ball on that one."

"They didn't really give me the nickname; my mom gave it to me forever ago," Sprite said.

"What's the story there?" Moto asked.

"Well, I guess it was actually the nurse. I was a premie. I think I came out at just over four pounds or somethin'; at least that's what they tell me."

"No way," Moto interrupted.

"Oh yeah, I'm serious. My mom was convinced that I was gonna die, and they were just racking up the bills. I was in the hospital for at least three weeks, and my mom never named me."

"That's terrible!" Brooke said.

"I mean, not really. She didn't want to get too attached to me knowing that I wasn't gonna survive. But the nurses had to call me something and put something on the chart." Sprite smiled to himself at some private thought before continuing. "When mom finally took me home, she officially named me after her pops. That got kinda confusing sometimes, though, so... Sprite it was."

"I was hoping you like drank soda on the sideline at your football games or something," Moto admitted.

"I do love me some Sprite," he laughed. "I swear it's the taste, not just the name, but no one ever believes me."

As they set to loading their things back into the truck, officer Sansom explained that he had heard all kinds of rumors about the goings-on around his neighborhood. The area had apparently gone to hell shortly after the outbreak, and the events of that morning were now a common occurrence. It was for that reason that the group gave up on their hopes of hiding out at or even making it to Brooke's old apartment.

After seeing how quickly the truck's resources were loaded back inside, they realized just how badly they needed to acquire more in the way of sustenance if they were serious about venturing out into the more desolate countryside. Sprite overheard John and Moto discussing the matter and interjected that he, too, had been working his way over to a nearby neighborhood store to load up on necessities when he'd found them. He had passed by the store the previous night and noted that it had hardly been touched because of the large number of undead trapped inside. Without any formal discussion, Sprite came along for the adventure.

Just as Sprite had described, they pulled up to find that the windows were still intact but filled with the silhouettes of staggering figures inside. In addition to that, though, it appeared that the noise from the trapped zombies had attracted even more to loiter around outside of the small building.

"Wow, I see why no one else has chanced a run at this place," John said. "You'd have to be crazy to try it."

"Ah that's nothing," Sprite scoffed. "We can handle that, easy. I mean, they're all so predictable. We've just got to plan ahead and execute. As long as we stick to the plan and don't do anything stupid, I can promise you won't end up pressing your face against those windows for the rest of time."

"You make it sound simple, but you kind of skimmed past the part where we come up with the foolproof plan," Moto said.

"We could probably take out a big chunk of them by just driving through 'em," Brooke said.

"The simplicity is good, but you're leaving too many variables," Sprite said, stroking his beard. "Why don't we avoid these guys on the outside altogether? The buildings are all so close, I say we just go rooftop to rooftop and stay off the ground."

"Wow, I never would've thought of that. I love it," John said.

"And from there, I think I can get us inside," Sprite said as he reached into the bed of the truck and pulled out Virgil's axe.

"Believe it or not, we actually have some experience in that part," Moto said.

Despite Moto's excitement, John nominated him to stay behind with the girls and left them with a pair of the guns they'd confiscated from the would-be carjackers. He and Sprite then walked down to a short building just a few lots from the store. Just as John had finished searching the perimeters for a fire escape or dumpster, Sprite emerged from a hardware store yielding an aluminum ladder.

"Hardly anything left in there, but apparently nobody wanted to drag this thing around. I figure we can use it to cross buildings without having to jump."

"Good thinking," John nodded. "I'm starting to think you might be worth your weight, which is saying somethin'. We might have to keep you around."

"Oh, no," Sprite said while holding the ladder for John as he climbed up. "I can't turn my back on my neighborhood like that. That ain't me."

"Well I hope you'll at least consider coming with us," John offered as Sprite joined him on the roof. "I hate to lay it out like this, but I'm not sure how long Moto and I alone can keep those girls safe."

The two pulled the ladder up onto the roof and laid it across to the next building as a make-shift bridge. Even with the other man holding it steady, the ladder wobbled significantly as they crawled over the alleys to each rooftop in sequence. Just as John had gotten comfortable with crawling along at such a height, they'd reached the void that housed dozens of the undead down below. Before they had even finished balancing the ladder to the store's roof, the zombies had already sensed their presence above and began to growl and reach for the two with an insatiable blood lust.

"Don't even let 'em bother you. It doesn't matter that they're down there or that they see us," Sprite comforted. "We didn't fall before, and there's no reason for us to fall now."

It sounded like empty encouragement to John when the words were spoken, but once he'd crossed the gap, he realized that the words had played a big part in his steady movements. While Sprite heaved the axe over to him, John tried to reciprocate the edifying energy to Sprite as he too crossed over, and the larger man also arrived without incident.

Once they had broken through the roof, and were able to see into the shop, the men realized that there weren't as many zombies trapped inside as they had anticipated. Sprite lowered the ladder down to the floor between two shelves, and John began his descent with axe in hand. They had guns available if necessary, but preferred not to use them if at all possible. For all they knew,

167

the outside zombies would be able to push through the narrow separation of glass if they were to be further provoked. John was amazed at how easily he was able to climb down to the concrete flooring, and calmly held the ladder while Sprite came to meet him. The two worked into a pattern of snatching the most useful of items into their bags, and then resurveying their surroundings. Occasionally, one would incapacitate an approaching zombie, and then the ritual would continue. Before long, they had collected everything they had hoped to, and calmly climbed back up to the roof, over to the adjacent buildings, and finally back down to meet up with the others.

John and Sprite separated the supplies evenly for their own group's bounty, but Sprite attempted in vain to sneak food back into John's pile when John's back was turned. The only disagreements came when one would argue that the other was in more dire need of a certain commodity.

"Just take it," Sprite said when they disagreed over who would keep a large bundle of antibiotics. "I haven't used that many z-packs in all my thirty years, and I doubt I ever would in the however many I got left."

"What about your family?" Hillary chimed in. "Won't they need medicine?"

It wasn't until then that John realized that Sprite had been bargaining goods for only himself during the entire negotiation. John and Sprite both contemplated Hillary's words silently for a moment while Sprite dodged the question.

"You don't have anyone left do you? You're on your own," Moto said.

"Listen, you don't have to concern yourself with me," Sprite responded. "I've got more than I'll ever need here, and I'm plenty capable. I'll be fine."

"Ok, I don't doubt you could survive, but what if you can help all of us and help yourself in the process?" John asked. "Is it really worth just surviving here all alone for the sake of surviving and being able to say you didn't give up on the neighborhood? I'm sorry man, but this neighborhood has given up on itself."

"God, why am I such a bad liar?" Sprite asked. "For being a cop and hearing lies all day, every day from people, you'd think I'd be better at it. To be honest, I'd already given up hope for this city--and every other city for that matter. After losing everyone..." he trailed off.

"Maybe we were the last ones that you were supposed to stay behind and protect," John said.

"Let's go make a fresh start somewhere," Moto interjected. "We can build our own something worth defending."

"You're right. Deep down, I know you're right," Sprite said. "I guess it just feels like quitting to me, and I never quit before."

"No one can make the decision but you," John said, "and I don't mean to pressure you, but it's easy for me to see that this doesn't even resemble giving up. Going with us wouldn't make life easier, taking on more mouths to feed, and whatnot. Quitters find ways to justify the easy. The low, broad road if you will."

"I didn't have you pegged for a spiritual guy," Sprite said.

"I've been exposed to it. I like a lot of the main points it communicates for sure. I've just always been too much of a control freak to admit that someone or something else is more in control of my life than I am. Oh, and I hate churchy people. They're the worst."

"Oh, come on. You can't let some bigots represent God for you any more than you'd let well... how about this. Don't blame God for things that people have done. The churches that God created as hospitals to sinners have been turned into museums for the dead. What I mean is you don't get to blame everything crappy on God just because it's convenient. God is consistent even when I'm not. And especially when I'm failing miserably at getting my point across."

"Not to encourage you to keep trying, but you're probably right. I just don't see how you can keep the faith considering what's going on around us." John motioned to the bodies strewn about the street.

"Well maybe we can dig a little deeper into that later," Sprite said with a slanted grin.

"Does that mean you're in?" Moto asked.

"I mean, if you guys are sure... absolutely. I don't want to invite myself along before you all have a chance to discuss it or anything like that."

"Hell no, man," John said. "We'd be lucky to have you around."

"Well I guess that's that." Moto grunted while loading Sprite's share of goods back into the truck. "But I'm warning you now; no Christian music."

Moto continued on with his numerous ex-girlfriend stories long after the group had grown bored of his attempt to entertain.

"Yeah, man she was something else," Moto said with a slight frown. "Despite everything, I still look back on our time together as some of the best days of my life."

"Aw, I doubt any of my exes would say that about me," Brooke said.

"That's always tough, man," Sprite comforted. "It sounds like she set the bar pretty high."

"Actually, the last one was my favorite," Moto smiled. "Pro tennis player."

John glanced up at Moto in the rearview mirror with a confused look. Moto opened his eyes wider toward the mirror in a way that said not to interrupt.

"No kidding, a pro tennis player?" Sprite asked with a raised inflection that suggested he was either impressed or suspected a lie.

"Yeah, that's the one that really broke my heart," Moto said seriously, before adding with emphasis. *"It was like love meant nothing to her."*

A groan rose up from the front of the car, while Moto laughed hysterically.

"Wait, were any of those stories true, or did we just endure this 10 minutes of rambling so you could set up a stupid joke?" Brooke asked.

"What? I don't get it," Hillary said.

"Oh, come on," Moto defended. "If we have anything, it's spare time."

"He's got a point," Sprite said, still chuckling.

"In that case, I've got one too," Brooke said. "It might even come in handy for getting food somewhere down the road."

"I can already tell this is gonna be good," John said with renewed interest.

"I'm going to teach you the best way to catch a polar bear." she said.

"This is gonna come in handy down the road?" Moto asked.

"Shut up, you had your turn," Brooke scolded. "It's actually really easy. You dig a hole in the ice and lay several green peas around its perimeter. Once it's all set up, you just hide and wait nearby until a bear is finally curious enough to come investigate. Finally, when the polar bear bends over to take a pea, you kick it in the ice hole."

The truck erupted in laughter, including Moto's, despite his bitterness for having been outdone.

"I still don't get it!" Hillary protested.

"Well, Brooke didn't say it quite right," Moto started. "It's supposed to sound like she's saying…"

"Moto!" John interrupted. "Shut up. She's just a little girl!"

"Ohhh," Hillary laughed. "You mean asshole!"

Brooke showed John a nervous grin that caused him to conceal his face from Hillary, though his entire torso visibly bounced with muffled laughter. Sprite tried to help in correcting Hillary about what words aren't nice to say, but he too lost his composure when the others all continued on with their snorting and chuckling.

As if the cruel, new world couldn't allow for such innocent joy to take place any longer, one by one each person's laughter was subdued into a horrified sense of awe. Just the type of inhumane cruelty that they had been attempting to evade was unfolding right before them.

From what they could tell, it appeared that a young, muscular man had flagged down a passing car that was driven by an older man and his wife. The old man was outside of his car and motioning his hands as if trying to explain something. When the group's truck rolled up on them, the dog began barking with a ferocity that none of them had yet witnessed. The young man glanced up at the approaching truck and pulled out a previously concealed handgun, firing several rounds toward the old man as he attempted to flee. The shooter leaned into the driver's seat of the car but resurfaced only seconds later to open fire on the woman before grabbing what he could of their belongings and fleeing. After he'd sprinted several yards, most of the stolen items had fallen from his grasp scattered across the pavement behind him. John was considering speeding toward the thief until the man dropped most of what remained clutched to his chest in order to point his gun toward their speeding truck. Seeing this, John

172

slammed on the brakes and everyone remained ducked down beneath a hail of powdered glass until John eventually peeked out and announced that the man was gone. Only a few bullets had penetrated the windshield, and none appeared to have struck anyone. Brooke checked Hillary up and down for injuries before simply squeezing the little girl to her chest. John sprinted from the truck toward the old couple's car with Sprite and Moto following close behind.

Beside the car, it was apparent that the husband was going to die. He had been struck by one bullet in the neck and lay lifelessly against the front quarter-panel, bleeding profusely. The bullet had struck an artery that now spewed blood across the fiberglass with each beat of his heart. The wife, however, was conscious and moaning.

"Why, why?" she muttered repeatedly.

The elderly woman desperately pressed one hand against her chest as blood drained out from between her fingers without resistance. Even with the supplies the group had recently acquired, they weren't optimistic that there was anything they could do to save either of the two. Knowing this, they still sprang into action. John pulled out some blankets from the back seat and laid them out on the asphalt while Moto and Sprite went to pull the old woman from the car and lay her down where they could more easily attend to her injuries.

Amazed that the man's heart was still beating, John unsurely placed his hand across the man's wound to try and slow the bleeding. Sprite unbuckled the woman and lifted her from the car. John considered sliding the old man into a more comfortable resting position but feared that laying him down would just rush more blood toward the gaping hole in his neck. John instead began wrapping bandages around the wound, but despite his best efforts, the bleeding continued unabated. Soon, the man's head slumped lifelessly. It was obvious he was gone.

Sprite and Moto continued attending to the woman and did their best to block the view of her deceased husband while fighting in vain to calm her enough to slow the bleeding.

Seeing that there wasn't much he could do to help with the now widowed woman, John decided to bury the old man's corpse in a section next to the road that had already been dug out for utility work. After getting the body covered with one slight layer of dirt, John was surprised when Brooke appeared next to him offering to help.

"I hate to do nothing," she said. "And I'd much rather be over here with you than having to watch that poor woman die."

"Not a fan of blood?" John asked.

"No, it's not that at all," Brooke said, gesturing to Hillary where she sat on the curb. "I just wanted there to be some level of censorship before I brought this one over with me. I'm sure as heck not gonna leave her alone in the truck after all that."

John heard a different tone in his brother's voice and listened in more intently. Apparently, the old woman was doing better as she appeared to be communicating with Moto while Sprite loaded some of the items from her car into the group's truck. John thought it was slightly odd, but he trusted Sprite's good judgment and elected to finish transferring dirt into the fresh grave.

Brooke and John talked as they worked while Hillary scribbled in her spiral notebook that would commonly emerge whenever she had any down time. John caught himself feeling something resembling guilt for the significant amount of joy he felt when talking with Brooke as they buried a man a few paces from his suffering wife. It'd started as his defense mechanism for trying to soften the horrific nature of the situation around them but had quickly developed into what he would later consider to be one of the best conversations he'd ever had with a woman--not that he could recall exactly what the conversation consisted of.

After several minutes of digging, John noted a new smile that would occasionally appear on Brooke's flawless, though sweaty, face at certain stages of their talk. It wasn't the smile that she typically used on Moto or when playing with Hillary. It was a smile that he hadn't seen from her before; one that carried all the way up to her paralyzingly green eyes. John did his best to make mental notes of what he'd done to earn these first genuine smiles from Brooke and made it his mission to find as many of them as he could in the future.

"Bad news," Sprite said to John as he approached the nearly filled grave, snapping John from his happy place.

"She didn't make it?" John asked.

"She's actually hanging tough for now," Sprite said. "The problem is... complicated."

"I'm all ears," John said, leaning on his makeshift shovel.

"Well, as you probably saw, we offered to bring her along with us once she kind of stabilized."

"Not ideal, but I can't imagine leaving her behind, either," John nodded.

"Well, so then she started listing off some of the things that we should transfer from her car to the truck," Sprite hesitated. "Most of it's in the trunk."

"I don't follow," John said. "Where's the problem?"

"Well, we'll need the key to get in."

"And you're telling me the key is at the bottom of this hole..." John said looking down at his nearly completed project.

"Don't most cars like that have a back seat that folds down and exposes the trunk?" Brooke asked.

"Yeah, we checked that," Sprite nodded. "No dice."

It took a lot more work to empty the hole than it'd taken to fill, but with Sprite's help the job was done in a reasonable amount of time. As they neared the man's body though, the dirt began to shift and rise as if on its own. It quickly became clear that the man had reanimated after being buried.

"Don't let her see this," John whispered to Sprite.

After Brooke had escorted Hillary from the immediate area and Sprite assisted in distracting the man's wife, John disposed of the thing with his shovel. After several nervous moments, he emerged from the hole with keys in hand.

"I hate to ask you this, miss, but had your husband been bitten?" John asked.

"No, I'm sure that he wasn't," she responded after Sprite had given her a sip of water. "Why do you ask?"

A gun's report echoed out through the forest. The desperate man who had earlier shot the old couple was now blindly firing shots in their direction as he re-emerged from the woods and sprinted toward their now unoccupied truck.

The men instinctively did their best to shield Brooke and Hillary as they all took cover behind the front of the old couple's car. Re-emerging from cover, John stepped out and gently dragged the blanket that the wife still lay on and brought her into safety next to them. Moto began returning fire as the young man climbed up into the truck and brought the engine to life. The crazed man accelerated the massive truck straight toward the car as Moto continued to unload round after round into the windshield. Everyone but Moto fled from behind the car and in a panic, sprinted toward the cover of the nearby brush. The truck's driver reacted by swerving toward them in an apparent attempt to run them down as he fled.

Moto surprised himself with a lucky shot into the truck's front left tire at just the perfect instant when the man had cut the steering wheel hard to the right. The truck's bare wheel shrieked as it dug into the soft asphalt, causing the truck to careen down the highway, tumbling violently and slinging plastic, glass, and sparks across a large area between the incapacitated old woman and those who'd fled. The truck's momentum carried it forward for a considerable distance as it flipped. Its back end narrowly missed Sprite who had slowed to pick up Hillary after she'd escaped Brooke's grasp. Seeing that everyone was unharmed but for the old woman who now lay motionless in a pool of blood beside the car, Moto calmly walked over to the wild-eyed man as he crawled out from the mangled wreckage. The man was bleeding badly but appeared to have miraculously avoided mortal injury. He groaned as he dug his forearms into the shattered glass in an attempt to crawl out through the truck's now narrow window. As Moto reached him and aimed the pistol at the man's head, the young man tugged at the loose seatbelt that restrained him by the armpit and pleaded between gasps for air.

"Wait, wait, wait," the man said, holding up his free arm. Without theatrics, Moto coldly squeezed the trigger.

Conjecture and speculation followed between the men after the excitement had passed, mostly with guesses as to why the old man had reanimated. The discussion grew even more heated after a more thorough examination from John revealed no visible bites or similar injuries of any kind.

"Maybe he got some infected blood in his mouth or eye or something," Sprite said.

"That's possible, I guess." John nodded as he continued to examine the body. "But Moto and I have seen this before. I'm starting to think it's more the rule than the exception. Not saying I can explain it any further than that, but we're going to have to be cautious of the recently or soon-to-be deceased."

John realized that the girls were back within earshot and Hillary's face indicated that she'd heard some of what was being said. He quickly steered the conversation to a tamer subject.

"Well, I guess we'd better go ahead and transfer what we can of our stuff from the truck over to their car," John said as he surveyed the wreckage.

"I don't know if that's gonna do much good, unfortunately," Sprite sighed.

John thought to himself that surely there would still be plenty of canned goods and clean water that would've survived the violent crash. He understood Sprite's meaning, though, when he turned and saw the fluids leaking from the car's engine. Several bullet holes littered the car's radiator and the front quarter panel where the group had taken cover. Two of the car's tires had also been destroyed.

John let out a long exhale, but did his best to hide his frustration. "Well, I guess we just grab what we can carry. But we have to be quick. We need to get off this road."

"Agreed," Sprite said while walking toward the mangled truck. "All that gunfire isn't going to attract anyone here that's worth waiting around to meet."

As they approached the truck, though, the old woman's discolored body let out a rattling groan and began to squirm and reach for Sprite as he passed.

"Ho, shit!" Sprite exclaimed as he jumped back. Though visibly relieved, it was obvious that he felt awful upon realizing that the woman was not a zombie but was somehow still clinging to life.

"Don't let me end up like one of them," she groaned. "Just shoot me. *Please!*"

Moto surfaced quickly with pistol in hand, and murmured softly to the woman before standing, and pulling the trigger. Instead of an echoing, merciful blast, though, there was only an agonizing click. The woman clenched her eyes shut and tears trickled down her cheeks. Moto turned the pistol to view it from the side, and saw that the slide was held back indicating that the ammunition had been depleted.

"Someone bring me another mag!" Moto yelled.

The group exchanged glances to see who might be running to his aid, but after a significant pause, still no one had moved. Finally, Sprite spotted a few spare rounds lying near the truck's wreckage, and brought them to Moto. As Moto fumbled to load a round into his magazine, the woman was finally granted mercy and breathed her last rasping breath. After several disgruntled whispers under his breath as he worked, Moto finally realized that the woman was already gone.

"Do I waste the bullet?" he asked.

"I don't see the need to attract any more attention than we already have," Sprite said.

"I wonder if she'll reanimate too," John whispered to Sprite. "She wasn't bit was she?"

"Would you effing do it already!" Brooke screamed with tears in her eyes. "Don't let that sweet woman become one of those things. What if it was your mother?" She stormed off to the truck and began dragging what she could from the inverted back seat.

They all flinched at the sound of the shot.

Everyone carried as much as they could handle of the items that were determined to be intact and most necessary for survival. The amount of things that were still going to be left behind was sickening to see. Even though they didn't intend to make a return trip, they decided it would be worth the time to disguise many of the goods which they were forced to abandon off among the trees near the highway. Sprite, being the strongest, was tasked with carrying much of the drinking water for the group. The others carried an assortment of items that they felt were important, including Hillary who filled her arms with a pair of dog food bags and the journal she refused to part with.

As they navigated down the narrow path deeper into the woods, Moto, John, and Sprite resumed their discussion about the occurrences of people reanimating despite not having been bitten. Brooke and Hillary lagged a short distance behind so that they could remain unseen, should the men walk up on some dangerous situation. They had started off with Sprite taking up the rear of the line in order to more securely protect the girls, but he'd eventually volunteered to take the over the machete duty. Moto and John's effectiveness at clearing a path had deteriorated as the forest grew denser and the blade duller. Brooke didn't mind being entrusted with holding down the rear of their formation or keeping a close eye on the ever tiring Hillary. She'd only wished that Sprite was still nearby after Hillary had grown too weary to carry both small bags of dog food any further; and as she was unwilling to call out for help, Brooke was forced to add the weight to her own already significant burden.

They were seeking out a safe place to bunk down for the night. Whether that would come in the form of a cabin, or a naturally defendable formation in the landscape had yet to be seen. As the sun's descent seemed to visibly accelerate, the group hoped that any option other than sleeping under the stars would present itself soon.

"I need to potty," Hillary said while tugging at Brooke's weakening arm.

"No problem sweetie. Just step off the trail a little, and I'll be right here by you."

Hillary took a few steps away, and squatted behind a bush near the trail as the men continued on ahead.

"Everything ok?" Brooke asked after the men's footsteps were no longer audible.

"I can't go like this," Hillary answered.

"You're gonna have to learn to use the bathroom outside, sweetie. We don't have any other option right now; I'm sorry."

"It's not just that," Hillary started, eventually returning to the trail. "I've never been able to unless everything is just right."

"How can I help make things better, sweetheart?" Brooke asked patiently. "We really need to catch up to the boys."

"I don't know," Hillary started, "make it safe?"

"You've got to be kidding me," Moto whispered after the girls had jogged to catch up. "That's the stupidest thing I've ever heard. It doesn't make a lick of sense."

Brooke was appreciative that the men had been paying enough attention to stop and wait for the girls to return to a close proximity before continuing on down the path. Once they had caught back up, though, their lack of empathy toward a little girl who had just lost her entire family was triggering her.

"I don't know what to tell you." Brooke shrugged. "She says that she'll try her best if we do that for her. What else can we do? And Sprite, what on Earth happened to your face?"

"Ah, I had a couple thorn bushes get the better of me. I didn't realize what they were in time," Sprite said while tenderly touching at the gashes across his face.

"Remember how Pop Pop used to ask if we'd been sorting bobcats when we'd come home looking like that?" John asked Moto with a nudge.

"Oh, man, Pop Pop. I miss him," Moto sighed. "Wait, that gives me an idea, let's try scaring her!"

"That's for hiccups, jackass," John mumbled.

"Pop Pop had more success with the one I meant..." Moto murmured.

"It really does seem like a lot of trouble for nothing. Is it gonna have to be like this from now on?" John asked to no person in particular.

"I don't know what you want me to say, guys," Brooke said, glancing over her shoulder at Hillary scribbling in her journal a short distance away. "She said she's never been able to pee unless her Dad was right there with her. She has to feel completely safe before she can go."

"Okay, but we have to line up in a circle around her?" Sprite asked. "That's just about the weirdest thing I've ever heard."

"Moto, Moto!" Hillary appeared tugging at his sleeve. "Look at this awesome tree I found!"

"Not now, kiddo; we'll talk later," he said without making eye contact.

"Look at her jumping around," Moto continued to the adults. "She doesn't even have to go that bad."

"Yeah, I think she'll find a way to go once her bladder's full enough," John said. "We just don't have time for this. We don't want to set that kind of precedent--that we'll drop everything and give her what she wants if she just whines enough. She might not be used to tough love, but she's gonna have to get used to it if we're gonna survive out here."

"She hasn't gone in forever, guys," Brooke said sternly, stomping her right foot for emphasis. "I don't think it's for attention. She just wants to know that she's not going to get surrounded by zombies, or left behind. We could've already been back on our way if we would just stop talking about it and do it. Who cares if it doesn't make any sense to you? It isn't about you. This girl has been through enough without some tough guys trying to push tough love on her right now."

Brooke walked over to Hillary, and by the time the two girls returned, the men were already forming a large circle with their backs turned, standing guard.

"What are the chances you guys could do this for me when I have to drop a deuce?" Moto asked. "I'd hate to get caught with my pants down."

"Brother, you're just gonna have to climb a tree or somethin'." Sprite answered.

A short distance down the trail, all three men slowed their pace at the sight of a grassy clearing to the right and a small spring with clear, flowing water to their left. With dusk rapidly approaching, there was little discussion before they were all in agreement that this was going to have to be their campsite for the night. After an evaluation of the resources available to them and a brief brainstorming period, a plan was formulated. The tasks were divided fairly in order for each person to be placed into the field that they were most well-equipped for. The small clearing was quickly transformed into a construction zone that buzzed with activity well into dusk until something resembling a safe zone had taken shape.

John, with his experience in splitting firewood was tasked with cutting down tree after tree for lumber. Sprite helped assemble the logs and move other heavy objects to the places where they were needed--along with every other situation that arose calling for muscle. Moto set to work carving edges of the wood into shapes that would pigeon-tail tightly together. This allowed for making a sturdy, raised sleeping area without having to pound nails, and potentially attract zombies. Since they already had a decent amount of drinking water, all agreed that making a shelter that would allow them a restful night's sleep comfortably out of reach of the insects and other critters, was priority over fire. When waiting on more logs, Moto also took to fashioning as many spears out of the smaller trees as he could for a makeshift barricade along the outer perimeter of their encampment. Brooke's experiences braiding her sister's hair during their late night talks paid dividends for interweaving vines and leaves into an almost impermeable roof for the shelter. Hillary was less than thrilled for her task of bringing water around to everyone as they worked. After it became apparent that Hillary's relentless clamoring for a more respectable job wouldn't end, Brooke finally dreamed up something to keep the girl occupied. Presented as the most important job of all, Brooke instructed Hillary to call out timber every time a tree was about to fall in order to warn every one of the danger. After one round of Hillary squealing at the top of her lungs, John had to intervene so that they weren't alerting every zombie in the county. Hillary attentively watched every swing of John's axe, anxiously anticipating the moment the wood would start to shift. Several times, the dog would leap up from the bed it had made in a pile of leaves and sprint to Hillary after she'd yelled.

"I think his name's Timber!" Hillary said after it had happened a few times.

"You might be right!" John said. "I think that's a great name for a dog!"

Spirits remained high as productivity continued, and no unwelcomed interruptions wandered up from the forest despite all of their noise.

The only danger that came was when Moto lost focus while cutting away at a log, and sliced a deep gash into his finger. He didn't expect the wound to be significant as it was only a finger, but the blood continued to pour out no matter what he tried. Once he'd bled through more than a few Band-Aids, he tore off some fabric for dressing, kept the wound elevated, and slowed his heart rate, but nothing worked.

"We should've brought super glue," Moto sighed.

"I remember an old trick my Dad used to do for us," Brooke said. "Did we bring the spices?"

"Um. I think maybe a couple are in that food box," John said curiously.

"Oh awesome, here it is," Brooke sat next to Moto. "Just hold still a sec."

"Tony Chachere's? Are you crazy?" Moto pulled away. "That's gonna burn like hell!"

"No, it really doesn't," Brooke assured him. "Well, I don't think it will. Dad always used Cayenne pepper, but I'm pretty sure this has Cayenne."

"What is it supposed to do?" Moto asked.

"It's gonna coagulate your blood, and fix you up better than stitches would," Brooke answered.

Brooke dumped a large amount of the seasoning onto Moto's finger before he was ready.

"Ow, dammit!" Moto pulled his hand back. "I told you!"

"Oh, I guess the salt might make it sting," Brooke read the label. "But cayenne pepper by itself is perfect."

"A lot of good that does me," Moto whined, grimacing.

John and Sprite did their best to control the swelling need to laugh, assuming that Brooke had played a trick on Moto. Unexpectedly to everyone but Brooke, the bleeding stopped almost immediately.

"How have I never seen that before?" John stared.

"I guess it really is good on everything!" Sprite laughed. "But don't everyone go testing it out. We've gotta save some for the food. I can't get enough of that stuff."

"Speaking of food, it's been forever since I've tried, but after some trial and error I'm sure I could get some working traps together," John said. "I'd hate to eat through all our canned stuff now and then have to rely on just hunting to eat. I think we'll catch something; there should definitely be some edible critters coming down to the spring for water."

"You're planning on staying out here for several days, then?" Sprite asked.

"I think we should be prepared to," John answered. "I'm sure we'll expand our search areas farther and farther out from the shelter each day, but there's no guarantees. I don't think we should assume that we're going to find anything better than what we have here anytime soon."

"It wouldn't have been my first option, I'll say that," Brooke said. "But I have to admit I'm starting to feel pretty safe out here compared to the city. No people means no zombies, right?"

"That's the idea, for a while at least," John said. "Sacrificing comfort for safety should definitely give us an advantage while all this stuff plays out past the early stages."

"Adapt to survive," Sprite nodded.

"C'mon Timber!" Hillary called while patting the wood floor next to her.

The dog ran over to lie between her and Brooke, taking up a significant portion of the shelter.

"I'll take first watch tonight," John said quietly to the men. "Just because we have a barricade doesn't mean that we're safe."

Moto sat up in a startle, covered in sweat. John was still awake, keeping an eye on everyone while they rested. Moto offered that he would take over watch. He then remembered that it wasn't just zombies in his nightmares that had gotten to him, but that Hillary had been taken. In the nightmare, he was frantically searching for her while also trying to avoid the countless undead. He remembered that he somehow knew exactly where to find Hillary. The closer he'd get to the building where she'd be, the more panicked he'd get that it was not going to be the sweet, innocent version of Hillary that he'd find there. He had awoken just as he swung the door open in his dream. He wasn't sure if he should feel grateful that he didn't have to witness what he'd expected to find, or if the not knowing was even worse.

Moto didn't intend to tell John about the dream, but was already halfway through the story before he'd decided one way or another. As he knew would happen, John began his diagnosis.

"Have you been worrying about her? I was kind of under the impression that you were more frustrated that she'd be putting us all in more danger."

"I don't know," Moto replied. "I'd definitely say that you and I would be better off alone out here as far as survival goes. Who adds in taking care of a little kid when they're mapping out their survival plan—not to mention making a human wall around her every time she wants to pee? Not exactly ideal."

"The dream sure seems like you're more worried about her than you are yourself though..." John left the statement open-ended, anticipating a response.

"It's just a dream, man. Not everything has to mean something. Not everything can always have some greater significance."

"No need to get defensive," John said without compromising his surveying of the trees which surrounded their camp. "If anything I'd be proud of you for putting others before yourself for a change."

"If I could choose between us finding her and not finding her, I think you know which one I'd take in a heartbeat," Moto said. "She doesn't exactly bring a lot to the table."

After a glare from John, Moto changed the subject and pressed that John should take advantage of Moto's adrenaline rush and catch some rest while he could. After sitting in silence surrounded by darkness, Moto startled back awake and realized that he'd fallen asleep during his shift. He was relieved to see that, though he'd slept for so long that shades of amber were already invading the sky to the east, no danger had come to the camp. It wasn't until he sat up that he realized Hillary was nowhere to be found.

-*Three*-

"The greatest accomplishment is not in never falling but in rising again after you fall." -Vince Lombardi

The rest of the group awoke to Moto's frantic barrage of questions. Timber had also gone missing. Moto couldn't stop his earlier nightmare replaying itself in his mind. He saw that Hillary had left behind her diary, which he snatched and quickly fumbled to the last page of. Finding no entry about her running away, Moto threw down the notebook in frustration and paced around the camp. John looked for Hillary's footprints or some sign left behind from Timber, but the forest's floor was covered in leaves that offered no help. After a few laps around the perimeter and a scolding from John for having fallen asleep, Moto stopped suddenly. He stared at the exposed page of Hillary's notebook for a moment before sprinting down the trail they'd come in on.

"Stay here in case they come back!" Moto called as he ran. "I might know where she went."

John examined the notebook's page where Hillary had drawn an unexceptional picture of an odd-looking tree.

Moto sprinted breathlessly through the overhanging brush which gashed him deeply and shredded his shirt. He tried to put the previous night's dream out of his mind as he ran. He caught a few glances of footprints from both Hillary and Timber in some lower areas along the trail and accelerated even faster. After only a few minutes, he was shocked to look up and see that he'd already made it to the hollow tree that Hillary had previously wanted to show him.

Moto screamed out for Hillary, and was somewhat disheartened when Timber ran up alone to greet him.

"Where is she, buddy? Take me to her," Moto said as he choked back tears.

The dog followed as Moto searched the ground expectantly for blood or possibly even a body as he approached the tree. He wasn't sure what emotion to feel when he saw a flashlight's glow poke out from inside the hollowed tree. The light blinded him as he turned to peek inside the tree before finally spotting a guilty-looking little girl. Hillary seemed to be fine once he got a look at her, but her face was covered in dirt that had been streaked away where she'd been wiping at tears.

"Don't worry. I can take care of myself," she said. "You don't have to keep me in your group if you don't want me."

189

"What are you talking about?" Moto asked. "You're a part of our group! I was so worried about you!"

"Nu-uh. I heard what you said last night. If you coulda not found me, you woulda liked that better."

"Oh, Hillary, I was just acting stupid. I'm sorry I haven't been very nice to you. Truth is I've been having bad dreams because I worry about you so much. I would do anything to keep you safe."

"What did I do to make you mad at me? I'm sorry. I can be better," she said, tearing up even more.

"Sweetheart, you don't have to do anything different. You've been such a big help for us. If anyone needs to change, it's me. And I will. I'm gonna be your best friend from now on, ok? Wherever you go, I go."

"Really? You mean it?" Hillary asked with a new glow.

"Absolutely, kiddo. I don't ever say this to anyone, but I love you. I want you to know that."

"I love you too!" Hillary smiled, rushing forward to hug Moto despite his ripped and bloodied shirt.

"But don't ever scare me like that again," Moto said, holding Hillary out with his arms extended and squatting to eye level. "You have to stick with me no matter what."

Hillary answered by thrusting her arms forward again, stealing another hug.

"Oh, thank God," Brooke said when she saw Moto walking back down the trail with Hillary on his shoulders. "John, Sprite, come back! They're okay!"

Hillary began tearing up again when she saw Brooke. One by one, they each hugged her tight and added in a light scolding about running off by herself. In a private conversation, Moto let John know that it had been his comments during the night that had caused her to leave. John was skeptical of Moto's pledge to treat Hillary as if she were his own daughter. The Moto he'd grown up with would've used such a situation as an "in" with Brooke. John didn't vocalize his thoughts, though, and scolded himself for how close he'd come to spitting out such a damning accusation.

John sat in silence as he loaded his extra magazines with ammunition. He fumbled with a lone round that remained and took advantage of the rare calm to sit and think. Each of them had undergone a significant transformation over the past several days. For Moto, the change was inarguably an improvement. John feared that his own internal transformation was one of pessimism and callous unlike the fruitful enlightenment the others had demonstrated. He allowed himself temporary forgiveness, considering that his personal descent could very well become the determining factor in the group's survival or otherwise.

John saw that one of Hillary's markers had fallen between the shelter's planks. Before returning it to her, he found himself considering the most likely way he'd come to experience his own demise. John decided to embrace his ever-growing pessimistic side and scribbled "Plan B" on the side of the lone bullet. He called out to Hillary who was already drawing in her notebook again and lobbed the marker back to her.

"I may not be able to control anything else, but at least I can control the way I go out," John thought to himself while he rolled the round back and forth between finger and thumb. Suspecting that Brooke was watching him, John tucked the bullet into the tiny pocket of his jeans. It was then that he realized he'd been habitually carrying his cell phone in its usual pocket for all this time. Perhaps in an admission to himself that the world wasn't going to go back to the way it was, John heaved his phone across the small clearing and into the creek.

191

"We could've used that!" Brooke said, proving that she had indeed been watching.

"It's been dead for a long time," John responded.

"When we find power again, we can charge them and use the alarms as a diversion or something. There are a million things we could find to do with them," Brooke said, flashing her own phone.

"Don't even think about it," Moto said. "As long as this thing can keep working, it's gonna be used for music. I wouldn't survive without it. You can take Sprite's."

Sprite grinned toward Moto and sat uncomfortably close to him saying, "Can we at least share earbuds if I let her use mine?"

Over the next few days, the group successfully fortified their remote encampment to the point where they could comfortably leave only one person on night-watch duty at a time. Aside from a few sporadic stragglers, there wasn't much threat from zombies. The occasional wanderer made for little excitement as the group consistently had more than adequate warning from Timber's growls. The dog had proven a useful addition to their family, even considering its constant hunger.

As the days dragged on, it became apparent that the biggest dangers they'd be facing in the near future were those of the less exciting variety. Complacency, boredom, and worries about the constant strain on resources occupied their minds for most of their waking hours. Even after they had voted to lessen their daily rations, what had once been an impressive mound of food was growing smaller and smaller at what seemed like an increasing rate. Shoes were wearing out, the weight of restless nights began to stack upon one another, and their vegetative cover from the outside world began to wilt away as temperatures plummeted.

Each person had their own way of coping with the sudden influx of spare time. Once there were seemingly no more conversations left unspoken, they each took on new hobbies to occupy the ever-slowing minutes. Some hobbies were more productive than others, but none of them was especially necessary, except in prolonging their mental stability. Hillary heeded Moto's advice and had begun drawing in the dirt in order to preserve the few blank pages that remained in her notebook. Moto spent his time obsessively carving out intricate shapes from spare planks of wood and occasionally sharpening his blades. Sprite had chosen to spend his time preserving his substantial muscle mass with constant pull ups, pushups, and other exercises around camp. Though it seemed like a waste of precious calories to John, Sprite never asked for any more food than even Brooke was allowed. John preferred to spend most of his time wandering off on exploratory hikes alone with Timber, canvasing the surrounding area. After reaching her fill of playing for hours on end with Hillary, Brooke took Moto up on his offer to watch the child and elected to join John on his extensive hikes. Sprite and

Moto couldn't help but notice that John's time spent in the woods increased significantly after she'd decided to go along.

"It might be about time that we hike back to the highway and get all the stuff we left out there," John said as he led Brooke down a narrow path he'd cut a few days prior. He'd purposefully left his paths as narrow as possible so as not to attract unwanted attention. The foot trails were quickly expanding into a winding labyrinth that only he could navigate.

"Why haven't we already?" Brooke asked.

"Seemed like an unnecessary risk, I guess. The stuff that happened out there, I don't know. I can't help but wonder about anyone that's survived this long. If I have any say in it, I'd avoid doing anything that'd risk crossing paths with 'em," John said between hacks from his machete. "The reward is starting to outweigh the risk though. We need that food."

"So I've been meaning to ask you," Brooke started, "do you mind me coming along on these walks with you? Cause I know it's kind of your time alone, but it's really become the highlight of my day."

Brooke skidded to a halt a half step after John had and realized that further up the trail Timber was growling quietly with his hackles standing erect. Peeking over John's shoulder, Brooke could see that a pair of zombies stood idly under a large tree where a third zombie hung from a noose. The hanging zombie had some sort of sign hanging from its neck and still attempted some feeble movements. The others had also shrunk into pathetic, hunched forms but for their significantly bloated midsections. Even from several feet away, the odor was repulsive to Brooke as she inhaled to speak.

"I think that one's the dad," she said gesturing to the male hanging by its neck.

"What makes you assume they're related?" John asked, trying to whisper softly as a hint that Brooke should do the same.

Brooke continued on without really answering. "I bet you anything that one hung itself after finding out that the rest of his family was already zombies. He might've even been bitten by one of 'em first."

"What is this? Is this how you're replacing your afternoon soap operas?"

"Shut up," she scolded though still in a whisper. "Sure, this is the most excitement I've had in a long time, but I still think that's what happened. And there's no one here that can prove me wrong."

"When I die, I shall rot," he squinted to read the man's sign. "What do you think he meant by that?"

"I guess he thought he was taking control. He didn't wanna wander around as one of them. He thought he'd just die instead of reanimating if he killed himself."

Subconsciously, John's hand was drawn to the 'Plan B' bullet poking out from his jeans pocket.

"We can't leave 'em like this," Brooke said. "There's only two of them on the ground. It's not even risky."

"I'm tempted to disagree, but we really shouldn't leave these two to wander up into our camp later on," John said. "Let's do it."

Sneaking up quietly, John approached the larger of the two standing zombies and struck its skull with his machete. The thing dropped to the ground instantly, but it took John's weapon down with it. It had wedged tightly into the thing's head, and John struggled to pull it loose. John put a foot on the dead thing's head and tugged at his weapon as the other zombie slowly shuffled over to him. John released his grip on the stuck machete's handle and began boxing at the other zombie to keep it at arm's length. He gave a few calculated jabs to the thing's face, while staying away from its dangerous teeth, until Brooke emerged with a small, dense limb and broke it over the zombie's head. Brooke stood calmly looking at John as he waited to confirm that the thing's movements had ceased completely.

"John," Brooke started, grabbing both of John's hands, "look at your knuckles."

"Oh, that's just my blood," John said. "It's not a big deal, it happens all the time when I fight."

"You can't fight like that anymore," she said loud enough to anger the hanging zombie. "That thing was covered in gore. Even if that is your blood, what if it got into your blood stream through

195

your cuts? You have to be more careful! Like you were saying about the food, it's all about risk and reward now. It doesn't have to be a bite that brings you down. You know that!"

"You're right," John acknowledged, and finally retrieved his weapon. "I'll be careful, I promise."

"Please..." Brooke said with watery eyes. It seemed as though she wanted to say something else, but no words followed.

"I actually think we're close to the road," John changed the subject. "Let's go grab some of our stash before the weather ruins what's left of it."

John tried to not show his appreciation for Brooke's concern, but he didn't release one of her hands as he led her through the trees.

"What the hell happened to you?" Moto asked John when they'd returned. "I didn't know you were going all the way to the road. Is that really all you could carry?"

"Don't worry about it, I'm fine," John said, laying down a few small cans of food next to Brooke's. "It's all we could carry, because it's all that's left. Some animal dug up half of it and tore through it. A lot of the stuff wasn't just damaged, but gone. This is all that we could salvage."

"Someone must've found the stash," Brooke said.

Though they were happy to have retrieved any food, it came as a blow to find out that the little bit they had was all they'd be guaranteed for winter. Moto didn't see any use of continuing the conversation and returned to showing Hillary how to build a fire without wasting multiple matches.

"Ok, so, after you dig the little trench, you stack some of the smallest sticks across it side-ways like this," he instructed the very attentive Hillary. "And, once that's lit, we're going to add bigger and bigger sticks and then limbs until we have a real fire big enough to keep everybody warm and safe. But, remember, it has to be wood dry enough that it snaps when you bend it. If it's wet, it's harder to light and it'll make a lot more smoke for people to find us."

"That's easy!" Hillary said excitedly as she pulled out the lone match Moto had allowed her to attempt lighting the night's fire. But after a few failed attempts at even lighting her match, Hillary offered that she'd let Moto take care of lighting the fire for one more night.

"Ok, fine," Moto responded. "But then you'll have to let me teach you about bear bags."

Sprite dropped from his dedicated pull up tree branch and approached John. "You get in a fight with the lady friend?" he asked, gesturing to the bloody rags covering John's hands. "I bet it was a knock down drag out."

"Ha, yes and no," John laughed. "Just resorting to my roots more than using my head I guess. It's nothing, though."

"Punching is my first resort too," Sprite grinned. "Don't sweat the food; it's nobody's fault. We'll find more."

"Yeah, I guess I'm glad we found out now instead of when we'd really be counting on it."

"Man, you wouldn't believe how much training it took before I'd remember to use my taser instead of just sitting a kid down the old-fashioned way," Sprite continued. "You can tell that I like to start with the south paw," he said, while petting the scars across his left hand's knuckles.

"Damn. It looks like you punched out a window," John said.

"I used to drink a lot. I don't remember much about that night, but the way the story is told, you're not too far off," Sprite said a little more softly.

"Don't worry, mine is worse," John smiled, pulling back the hair that had covered his brow to reveal a large scar. "I walked right through the sliding door to our back patio."

"Oh, God I remember that!" Moto chimed in. "He was sprinting for a cut of cake on my 5th birthday. Still the funniest thing I've ever seen."

"I was hoping you couldn't hear us," John said. "I can't believe you still joke about it. I could've died, man."

"Oh, whatever. You just remember it that way 'cause you were a kid. That's nothing compared to this," Moto said, pulling up his pant leg to reveal a large, deep scar extending the length of his leg. "All the little ones are actually from zombies, but the deep one is from when I had to lay my bike down."

"Oh, okay." John scoffed. "You couldn't figure out how to change lanes going over 40, and you nailed a curb."

Everyone laughed before Moto had a chance at his rebuttal.

"I gawt wun!" Hillary said proudly with her tongue protruding from her mouth. "I bit off my tongue when I slipped in the shower."

"I guess I'm just too coordinated," Brooke said. "I don't have anything impressive, maybe a scrape on my knee from softball; oh, and this one on my arm from donating plasma."

"People still do that?" John asked.

"Oh, it's definitely worth it if you have whatever I have," Brooke said, showing her arm. "I got paid more for my plasma than I could've gotten at any part-time job on campus."

The scar comparisons made for a pleasant evening of forgotten stories that had previously faded from memory. Each story seemed to plant a seed of remembrance for someone else's experience that they never dreamed they could've forgotten. Until the darkness descended, everyone laughed and carried on for the first time in days, and the small campsite resembled something of a home. The men all took turns comparing the lengths of their post-apocalyptic beards and marveling at their mountain man appearances as best they could by the reflection of the stream. Once things had finally grown quiet, John realized that he was the only one still awake and had, by default, been nominated for first watch. He sat alone beside the dimming fire and thought about how happy he'd grown with his small group of survivors. He couldn't allow himself to dwell on the pleasant thoughts, though, and eventually deviated to those of dread at the realization that he would, more than likely, lose one or all members of his new family. The weight of the responsibility he felt for them all was ever-present and, at times, overwhelming. He couldn't imagine the punishment he'd endure if anything were to happen. Especially if it was something he could've prevented—or something he'd caused.

John wasn't sure if Brooke had just awoken or had never been asleep, but he was comforted when she slid over nearer to him for warmth. Instead of focusing on the pressure to keep her and the others safe, John embraced the opportunity and wrapped his arm around her. Brooke nuzzled her head against his shoulder, and it wasn't long before she was sleeping peacefully.

John snapped upright and realized that, though he'd been able to stay awake, he had been zoning out for some time. Out in the woods, on what he presumed to be one of his freshly cut trails, John heard the distinctive sound of a large animal walking slowly on two legs. He had gotten used to even the smallest of forest wildlife sounding monstrous at night when traversing across the dead leaves of the forest floor. Whatever was approaching, he was sure, had to be at least the size of a grown man.

Thankful that he hadn't re-illuminated their camp by adding fresh wood to their now dim fire, John grabbed his gun and snuck over to the tree line nearest to the sound of the approaching footsteps. The previously overcast sky had cleared and allowed for the large moon to light up much of the ever thinning forest. A short way down the path from camp, John laid flat and waited until finally spotting a human form stumbling around the final bend in the trail. John began to lower his gun, sure that the creature's gait meant that the intruder was only a singular zombie. He normally dispatched the lone zombies in a quiet manner both to preserve bullets and to allow everyone else to remain sleeping. Suddenly, though, the creature called out to him.

"Hey, you. I see you!" The silhouette spoke.

John raised his aim again, finger pressed against the trigger while remaining silent. A dozen thoughts ran through John's mind in a matter of seconds. What if they go back and tell their people where we are? Has he been watching us? Do we have the resources to fill another mouth? If something were to happen, what would become of the girls?

A loud pop rang out from the direction of the man, and John instinctively pulled the trigger.

A feeling of panic struck John as he realized what had happened. Amidst the screams from Hillary back at camp and the final fading moans from the stranger, John realized that the popping sound he'd heard had only been a snapping twig at the man's feet. After a brief moment of consideration, though, John stood by his decision. He didn't want to admit it to himself, but given another chance to face the choice under identical circumstances, he presumed that the scenario would play out in the exact same fashion. He had made a decision that his new family came first, and to accomplish that meant making hard decisions. Though he had already come to terms with that fact, he decided it was best to hide his actions from the rest of the group, regardless of his pure intentions.

After closer inspection, John realized that the old decrepit man was already dead. John was relieved that he had hit his target in a way that ensured that the man wouldn't have to suffer and that there wouldn't be any danger of reanimation. By the looks of the man's skin, John would've guessed that the man had been severely infected already, and he had saved everyone a lot of grief over how to deal with the potential threat. Still, though, he planned out how to best conceal his actions from the others.

In the time it took for John to turn and leave the evidence of his mistake, Moto and Sprite were already upon him.

"What happened? Are you ok?" Moto asked as he approached.

"Yeah, yeah, sorry for the scare," John said slowly, buying time to think. "I've been tracking a, uh, skunk, and finally had a chance to get him before he sprayed one of us or Timber. Who knows if the zombies are big on smells or not, but I figured it was worth the risk of a gunshot."

"Oh," Sprite said, a skeptical countenance communicated through his brow. "Glad everything's ok."

After settling the girls back down for the night, John waited anxiously for everyone to go back to sleep so that he could bury the stranger's remains before the cloak of darkness had lifted. It hadn't been long before silence had reclaimed their shelter, and John crept down the trail where he eventually stumbled over the dead body. He paused for a moment to compose himself and do his best to avoid completely covering himself in the man's blood. In his silence, John heard obvious footsteps given away by the crunching of dry leaves along the same path he'd just walked.

"You really think you can lie to me after all these years?" Moto asked.

"Fine," John whispered, "but keep quiet."

"What really happened?" Moto asked.

John gestured behind him where Moto could barely make out the dead man's outline. Moto opened his mouth to whisper a response, but instead heard a much deeper voice.

"Are you sure he was alone?" Sprite asked without having been seen.

"Damn, you're stealthy for a guy your size," John whispered loudly. "I don't know for sure. I thought he was a zombie at first."

"By the looks of him, he would've been one sooner than later," Moto observed.

"We'll have to keep an extra close eye out tonight," Sprite said. "If any of his group is around, they'll definitely come poking around where the shot came from after he doesn't come back."

"How'd you know it wasn't a skunk? Am I that bad of a liar?" John asked.

"I'm country, man," Sprite answered. "Skunks still spray if you shoot 'em. Only way to prevent it that I know of is to trap 'em and drown 'em."

"You can't be serious," Moto said.

"Oh yeah, man. It works. It's like boiling a frog in a pot," Sprite answered.

"You're a scary kind of dude, Sprite," Moto said.

The men settled for digging only a shallow grave after encountering the relentless root system just below the earth's surface, and rested the unlucky old man in his final resting place without waking the girls.

Both Moto and Sprite told John that he had done the right thing, though they doubted that they themselves would've been able to follow through in a similar situation. Though Sprite and Moto offered to stay up for the rest of the night, John laid restlessly in the shelter. Even more disheartened than before, his mind ran wild about the unavoidable deaths that surely awaited him and his new family. If they were still encountering people out in the middle of the woods, he wondered how he could ever be confident in his ability to keep them all safe and fed. He wondered if he'd die alone, like the old man, and buried in a shallow grave, or if he'd end up laying down his life for the preservation of another's.

After hours of reflection on his life to this point, and contemplation on the future, John realized that he was prepared for his days to be cut short. The thing he was not ok with was losing his humanity altogether, and living only for the sake of living. He didn't know if he really and truly regretted the decision he'd made that night, but he wanted to make it a point to also try and nurture his human side whenever possible. Unexpected to even himself, his first course of action in preserving his humanity came in the form of seeking out someone to love and be loved by. Though it would undoubtedly end in an even more painful departure for one or both of them, he had to let Brooke know of his growing feelings for her. For the first time since being deployed, he fully let his mind drift to a place of daydreaming about happiness and selfless love.

The next morning, John was shocked to see that the sun had already risen high above the horizon, and all of the others sat quietly around the fire finishing their inadequate breakfasts. Each one was taking turns talking about what their first meal was going to be after the world was rid of the undead. Only a few hours previous, John would've scolded them all for losing focus and wasting time fantasizing about something that would never happen. This morning, though, John struggled to find a reason not to be joyful and walked straight to Brooke by the creek where she was rinsing off her Styrofoam bowl.

"Well, look who woke up!" Brooke said cheerfully. "None of us could bring ourselves to wake you."

"Thank you for that," John said. "I can't remember the last time I felt so rested. So listen, can we talk?"

"Well sure, but why not eat a little something and we can just talk on our hike?" Brooke asked.

Happy to wait for an opportunity to talk in private, John prepared a bowl of dry cereal and some bleach-treated water with a modest addition of lemonade powder to mask the taste.

"Man, remember dishwashers?" Moto asked. "Or even running water? I'm so tired of having to walk down to the creek and hunch over just to rinse my dishes."

"We had no idea how good we had it," Sprite agreed. "If I could go back, I'd slap myself around for taking it all for granted."

"I used to flush the toilet just to get rid of my gum," Moto recalled. "What I wouldn't give for one working commode."

"I had a thing for stray hairs," John laughed. "I would throw out my whole bowl of cereal if one of my *own* hairs fell into the milk."

"Oh, yeah," Moto laughed. "He'd throw the biggest fits whenever mom made him eat around it. Even if she took the hair out for him, he would work himself to tears."

"Easy, Ivory Coast," John threatened.

"Wait, Ivory Coast?" Sprite asked. "I've gotta hear this one."

"So, they let us watch that last World Cup when the U.S. beat Spain; so, keep in mind, this is like two years ago," John started with a grin. "Well, the guys are all talking about the next match with Ivory Coast, and Moto is just completely baffled."

205

"Shut up," Moto said. "I'll do anything."

John continued without pausing. "Moto had gone for over twenty years thinking that Ivory Coast was a brand of *bar soap*."

Everyone laughed, including Hillary after feeling left out.

"Ok, ok. Everyone pretend that you've always known every country ever," Moto said.

"How did you even graduate?" Sprite laughed.

"I cheated," Moto answered. "What? I'm sure you cheated your way through Spanish or something."

"But I still don't get how you never picked up that little bit of information outside school," Sprite continued. "We've failed you as a society."

"Well of course *you* know where it is, you're African American," Moto said.

"Whoa, whoa," John interrupted.

"No, I got this," Sprite said. "If you wanna get technical, I'm Native American."

"Holy shit, for real?" Moto asked.

"Well, not like you're thinking, but yes. The people you're thinking of are actually indigenous Americans. Native just means you were born there. I'm native, I just happen to be black as hell."

"Ok, awesome," Moto said. "Black is so much easier to say than African American."

Sprite laughed out loud. "Yeah, let's just go with that."

John caught a subtle gesture from Brooke and stood to follow her out for their walk. He was frustrated when, after only a few steps down the trail, Moto predictably came running up behind them and spoiling John's best chance to follow through with his promise to himself. Mercifully, though, Moto had only come to give John a rifle for their walk, considering the uninvited excitement from the previous night.

"I guess I just want to talk for a little bit and finish my spiel before you answer, is that okay?" John asked uncomfortably after Moto was out of earshot.

"Of course, what's up?" Brooke asked with an interested but otherwise indiscernible look on her face.

"So, I've been thinking a lot lately... like a lot. I think it's important that you know how I feel, because it wouldn't be fair to either of us for me to just keep acting like nothing has changed. Whatever your response is is completely fine, but I just have to get it off my chest for both our sakes."

John hesitated when Brooke's only response at this point was, "Okay...", even though he'd asked her to hear him out. He felt the rifle begin to grow slippery in his hands and panic set in that Brooke might not have any interest in what he was about to divulge.

"So the truth is, and the way I'm going to say it probably won't do it any justice, but I really want to express to you..." John paused.

Brooke stopped mid-stride and turned to look at John who had frozen with glossy, expectant eyes looking past her.

"... how hungry I am," John said.

Only then did Brooke realize that she'd been consumed with anticipation for what John might be leading up to but forced herself to refocus and turn to see that John was staring at a large buck grazing out on the next hillside. She wiped away the moisture from her eyes and whispered that she too was starved.

"Keep an eye out for zombies," John whispered as he raised the rifle. "I'm gonna take the shot."

John was positive that the bullet had struck its target but feared that he may have missed the kill spot directly behind the buck's shoulder blade. Fueled with adrenaline, the buck tore off into the woods along the creek and out of sight.

"Did you miss?" Brooke asked cautiously.

"A little bit," John answered. "Now I have to track him down. Hopefully he didn't go too far."

Brooke cursed her decision to wear shorts for the hike when the crisp air of fall had already arrived. She wasn't cold, now that her blood was flowing, but her legs took a beating as she followed John's lead across the creek and navigated through a maze of bramble briar, poison ivy, and stinging nettle. The conversation as John tracked the deer was awkward and forced, as John elected not to continue on with his declaration of love until a more convenient opportunity arose. Finally, the periodic blood drops ended at the corpse of the large deer.

"Make sure you rinse off in the water," John pointed to the creek. "If you catch it fast enough, the poison ivy won't be nearly as bad. I've always heard it's water soluble."

"And what can I do about the cuts and stinging?" Brooke joked as she splashed water across her bare legs.

"I think a full belly of venison will help with that," John grunted as he cut open the deer's throat and spilled its blood.

Brooke gagged and directed her attention back to treating her legs. "We can walk back on the other side of the creek, can't we?" she asked. "It looks a lot more clear on that side."

"I don't see why not," John answered, as he carefully cut circles in the deer hide just above each hoof. "You might actually want to go ahead over there and keep an eye out while I do this next part."

Not requiring any additional details, Brooke took the rifle and waded most of the way across the shallow water where she waited patiently atop a smooth rock.

After doing her best to not let her gaze wander over to the other bank, Brooke finally heard John's footsteps approaching in the water. She looked up to see John carefully stepping his way across, while clutching the carcass's front two legs over his shoulders and the gutted torso dripping all down his back like some kind of repulsive backpack.

"I think I'll stay up front and upwind," Brooke said as she took off walking up the creek.

John was grateful for an excuse not to talk much on their walk, as he'd lost some of his confidence that Brooke would be interested in any kind of romantic relationship. He caught himself over-analyzing every little comment that Brooke made as they walked and began to psych himself out that putting his feelings out there would be the worst possible thing he could do. John hated himself for thinking such a relationship could ever work in the new world, and plotted how he could get out of the conversation that he had obviously intended to have.

After his legs told him that they'd traveled a long while, John noticed that the sun was no longer in front of them and that it was starting to descend rapidly.

"We should be about back by now, right?" Brooke asked from up ahead.

"Yeah, something's definitely not right," John said as he shrugged the deer over onto a rock. "I don't think the creek was ever quite this deep, and I don't think we've been walking toward the sun for a while now."

"How's that possible, though?" Brooke asked. "We've stayed right next to the creek the whole time," she continued as she walked back to where John was resting. "My God, that smell!"

"I think we might've missed our window on getting this meat cooked," John said, smelling under his own arms. "And I think we missed our turn. We must've come up on a fork that we couldn't see either coming or going."

"All that for nothing? Are you sure we can't just cook it really good?" Brooke asked while sniffing at the carcass from several feet away.

"Not the time you want to get food poisoning and dehydrate yourself," John sighed. "It's only gonna get worse by the time we find our way back."

"Ok, so do we just cross back over and walk southwest until we hit the other little branch of the creek?" Brooke asked.

"That would make sense, but there's no guarantee it'd work," John said as he surveyed their surroundings. "We've been walking for a long time in the wrong direction. If we just take off trying to walk in a straight line for several miles with no sun, we'll just wind up walking in circles and getting even more lost."

"So we follow the creek back down? Or we just set up camp right here?" Brooke asked.

"I'm gonna run up to the top of that hill while there's still some daylight and see what I can see," John thought aloud.

"Ok, Zacchaeus," Brooke said as she sat. "But hurry back."

Brooke raised the rifle at the sound of something large quickly approaching from out of the darkness.

"I found the highway!" John exclaimed.

"God, you scared me," Brooke sighed. "What kept you?"

"Well, I couldn't really see much through all the brush, so I took your Zacchaeus advice and climbed a tree. The highway we were on isn't too much farther from the top of the hill. It's not the safest place ever to hike, but at least it's a sure thing. If we just follow alongside the road until we get to the spot where the truck wrecked, we can definitely find our way back."

"You're a little too excited about the prospect of hiking for miles in the pitch black. It's a good idea, but we're not exactly home free."

"I mean, unless you'd rather just wait it out here 'til sunrise?" John asked.

"Wait, wait! I knew this would come in handy!" Brooke paused before blinding John with a bright blue light. "I took it off the old couple's keychain. I was actually gonna give it to Hillary. Thank God I never did."

As they walked, Brooke would occasionally conserve her light's battery by judging the road's path through the visible stars whenever they weren't blocked out by the towering trees on either side. The optimism that the truck's wreckage could be around any turn at any moment diminished and gave way to the fear that they may have already been past the truck, if they were even on the same road. It seemed as though every elevation change was an incline, and their thirst became impossible to ignore. As their hike dragged on, Brooke lost her ability to judge time or distance and the two continued to endure the monotony of one foot in front of the other. Even the mysterious rustlings of leaves from the forest that had previously produced rushes of adrenaline for Brooke had now become monotonous.

All thoughts of thirst, hunger, and boredom were gone, and a new life was breathed into the two when they came upon a sign that read French Broad River.

"I know where we are! We're close!" John exclaimed as loudly as he dared.

Brooke let out a sigh of relief, and called back to John with heightened spirits, "Did you know this river was named after Joan of Arc?"

An awkward moment dragged on until Brooke wondered if John had even heard her joke and contemplated calling out to make sure he was still nearby.

"I actually learned that while studying abroad!" John said, breaking the awkward silence.

"Wait, you know I was joking, right?" Brooke asked. "I meant French Broad, like, French chick."

"Oh, I know," John grinned to himself.

"So what did you mean by..." Brooke stopped walking. "Were you checking me out?!"

"I'm loving this side of you," John laughed.

Brooke turned and put her hands on her hips in contempt.

"Wait, no. That one wasn't a pun," John said. "I promise I meant your sense of humor, not your posterior."

"I have my moments," Brooke smiled back at him. "You should keep finding time to spend with just me. Maybe you'll finally realize that I'm a pretty decent catch--especially considering your current options."

The words alone might not have done it, but the moon had peeked out just enough at just the right time to reveal that kind of look a girl gives a guy that leaves little doubt as to her intentions.

"And there it is," Brooke said gleefully as she turned to see the truck's headlights reflecting her light's blue glow just before it faded out.

"Wait, turn that back on," John said. "I think I saw some movement up there."

"I'm trying," Brooke whispered. "I think it's dead."

"Stay here," John said before trotting ahead and disposing of the lone zombie with nothing but his buck knife and the fleeting light of the moon.

"Um, John, do you hear that?"

John slowed his breathing to listen, and shuddered at what he heard. The sound of numerous hungry dogs from behind the cover of the tree line was obvious. Without further warning, the pack sprinted out onto the road toward them.

"Get to the car!" John yelled as he reached out toward Brooke with one hand, and swung the butt of his gun toward the sounds of growling with his other. He was surprised when they were actually able to reach the dead couple's car safely. Squinting, John could see that the dogs had elected to go for the easier meal, and were ripping apart the recently incapacitated zombie.

"Do you think they're just hungry?" John whispered. "Or are they infected?

"John..." Brooke said softly. "One got me."

"What? Where?" John asked frantically. "Are you bleeding? How bad is it?"

"Not too bad," Brooke said. "But it broke the skin. I think I'm infected."

"No you aren't!" John scolded. "Dogs aren't carriers. You're gonna be fine."

"They've been eating zombies, though," Brooke said in a defeated tone. "They definitely have the virus, or whatever it is, in their mouths from eating the infected."

"You don't know that," John said. "We're gonna get you out of this, and you're gonna be just fine. I just need you to stay calm and focused."

"How exactly are we going to get out of here?" Brooke asked him, clutching her hand.

John sat for a moment without speaking a word. He considered the small round he'd placed in his pocket what seemed like months ago, but couldn't think of any use for the bullet labeled "Plan B". He had resources all around him; John just had to put the pieces together into something that would walk them out of the situation without further harm.

Brooke saw John's eyes light up, and he sprang into action. First, he grabbed a loose coat from the back seat of the car, and then tugged loose half of the telescoping clothes rod that hung there. He tightly wound and tied the coat around one end of the rod, and then wrapped a second jacket on top of the first.

"I've gotta run out there real quick," John explained. "I'll be *right* back."

"John, they'll smell the deer blood on you. Don't leave."

"I promise," John said. "I'll be back before you know it, and then we're gonna walk right out of here."

The look on Brooke's face told him everything that she was feeling. He cupped her face in his hands and looked calmly into her eyes.

"Do you trust me?"

Brooke took a breath. "I trust you."

John nodded and crept out of the driver's seat. He scurried silently over toward the wreckage of the rental truck. Brooke lost sight of him for a while but could tell that most of the dogs were still tearing at the zombie's corpse. Finally, John reappeared yielding a glowing torch in one hand. He hastily led Brooke from the car and swung the large flame at any dogs that dared to come close. The two rushed as fast as they could down the now familiar path toward their campsite without regard for the possible dangers lurking just out of view.

"What the hell happened?" Moto's voice greeted them after Timber's growling had alerted him of an intrusion.

"It's fine. She's gonna be fine," John answered as he guided Brooke to the flowing creek.

"She? What about you? You're covered," Sprite said.

"Brooke?" Hillary was on the verge of tears. "Brooke, are you ok?"

"We're both fine," John said sternly. "Everyone calm down. Somebody bring Brooke some water."

Hillary began crying to herself and Moto went to comfort her as Sprite poured some treated water for Brooke. Once things had calmed, John decided to go over to Hillary and apologize for how he'd snapped at her and was relieved to find that Moto had already calmed the young girl, at least until he approached.

"Ewww," Hillary exclaimed. "You're covered in bleed!"

Laughing, John apologized, "Sorry, sweetie. And I'm also sorry I snapped at you earlier. I'll go clean up and we'll talk."

John cleaned himself as best he could while sharing his adventure with Moto.

"Genius," Moto said. "Wait, how did you get the torch lit?"

"I just used some diesel from the fuel tank, and lit it with the truck's cigarette lighter. Thank goodness the battery still had some charge on it."

"Well met, man," Moto said. "I'd still be sitting in that car right now."

The two brothers returned to the light of the camp to see that Brooke was sitting off by herself with Sprite and Hillary already sound asleep.

"I'll leave you to it," Moto said, slapping John on the back. "Glad you're ok; we'll find another deer."

John took a brief detour before approaching Brooke, and was glad to see that she had not yet fallen into slumber. He forced a smile even though she didn't reciprocate and presented some weed-like flowers from behind his back.

"I've been anxious to show these flowers how beautiful you are," he said.

Brooke was somewhat annoyed that the gesture forced a smile from her, even though she'd given her best effort to resist. "So you really are a big reader!"

"Huh? Oh, yeah, I guess." John tried to play it off as he sat next to her.
"Why are you over here by yourself?"

"Wait. I call B.S. Tell me the author." Brooke questioned.

"I have no idea what you're talking about. I guess I just heard it somewhere," John said dismissively. "Stop dodging my other question. Are you okay?"

Brooke held up one hand to reveal that she'd tethered her arm to a tree.

"I'm fine. I just think it'd be irresponsible to be optimistic to the point that I endanger any of our group. I refuse to put Hillary's life in jeopardy if I don't absolutely have to," Brooke said.

"Your hand doesn't look that bad," John observed. "And remember how we told you that Moto had his legs completely shredded by zombies in the ocean when the outbreak first started. You really are gonna be ok."

"I'm sure you want to believe that, but we still don't really know the rules of all this. It's fine, but this is just something I need to do," Brooke said with a tone that indicated the decision wasn't up for debate.

Brooke forced herself to remain stern with John--though she'd developed a youthful butterflies-in-the-stomach feeling each time John continued to live up to her expectations. His presence was the only thing that could distract her from the possibility that her days could be coming to an end. Even with the deer's blood still caked behind John's ears, Brooke had to make a conscious effort to not smile each time the two made eye contact.

"Well I can't stop you from tying yourself up, but I'm not gonna leave you out here by yourself all night," John said, sitting more closely to Brooke than before.

Brooke's hands slid down from her leg and grazed John's. His initial reaction was to pull away and play it off just in case the gesture hadn't been intentional. Glancing up to her face revealed that the move was no mistake. It was a look like the one he'd caught on the road earlier, but this time it was obvious that Brooke wanted him to see it. John realized that he was actually smiling, not just on the inside. Trying to look more confident than he felt, John took Brooke's hand and held it in his own against his leg as he comforted her.

The two continued to talk well into the night after the others had long since succumbed to sleep. John was exhausted but wouldn't allow himself to lie down as he knew that Brooke wasn't going to rest that night.

"Thank you for staying with me and not letting my imagination run wild," Brooke said. "I don't know where I'd be without you, honestly."

"Of course; I don't know where I'd be without you either," John smiled.

"Oh, please. Everyone knows you can't just repeat what the other person already said. That's totally unfair."

"Calm down, at least I brought you flowers!" John said. "I'm doing my best."

"AKA weeds," Brooke said with a laugh, holding up the pathetic bouquet, "and a stolen pickup line to go with it."

"But seriously, I meant what I said," John took a serious tone. "I was tailing off into a pretty dark place before. I caught myself wondering if I'd be better off leaving all the kids and weaker people to fend for themselves. I realized it's not worth living just for the sake of living, but the rest of the context didn't really take shape until you. I tried not to like you in that way, believe me. I thought a new love interest in this kind of world would only result in more pain."

Brooke's eyebrows rose when John rolled off the "L" word without hesitation.

"But, then again, I guess that was kind of true in the old world, too, and people still made the choice. And I guess I'm kind of hoping you're wanting to make that same choice."

Without thinking, Brooke found herself smiling and nodding at John. She wasn't able to come up with the right words until John leaned in for a kiss.

"Ok, yes, but you have *got* to clean off a little better," Brooke said with one hand against John's chest. "You kind of reek."

Moto was tempted to be jealous of John when he awoke to see that he'd fallen asleep cuddling Brooke away from the shelter. He chose instead to be happy for the two, as he could easily admit that they made a much better couple than he and Brooke ever would've. Moto decided to quietly prepare some of the little remaining food for himself and Hillary as the rest of the group remained sleeping peacefully. Even once they'd finished eating breakfast, they were still the only ones awake. In order to allow the others to sleep while also keeping Hillary entertained, Moto decided to take Hillary and Timber to go exploring, while also searching for any sort of food that he could find. Once he'd established that Hillary had to keep Timber on their make-shift leash at all times and that she had to stay just beside him no matter what, Moto led Hillary down a new trail.

Moto kept an eye out for tracks, whether human or otherwise, but found none. They walked on until the sun had climbed high into the sky and Hillary's legs had fatigued to the point that Moto was forced to carry her. Despite his best efforts, Moto found nothing to show for his time.

"Let's rest for a bit at that creek up ahead," Moto said, growing tired from carrying the young girl. "Timber could use some water. If we don't spot any other animals coming down for a drink after a while, I guess we'll just head back."

"But we haven't found any food," Hillary said. "Don't we need to find some?"

"It would be nice, but I think I'm burning more calories carrying you around than I'd find if I stayed out here all day. I might try again tomorrow without Timber. His scent might be scaring the deer off."

Instead of wagging his tail at the sound of his name as he usually did, Timber began to growl ferociously, with the hackles on his back standing on end.

"What is it boy?" Hillary asked as Moto set her down. "Is it a deer?"

Timber unexpectedly yanked hard against the leash and snapped the tethering twine. Ignoring the shouts from Moto and Hillary, Timber tore off into the woods across the creek.

"So much for my break," Moto sighed, picking up Hillary and his rifle.

Fortunately for Moto, he didn't have to run far before he came upon Timber in a clearing. Timber was holding his ground, snarling at three sickly looking dogs that had lost much of their hair. In another setting, Moto thought, the dogs could've been mistaken for the fabled Chupacabra. Their stomachs were sunken and every rib and muscle jutted against the graying, scabby flesh to such a degree that it appeared the skin might rip. Moto wasn't sure if the diseased-looking dogs just had mange or rabies or if the zombie virus could, in fact, transfer to canines. Moto's calls to Timber were futile, and he watched helplessly as the decrepit mongrels began to slowly surround the outmatched dog.

Moto took a brief moment to process his only two options. At first, he felt that the responsible decision would be to take Hillary and run, abandoning Timber. As hard of a decision as it was, the only thing giving Moto further pause was the knowledge that fleeing wouldn't guarantee that the pack couldn't easily run him down after they'd pulled Timber to pieces. Without further time to plan or process, Moto acted. He first passed Hillary up onto the lowest branch of a tree, safely out of reach of the animals, and then took aim at the most aggressive of the three dogs. Moto steadied his aim and let out a slow, steady breath. Just before he'd let the bullet fly toward the alpha dog's ribcage, though, Moto thought better and adjusted his aim to the animal's head. Praying that the other two dogs would flee, Moto pulled the trigger. For a moment it seemed as though the plan had worked to perfection. The lead dog dropped instantly to the ground, and the two remaining dogs cowered back. Moto whistled to Timber but was answered instead by a moaning zombie as it stumbled out from the trees several paces behind him. Ignoring Hillary's screams as the thing approached her tree, Moto spun around and dropped the zombie with one shot to the head. The two diseased dogs then ran past him and began tearing at the flesh of the zombie, dragging its lifeless body even closer to the tree where Hillary sat.

Moto did his best to block out the distractions of the crying, barking, and tearing of flesh as he took aim at another of the dogs but then paused at the sound of another zombie's groan. One groan turned into two, and then three. Moto froze in place as the groans and shuffling footsteps around him multiplied into a chorus of the undead. He turned to see that a growing horde of zombies was approaching from just beyond the clearing. Moto estimated that he would have plenty of time to dispose of the two remaining dogs, retrieve Hillary, and jog to a safe distance from the staggering horde. However, to his horror, Hillary lost her balance on the narrow branch and fell to the ground just feet from the hungry dogs. Moto watched in dismay as the worst possible scenario played out before him in slow motion. Adrenaline coursed through Moto's veins as one of the dogs looked up from its meal and began to creep toward the hysterical little girl. Even before Moto had begun to raise his rifle, Timber was already sliding to a stop between the dogs and Hillary, snarling and baring his teeth to hold the two dogs at bay.

Moto pointed the rifle and wounded the dog nearest Hillary with a hurried shot as he began to run toward her. Slowing only slightly, Moto tried to anticipate the bouncing of his crosshair and fired off another shot in the direction of the second dog. Missing badly, Moto forced himself to slow to a walk and was able to strike the dog just above its hind leg. Though neither shot was fatal, both dogs were severely hobbled, and Moto took off in a full-on sprint for Hillary.

Unsure what else to do, Moto left Timber to fend for himself as he scooped up Hillary and continued his sprint into the wooded area away from the approaching horde. After only a few steps, though, Moto slid down hard onto his rear after seeing several more zombies just ahead of him. The fall wouldn't have been serious but for Moto's efforts to keep Hillary from injury. Moto's focus was solely on protecting Hillary, and he landed hard along the edge of the path. He fought to make his way back onto his feet but felt the familiar twinge of throbbing pain in his wrist due to a severe sprain. Before he was able to stand, a zombie thrust itself upon him so quickly that Moto couldn't lift the rifle up between them. Moto fell to his back and tucked one knee up against the zombie's chest, pushing with the butt of the rifle to keep the ghoul's infectious teeth out of reach. Blood and ichor dripped onto

Moto from the thing's gaping maw, and the incredible stench of death overcame him.

Out of nowhere, the zombie was tackled away in a blur of motion and rolled down a steep embankment next to the trail. Moto looked down the hill to see that it was Timber that had miraculously attacked the zombie with enough momentum to force the thing off of him and Hillary.

Completely exhausted, Moto forced himself to keep moving forward. He stood to see that he was still cornered by zombies approaching from both sides, now only a few paces away. Moto raised the rifle with his one injured arm as he clung to Hillary with the other and fired wildly at the nearest of the undead, striking it in the chest. The pain from raising the gun was blinding, but the pain that came after the rifle had recoiled was too much, and Moto dropped the gun.

Every semblance of a path was completely blocked, and more zombies appeared out of the brush with every passing second. Without using the injured hand, Moto wrapped both arms tightly around Hillary, and Hillary clung snugly against Moto's torso like a young monkey to its mother. Tucking his chin to his chest, Moto covered Hillary as best as he could, pointed his body straight into the thick forest's bushes and thorns, and let gravity guide him down the steep hill. On the first step, Moto felt a hard pull against his back leg just as he was pushing off to run and caused him to tumble out of control.

When they'd finally come to rest, Moto checked that no zombies were near them and began to inspect Hillary for injuries. Finding only a few superficial wounds, Moto fought to stand and realized that he'd now also injured his ankle. Pulling at his pants leg, Moto realized that he hadn't just pulled a muscle or sprained another joint. The bottom of his pants were completely saturated with blood. Praying that he would find that a sharp stick or thorn had stuck him, Moto pulled at his sock to find what he thought to be the teeth marks from a dog's bite. Having already endured the possibility of infection several times before, Moto forced himself to stay calm until he'd returned Hillary to safety. Even if one of the dogs *had* bitten him, that wasn't necessarily a death sentence. Brooke herself had been bitten by one that had likely fed on a zombie's corpse, and she'd shown no symptoms of contracting the virus. Relieved that he was still able to walk, Moto lifted Hillary once again and set off in what he thought was the right direction.

It didn't take long before Moto had found a path, but the way seemed like more of a game trail for deer than one of the paths John had been using to navigate near the shelter. Moto chose a direction and began walking a short distance until he heard the growls of another dog. Moto stopped, hoping that the dog had not already sensed his and Hillary's presence, and tried as best he could to keep Hillary from crying. Moto crouched down and grabbed the sharpest stick within his reach, waiting silently. Just then, an unexpected gunshot echoed through the hills, and the growling ceased immediately. Moto's initial relief that the threat had been eliminated was quickly replaced with the fear of knowing that someone with a gun was very near. His thoughts went back to the lone man that had been shot after wandering into their camp. Moto froze at the sound of rustling leaves just around the curve in the trail. Something large was near.

Timber rounded the turn and sprinted up to Hillary, licking her face incessantly.

"It's Timber!" Hillary cried gleefully.

"Stay quiet, sweetie," Moto whispered. "There's still someone out here that we need to hide from."

After a few moments of silence, Moto could barely make out the sound of footsteps up above them on the ridge. He could also hear the voices of more than one person, though he couldn't make out their dialogue until they were almost upon him.

"No, I'm positive, that was Timber!" a familiar voice whispered loudly.

Moto paused long enough to be absolutely sure who the voice belonged to before he called out, "John, is that you?"

"Moto? Oh, thank God," John answered.

"Do you have Hillary?" Brooke yelled out.

"Yeah, we're ok!" Moto said, standing to see the others making their way down the hill. "That was you that shot, right?

"Yeah, Timber was standing off against some stray dog," John said, giving Moto and Hillary a stronger than usual hug. "I was worried my shot had scared him off."

Brooke jogged up and pulled Hillary out of Moto's arms, rocking her back and forth with an extended hug, kissing at her cheeks. "I was so scared we weren't going to find you two! Where have you been?"

As they all walked, Moto caught them up on all of the excitement that had taken place during their eventful day. He decided to wait until Brooke and Hillary were out of earshot before disclosing the bite he'd suffered. John reassured him of all the things Moto had already been telling himself, but the words did little to give Moto optimism.

Sprite had stayed behind at the camp in case Moto and Hillary should return before John and Brooke. John hadn't really begun to worry that morning about the length of time the two had been gone, despite Brooke's constant intuitive warnings. That is, until he heard the gunshots.

"At that point," John said, "none of us could do anything else until we'd found you. I might have been a little nervous that you'd been gone so long but saw that you'd taken the gun and figured you could handle yourself. After we heard more than one gunshot, though, I knew you weren't just hunting. We all freaked out just a little bit."

"Oh, poor Sprite," Brooke thought aloud. "We need to get back and let him know you're both ok."

Moto did his best to stick to the back of the line in order to conceal his blood-soaked pants from the girls as they all made their way back up to the trail. They all walked together in high spirits, with Moto struggling to keep up in the rear. He tried not to focus on his dilemma, but the sharp pain in his leg was a constant reminder to Moto that he might no longer be in control of his own destiny. He'd occasionally laugh with the others ahead of him, but Moto mostly ran the events of the day back through his mind, wondering if there was anything else he could've done. A way into their walk, Moto recalled a brief prayer that he'd offered if God would just preserve Hillary after she'd fallen from the tree. Moto forced himself to refocus and to thank God that Hillary was indeed protected but also selfishly added another request for his own survival. When he lifted his eyes to the heavens, though, Moto took a second to process an unexpected sight.

"Is that smoke coming from our place?" Moto pointed.

Above the trees, a huge plume of black smoke was rising up from not too far down the trail, just where their encampment should've been.

"Wait here," John instructed. "Let me go check on it."

The other three waited where they stood, brainstorming what explanation there might be. Moto wouldn't bring himself to mention it, but he became more and more concerned that the other members of the dead man's group had finally found those responsible for his death. Hillary smiled and played with Timber in blissful ignorance of the events unfolding around her while Moto and Brooke whispered and feared the worst. After what seemed like hours, John came jogging back down the trail. He was covered in sweat, and his eyes were opened wide.

"We've gotta go," John instructed.

"Go where?" Brooke asked. "What about our food?"

"What'd you see?" Moto talked over her.

"It's all gone," John answered in a stern whisper so that Hillary couldn't hear.

"It's all gone, and there are zombies *everywhere.*"

With only a rifle and the ragged clothes on their backs, the group found themselves scrambling into an unexplored section of forest. Moto silently mouthed a question to John as to Sprite's fate, but John's response was only an ignorant shrug. Each time they assumed they'd traveled far enough to achieve some sort of sanctuary, more evidence would arise indicating that they had not yet escaped the increasingly present threat of zombies. Sometimes a snarl from some unseen source served as their warning to keep moving--other times it came in the form of the barely audible shuffling of feet. After enough instances, just a slight showing of aggression from Timber was heeded as enough of an indicator that they weren't safe. Their aimless hiking along the path of least resistance continued on until the sun began to threaten concealment of its life-giving light.

"Ok, really quick pow wow," Moto gasped as he halted their ever-slowing pace. "Pee, or rest, or whatever you've gotta do."

John observed Timber who walked in a tight circle before plopping down with a heavy exhale.

"We're not going to have the time to build any kind of shelter or perimeter for the night," Moto said softly.

"Hell, we don't even have the tools," John grumbled. "We've got to find something, and soon."

"Should we just climb up in some trees to get away from 'em?" Moto thought aloud, while looking up. "That seems like it could work for one night."

"What happens when we get surrounded?" John asked. "I don't have near enough bullets. We'd be screwed."

"I don't know, we could grind off some sharp branches and stab down at their heads until they're all dead," Moto offered, nodding at his own idea.

"I'd just be so paranoid that someone would start dozing off and fall," John said, looking over his shoulder at Hillary. "Wait, where did Timber run off to?"

"He probably just went off with Brooke; I saw her walk off that way," Moto pointed without concern.

A moment later, Moto and John halted their planning when Brooke returned with no knowledge of Timber's whereabouts.

Hillary began to call loudly for him, but John shushed the girl, still aware that zombies were likely not far off.

"I see a few paw prints over here," Brooke pointed and began tracking the dog's steps. Occasionally, the fallen leaves of the season would make the trail next to impossible to find, but the dog's path predictably continued straight down the gentle slope.

"Wait, do you hear that?" John asked after several minutes of tracking. "Flowing water! Thank God."

They all continued directly toward the sound of rushing water, occasionally spotting evidence of Timber's path. Finally, Moto made out the sunset's pink reflection from through the trees. Lying in a shallow section of the cool, flowing water, Timber appeared to be smiling.

"Come on sweetie; let's get a drink of water," Brooke led Hillary. "We don't know when we'll come across more, so drink a whole lot."

"You think it's safe?" Moto asked John, shuddering slightly in the cool, evening air.

"Safe to drink? Probably. It's cool, clear, and flowing," John said. "But I think it might be even safer than that."

"Wait, what do you mean?" Moto asked, looking up after several large gulps.

"Look over there," John pointed to a moderate island in the middle of the deep creek. "It's big enough for us to all sleep on."

"Oh my gosh, that's brilliant," Moto nodded. "The zombies aren't coordinated enough to wade through the current without be swept downstream."

Though their stomachs were empty, they all rested comfortably on their own private island that night. John dug out shallow dips in the rock and dirt to conform more comfortably to their bodies, and Moto carried across huge piles of leaves in his jacket to soften their nests. Though they couldn't dig deeply enough to completely block the cold winds of fall, the setup was much better than they'd expected to find, given the circumstances. John worried that zombies might still accumulate on the shores around them rather than wandering far enough into the water to be carried away by its current, but decided there was nothing more he could do.

Moto lay as still as he could, shivering in the cold, and struggling to sleep. He did his best to not rearrange himself because the dried leaves crunched loudly with each tiny movement he made. After a long while, he considered waking John to see if he might switch spots so that Moto could be protected from the northern wind for a bit, but couldn't bring himself to ruin anyone else's sleep. Unsure if he'd slept or not, Moto jolted awake, feeling a few large raindrops strike him in the face.

"John," Moto shook him awake. "It's raining."

"Mmh," John groaned. "There's nothing we can do about it. Just put your jacket over you."

Long after the others had fallen back into a deep sleep, Moto continued his unending fight to get comfortable. With the sounds being drowned out by the heavy rains, Moto continuously repositioned himself in the damp hole, fighting to hide from the frigid air. A solution finally presented itself when Moto felt the warmth he'd been praying for descend into the hole with him in the form of Timber when the dog came to lay with him. Moto finally slept.

Later in the night, Moto again found that he was the only one awake. Even Timber seemed to be resting comfortably at his side. Moto shivered after being soaked by the even heavier sheets rains that had rolled in. He wasn't sure how long he'd been asleep, but there was still no sign of sunrise. Frustrated, Moto laid his head back down and realized that it wasn't just the rain that had awoken him. The water level had risen to the point that it was now creeping up onto the island, and the hole for his head had begun to fill.

When it became clear that the water would only continue to rise, Moto woke the others and alerted them of their predicament. They stayed for as long as they could on the ever-shrinking island, forfeiting any hopes of rest, until their stake of land had been fully reclaimed by mother nature.

"Dammit, can we get a break?" Moto griped after stepping down into a large puddle.

"Alright, everyone hold hands," John instructed, reaching out in the dark. "There's no way we can stay here until daybreak. We'd better get out while we can still do it safely."

Stumbling in the darkness, John regained his sense of direction by the water's flow and led the group safely to shore. Fear overtook them all, as the relentless onslaught of deafening raindrops pounded the earth around them. Everyone held hands, with Moto and John on either end of the line swinging large sticks in front of them in order to discover any unseen dangers, whether inanimate or undead. Occasionally, they would freeze upon hearing Timber growl, and sometimes even hearing the footsteps of a nearby wandering zombie. Fortunately, the zombies were as handicapped as the survivors by the thunderous percussion of raindrops and the non-existent visibility.

The storm worsened, and only the occasional strike of lightning assisted the men in finding their way. Just as they began to wonder for how much longer their luck would hold out, the sun began to creep up across the eastern horizon. Though blocked by clouds, the light that did penetrate was more than enough to help them negotiate the terrain safely.

It quickly became apparent, though, that the zombies were also being aided by the additional light. The radius of distance the group had to maintain between themselves and the undead grew as the light intensified. When avoidance became impossible, Moto and John fought to stab at the nearest of the approaching threats with their sticks, incapacitating many with ease. As the rains slowed, though, more and more zombies began to appear from all sides, alerted by their brethren's cries.

"We can't keep this up much longer," Moto said through his shivering jaw. "Time for my tree idea?"

"We just might have to," John said, taking in the terrain around them and the looming horde.

"Timber, no!" Hillary scolded the dog as it threw chunks of mud up at her.

The others looked down to find him digging ferociously until his front half had almost completely disappeared down into the earth.

"Wait a second, look," Brooke paused. "The water is flowing somewhere. Is that a cave?"

Moto quickly squatted down and looked into the narrow hole which now housed almost all of Timber.

"Holy shit, it's huge in here!" he said ecstatically and began prying at the large rocks on either side of the hole. "John, give me a hand!"

Soon, they had widened the hole to the point that their shoulders could pass through it easily. One by one, each person laid flat on their belly and slid themselves down feet first into the cavern with some assistance from Moto below. The hole continued to widen as the flowing stream of rainwater poured down into their shelter, eroding away their defensible hole. After disposing of several zombies while all of the others made their way inside the cave, John finally ran over and slid down into the hole as if careening head first down a slip and slide. He soon realized that he'd underestimated the depth of the cavern and rotated a perfect half somersault in the air before landing hard on his back on the cave's floor.

The cavern felt spacious, considering the tiny hole that had led them there. Moto estimated it to measure over fifteen feet in diameter, and at its highest point, the roof was well over ten feet high. Moto was happy to see that the water inside the cave was draining slowly out the other side through a smaller hole, quieting his fear that they might've been in danger due to rising water levels. Less encouraging, though, was the fact that the small hole was completely comprised of rock, and there didn't appear to be an alternate exit point through which they could escape.

Suddenly, Timber alerted them to the presence of danger yet again. Moto looked up to see that a zombie had pursued them to the hole just as it lost traction and completed its long fall flat onto its head. Even though the fall had seemingly incapacitated the zombie, Moto didn't hesitate to stab it through the brain.

"Quick, help me find something to plug up the hole," he pleaded, searching around with his hands beneath the shallow water's surface.

When another zombie appeared by the hole, John stabbed it through the eye socket with his long, sharpened branch, rendering the thing lifeless before it had even extended half way through the opening. When another tried to pry its way into the narrow opening next to its motionless partner, John struck that one dead as well. Before long, the water at their feet was darkened with the blood of their dead enemies, but the solution for plugging the hole had presented itself. A mound of corpses sealed the only passable opening almost completely.

"I guess that works," Moto sighed, sitting on a high, dry spot along the edge of the cave and watching as one zombie pushed its hand through a small space above them. "It's like something out of a nightmare," he continued, watching as the thing grabbed futilely at the unseen survivors.

"My God it smells," Brooke said after a while, holding her index finger up to block her nostrils. "How long do we have to stay in here?"

John quietly pulled down one of the motionless corpses from the hole above them, allowing two others to take its place.

"Well, we might have to stay for a bit," John sighed, stabbing at the new zombies and effectively re-plugging the hole. "They don't seem to be interested in moving on."

Slow, uneventful hours passed, and John and Moto's stomachs began to cramp with hunger. Suddenly, and completely without warning, the group all looked up at the sound of jets soaring overhead, followed shortly by the rumble of what they assumed to be an airstrike. Listening attentively now, they heard numerous other soft, more distant explosions.

"Are we gonna die?" Hillary asked.

"No, sweetie, they're just cleaning up the cities," Brooke answered without missing a beat. "We're not close enough to a city that *we* should be scared."

"This is good right?" Moto whispered to John. "Still a government, still a military?"

"I guess you could say that... as long as they're not stupid enough to use nukes, and we're able to avoid the napalm," John answered. "I'm not gonna hold my breath for them to come pick us up and take us to some happy little village that's unaffected, but, if they're cutting into the number of zombies, I guess I'll take it."

"You think the noise from the explosions drew the zombies away from here?" Brooke asked.

Not hearing anything above them but for the explosions in the distance, John cautiously pulled two more bodies down into their growing pile. His guarded optimism was quickly disproven when a new chorus of moans from the undead echoed down.

"This is bad. Like really bad," Moto grumbled as John re-plugged the hole. "There were dozens of 'em up there; they're just waiting for us."

"I never would've dreamed they'd still be hanging around after that long," Brooke said. "With all the rain, I really doubt they're still able to pick up our scent out there. If we can't hear them, then there's no way they hear us."

"I really thought they'd be attracted to the fires," John groaned as he pushed the corpses over to the side of the cave. "I guess we can give up hope that they'll be leaving on their own."

Moto re-took his squatting position on his rock and tucked his knees up against his chest. The entire time they'd been trapped in the cave, John had quietly observed as Moto hugged himself and sat quietly. John would've feared that Moto's bite was beginning to turn him, except for the fact that Brooke had endured a much more severe dog bite and appeared to be completely healthy. John leaned against the nearest wall and quietly observed Moto's pathetic condition as he considered the possibilities. Even *if* the graying skin and lethargic demeanor weren't only due to the lacking heat and food, there was little that John could do to help Moto or ensure the safety of the others. His only option was to continue to monitor Moto carefully. As John watched, a large dirt clod was jarred loose from a nearby missile strike and broke across the back of Moto's head.

"You'd better find another spot," John whispered. "The next one might not be a dirt clod."

John looked up to see if there was a rock above himself that might have loosened from the explosions. He considered that perhaps the cavern wasn't composed entirely of stone. He'd already circled around the cave dragging a hand across every section of wall within reach, finding only rock, but he hadn't considered other sections of the ceiling. At the spot where the dirt clod had fallen, John noticed a small discolored area with exposed roots. Unsure what he was hoping for, John thrust his long tree branch up into the rooted area and found almost no resistance.

"You seeing this?" John asked, kicking at Moto's foot.

"Yeah, so?" Moto shrugged. "You're just gonna open another hole for the zombies to come through."

"I'm not so sure there are zombies on this side," John explained. "Wouldn't this part over here be off on the other side of the hill from the creek? There might be a good chance they wouldn't be able to see us at all from over here."

John stabbed at the spot again, and a chunk of soil fell to the ground, allowing muddy water to flow in. With a slight wiggle of the branch, sunlight dripped in with the water.

"Let me on your shoulders," John motioned to Moto. "I wanna peek out."

"How about you let me on your shoulders?" Moto stood sluggishly. "I'm not feeling that great."

John understood and, above that, didn't want to draw any more attention to Moto's worsening condition in front of the girls. Considering that fact, John ducked down and lifted Moto up onto his shoulders while Moto pressed the large branch to the ground to help himself balance.

"Is there any way to get higher?" Moto asked. "What I can see is clear, but I can only see so much from here."

John struggled to grasp the bottoms of Moto's shoes and lift as best he could while Moto pressed down on the limb as if a pole-vaulter, relieving some of the weight. A loud snap echoed as the branch broke, and the brothers tumbled hard into the contaminated water below.

"I think we could still get out that way," Moto said, looking up at the small hole from the flat of his back. "We just need a little bit of a boost. Once one of us is up there, it'll be easy to pull the girls up."

"Maybe," John thought for a moment. "How are we gonna get that extra little boost?"

"What if you both lift me up together?" Brooke offered. "I bet we could reach. And, for the last person, we could tie our belts and jackets into a rope to hoist them up."

"Absolutely not. We don't even know if the coast is clear up there yet," John said.

"I thought it was a great idea," Moto said, shrugging.

"Yeah, at least let me poke my head out and see," Brook argued.

"Alright, let's give it a shot, I guess," John said reluctantly, "but stay as quiet as possible."

Moto and John set up a standing pyramid base with their knees bent, allowing Brooke to climb up by stepping on their thighs and then shoulders, grasping tightly to their hair with each hand for balance. Once stable, John and Moto attempted to straighten up and lift Brooke through the hole. Moto struggled to control his balance as his feet slipped badly on the sloping rocks where he stood.

"I can't reach. Bring me down," Brooke whispered and squatted down as their pyramid began to shake noticeably.

John reached up, secured Brooke by her hips, and helped her to the ground safely.

"Sorry, I thought I was tall enough," Brooke said.

"Okay, I have one last idea," Moto said. He spoke as if he was about to disclose the last thing anyone wanted to hear. "You know that riddle about digging yourself out of a hole?"

"Yeah, where you dig out stairs or whatever? I already thought that, but we don't have any dirt to work with, really," John thought out loud.

"Yeah, well, you'll have to bear with me on that part," Moto said, glancing over at the pile of corpses.

For what it lacked in glamour, Moto's idea made up in simplicity. One by one, John continued to pull down a motionless corpse at a time onto their growing pile of bodies, allowing another ambulatory one to take its place before repeating the process. It didn't take long of continuing the pattern until a significant pile of bodies had been assembled beneath the second hole of the cave.

Brooke's idea with a cell phone alarm acting as a distraction was given a chance by poking Sprite's ringing phone up through the plugged hole as his was the only phone with some battery charge remaining.

"That might do 'er right there," Moto said, eyeballing the distance between the top of their pile and their escape.

John was glad to sense a little bit of normalcy to Moto's voice. Though, he was also a little frustrated that Moto was perking up now that the work was finished. John was completely covered in gore from stacking bodies to the top of the pile and took great effort to spit out a full sentence. It's wasn't just the exhaustion. It was the repulsive, inescapable odor that now enveloped him.

After gathering his composure, John insisted on going first and stumbled up the awkward, shifting pile of decomposing bodies. Some of the undead had degenerated to the point that their skin easily peeled away from the bone under John's weight as he climbed.

"Good God, this smell," Brooke muttered.

John fought back several gag reflexes and was eventually forced to hold his breath entirely in order to reach the top of the pile without vomiting. Even his own scent couldn't compete with the fumes that escaped from intestines and bowels as they ruptured under his weight. From atop the pile, John peered out from the hole with a full view of their surroundings.

"Coast is clear," he whispered down before leaping up through the narrow hole. His head reappeared upside-down alongside an extended arm. "Who's next?"

"Hillary, are you ready?" Brooke asked while approaching the mound. "I can hold your hand while you climb up to John."

Tentatively, Hillary walked up to Brooke and eyed the tall pile of gore. Without speaking, the young girl calculated her path, and began to step softly on the corpses and climb unassisted.

"I can do it by myself," Hillary said. "It's easy if you just step on their jaw."

Brooke was equally as encouraged as she was repulsed by the little girl's ability to adapt and continue to move forward despite everything. She tried to picture what type of person the little girl might become if she were to survive until adulthood in this new world. The person that she began to imagine was not an entirely promising one, and Brooke quickly shook the thought.

"That's good sweetheart, you've got it!" Brooke said with hands raised at the ready like a parent spotting their child as they ascended the ladder of a slide.

Hillary's smaller stature made for less shifting of the lifeless bodies, and she easily navigated her way up the pile until she was within reach of John. Once she'd been hoisted up safely, Brooke began to make her way up with a little help from Moto. It didn't take long for Brooke to realize the value of Hillary's advice in utilizing the jawbones as footholds.

John caught himself hesitating for a split second at the sight of Moto waiting impatiently after already passing up the mortified dog. Despite the occasional glimpse of normalcy, Moto looked awful. John admitted to himself that Moto wasn't well. He considered the validity of his logical temptation to protect the girls and teased the thought of leaving Moto behind for so long that Moto noticed his hesitation, waiting with arm raised. John shut off his "rational" thinking and forced himself to reach his hand down into the hole and take hold of his brother.

Back outside, the world seemed unbearably bright. The rain had dissipated, but the cold remained. During the few hours they had been underground, the temperature had seemingly dropped by twenty degrees. Though they were all improperly dressed and freezing, the group moved on as quietly as they could from the growing hoard across the hill. Once out into an opened clearing, they paused to rest and plot out their next move.

Brooke listened as the brothers bounced several ideas off one other, none of which seemed very appealing to her at all. The unfortunate sequence of events had significantly limited their list of available options. She loathed the fact that all of their careful planning and execution had landed them in a place perhaps no better than if they'd wandered aimlessly in the wilderness in the first place. She thought to herself that, ultimately, their only option was to wander in search of food and warmth. Feeling as low as she had since her sister's death, Brooke sat silently and hugged on Hillary, trying in vain to keep them both warm. Smelling smoke, Brooke looked up through the gap in the trees above, fully expecting to see smoke plumes from a rapidly approaching wildfire. Brooke was instead greeted by the most vibrant rainbow she'd ever observed. Hillary saw Brooke staring up, and was thrilled with the sight.

"Hey, look," the young girl pointed up. "Do you think it means God is gonna help us, like after the flood?"

"Unfortunately, kiddo, God didn't choose to do this like he did the flood," John said. "People did this, and I don't know if God is very happy with all of us right now."

Hillary looked to Brooke for confirmation.

"I sure hope He helps us," Brooke said. "We could really use it about now."

"You want to pray with me?" Hillary asked Brooke. "Whenever we need God, we're s'pose to pray."

"Sure, I don't see why not," Brooke smiled. "But we have to be really quiet while the guys think, okay?"

Hillary smiled and bowed her head, folding her hands in the most stereotypical prayer stance. Brooke watched Hillary until the girl looked up to confirm that she too had closed her eyes. Together, the two sat silently with heads bowed.

While they still prayed, a faint squeaking noise became audible. Timber growled but remained relatively calm as the slow, consistent squeak was seemingly just out of sight and approaching. Brooke anticipated that the sound was soon going to emerge from the trees just down the hill from where they sat and abruptly halted Hillary's prayer. The group all watched anxiously as a lone zombie emerged from the brush and wandered aimlessly, still not having sensed them.

245

The zombie wore nothing other than its hiking boots, tattoos, and large backpack. John couldn't envision a scenario that would've resulted in the zombie losing all of its clothes while managing to keep the pack on, except that the hiker had been naked even before death. Hillary stared curiously at the grotesque sight until Brooke instinctively covered her eyes. The effort seemed vain, considering the other atrocities Hillary had already been calloused to over the past several weeks. This one, though, was particularly disturbing. One arm was dragging a hiking pole by the wrist strap, and the other arm had been severed at the elbow. Its previously slender stomach had puffed out significantly from the gaseous buildup of decomposition. The belly landed, in John's estimation, somewhere between that of an impressive beer belly and that of a nine-month pregnant woman. Perhaps most notable of its injuries was the gaping hole in its head. An apparent gunshot had blown off a portion of the thing's skull, leaving a gut-wrenching black ooze of a crater. The wound was significant, but somehow the thing still walked.

John quickly finished the job and disposed of the lone zombie after he'd confirmed that no others were in close proximity. Moto walked over and began rummaging through the thing's backpack. Inside, he found a few much needed granola bars, matches, moleskin, water purification tablets, some headphones, and a journal.

The group shared a modest lunch while dividing up the man's belongings amongst themselves. Moto claimed the headphones to go along with his own phone, should he find a way to charge it. Brooke applied moleskin to her and Hillary's blisters. John thumbed through the journal, noting a few interesting posts of observations and speculation about the outbreak and decided it would be worth keeping. As he finished flicking through the pages, John spotted a hand drawn map inside the book's back cover. Though the drawing had been significantly smudged by rainwater, the remaining legible sections showed landmarks, a dotted line, and an X--just like a treasure map.

"Check this out," John said, rotating the book toward the others. "What do you think it leads to?"

246

"I think I can read some of it," Moto squinted at the unintelligible blotches of text. 'Reoccurring dream where I'm one of them... can feel the pain they must feel... in my joints, my stomach's relentless ache, my absence of a heartbeat...considering ending it just so I can be sure that... family is surely gone... don't intend to find out if the nightmares were a foreshadowing of my ultimate fate.'

"None of it is about the map?" Brooke peered at the page between the brothers.

"Nothing," John frowned. "Just a note from before he uh..."

"The zombies still hurt?" Hillary asked. "Is that why they're always groaning?"

"No, no they're completely gone," Moto turned to comfort the eavesdropping little girl. "The real person is already in heaven. It's just an empty body walking around."

"Hey, do you think that's the three peaks above the river that we saw before? When you were tracking the deer?" Brooke asked John, pointing to one of the few surviving landmarks indicated on the map.

"If it is, we might be able to find our "X" after all," John nodded. "Even without the other clues, this will give us a solid point of reference with the hills in relation to what I can only assume was supposed to be the river."

"C'mon, Hillary!" Brooke called out with a renewed optimism. "Let's go find your answered prayer!"

After a grueling hike, they all stood looking down from atop the "trinity hills", as they'd come to refer to the formation next to the treasure map's final destination. From there, they not only found the reason they'd been smelling smoke all day, but it was also possible for them to look out across the expansive terrain, surveying the area for what the map's "X" might have been indicating. In the distance, massive plumes of smoke could be seen rising up and suffocating the majority of the sky. In some sections, a warm orange glow flickered from below the looming darkness, in all likelihood indicating that the fires were still actively expanding and engulfing the countryside. What had previously felt like a typical overcast fall sunset now loomed as an ominous floating mountain of ash blotting out the late afternoon sun. Though they didn't appear to be in immediate danger, the fires did indicate just how bad things were becoming around the larger cities that had been targeted.

"Is that fire from the airstrikes you think?" Moto asked between violent coughs. "Is it just gonna keep spreading?"

"Until it burns itself out, I suppose," John said. "I don't see anyone intervening. And why would they? It's just burning out all the zombies as far as the people in D.C. are concerned."

"Well for our sakes, I guess we just pray for more rain," Brooke said. "Thank goodness the ground here is as wet as it is."

"You're dead on," Moto said. "Remember those wildfires a few years back? The ash from California covered up half the country. Imagine the damage if they strike up fires in all the major cities and just let them burn free. There won't be any crops to find or any animals to hunt before long. The world would become a pretty impossible place to live.

"In the short term, I just hope that fire isn't going to drive all the zombies toward us," John said softly enough that Hillary couldn't hear. "I wonder if that's why so many were coming up on us at the cave."

"Well, let's find this 'X' first off," Moto said, pausing to cough. "At least maybe that can help us with one of the impending dooms on our list."

"I knew there wasn't a house anywhere out here," John said with a sigh, surveying the lower area behind them. "We would've seen it before if there was anything that size. I just figured there must be *something* worth finding if it's worth drawing out on a map."

"Maybe it was just a weapon or food stockpile that someone else already found," Moto said. "There's no telling how long that hiker had been dead."

"Well, standing up here and flapping our gums isn't gonna answer any questions," Brooke said as she worked her way down the hill with Hillary in tow.

Before following, John and Moto took one more look with the map from their high vantage point to pick out what area they'd use as the center of their search.

They could tell decently by a distinct curve of the river that they were very near their target area but found nothing more than a few small clearings in the trees. An extensive search of the immediate area surfaced nothing of note, and as their stomachs began to grow into knots from hunger, their emotions also began to tighten.

"The whole thing is so smudged we could be miles away for all we know," Moto grumbled. "That freaking map could be pointing to a damned dog house the next county over, while we're out here digging through the leaves."

Moto stopped his rant abruptly upon noticing a few flecks of white stuck in the hairs of his arm. He looked up, along with Brooke and John to see that the smoke was inching ever closer, and the ash had already begun its descent back to earth.

"Does this mean the winds changed?" Moto asked with wide eyes.

John and Brooke made unsure eye contact and gave Moto no response.

"Snow!" Hillary exclaimed, with her chin raised and her tongue extended.

"No, sweetie, stop. That's ashes," Brooke said, brushing the flakes off of the little girl's hair and jacket.

Unfazed, the little girl shrugged and skipped over to a small limb to initiate a game of fetch with Timber as the adults reconvened. Before long, one of Hillary's throws wound up in a thicker patch of vegetation that even Timber didn't deem worth the effort to retrieve. Instead of simply picking a new stick, though, Hillary slowly trudged her way through the wall of sticks and leaves in order to reach their toy. Suddenly, she jumped back and began sobbing, as Timber looked on with visible concern.

"Was it a snake?" Brooke asked, rushing over.

John inspected the small wound on the girl's shin. "Probably just some bramble briars."

"Try again," Moto called from where Hillary had been injured. "Barbed wire."

Closer inspection of the area revealed large amounts of sharp wire, and even trip lines attached to empty soda cans. Though their efforts were slowed without the benefit of gloves, it eventually became clear that the wall of vegetation was also placed intentionally surrounding a decent sized area. A mound of bricks hinted at a fallen chimney. In the center of it all was a small square section that didn't fit with the area surrounding it. The reason became obvious when Moto reached down and swiped away at the flat section of ash and leaves to reveal a square area of particle board. Beneath the board was a metal, hinged door with a small handle.

"Please, God, be a prepper," John said, before Moto yanked at the heavy door.

An awful concoction of aromas arose from the hole which housed a ladder similar to that of a manhole.

"Sewers?" Brooke asked, holding her nose.

"Out here? Doubt it," Moto laughed before succumbing to a coughing fit.

"I'll check it out," John said, with his shirt collar pulled up over his nose, already putting his foot to the ladder.

Moments later he returned with a large smile spread across his face.

"It might have to air out a little, but I think we found what we've been looking for. It's a sure 'nough bunker full of supplies and everything."

John fielded their excited questions as best he could while searching through some limbs and leaves several feet from the hatch before merrily shoving away a large fallen tree branch from a pipe protruding from the soil.

"It has an exhaust vent," he explained, "but there's no power to the fan. Hopefully, just opening up this pipe will give it a chance to air out some."

"Did the food all go bad or something?" Brooke asked.

"I don't really think so," John frowned. "It looked more like the last tenant chose not to come outside... at all. So you can imagine the buildup of a mess he left."

"I hope you mean trash," Brooke said.

"Well, yeah, there's that. And then there's the matter of the poop."

"Not it!" Moto said with a smile and a raised hand, despite his deteriorating condition.

"Not it!" Hillary mimicked.

John and Brooke exchanged an uncomfortable glance.

The amount of ash falling in the area slowed, and once John had emptied the buckets of excrement, the putrid aroma dispersed rather quickly. The group shoveled food into their faces by the fistful until their swollen stomachs were repulsed by the offer of another bite. They began sorting through some of their new embarrassment of riches with one the working flashlights they'd already come across in the bunker. Many of the items would've been a tremendous help if there'd been electricity, such as a radio, satellite phones, fans, and space heaters, not to mention lights. John knew the cell towers would quit working without power, but was unsure if the satellites were self-sufficient enough to have lasted this long.

Shockingly, John's ears perked up to the sound of an all too familiar *ba da ding* which indicated a cell phone had begun charging. He turned to find Moto standing by the edge of shelves with his child-like grin being illuminated by his cell phone's glow.

"Dude, I'm gonna get to listen to my music for the first time in *forever!*" Moto said without breaking the smile.

"Where did you find power?" John asked.

"I just plugged my phone into this big battery with an AC outlet. Somehow it's still holding a charge!"

"There's no way," John said. "No way that battery hasn't died down here in the cold."

"Tell that to my phone," Moto said.

"Well, okay. We'll take what we can get, I guess," John said happily as he began inspecting the battery more closely. "Wait a second. Where does this wire run to?"

John climbed back up to the surface and found where the battery's wire resurfaced inside a small PVC conduit. The pipe ran along the ground some ways before ending at a decent sized solar panel that had been covered by ash. Laying down in the brush nearby was a yellow traffic sign with two caution lights. Someone had repurposed the sign's solar panel and battery to bring electricity into the bunker.

"Don't waste all the juice!" John yelled down to Moto. "I know you think of music as a priority, but it's only a small solar panel. We're not gonna be able to re-charge the battery until all these clouds and ash move out. Let's save it for a heater or light or something."

Moto glanced down to see that his phone had been charged more than enough to listen to his music for a bit and unplugged the phone without argument. Moto plugged in the hiker's earbuds and walked to the next room where he took full advantage of a vacant cot and was soon sleeping soundly. After finding nothing stored in the bunker that was of any interest to her, Hillary followed suit by climbing into a small bean bag in the corner and immediately fell asleep with Timber curled up at her feet.

While familiarizing themselves with their new shelter and sorting out the still useful items, John and Brooke's stomachs recovered enough that they decided to raid the stock of alcohol that had been stored in a locked cabinet above the now useless microwave. While quietly re-locating an armful of useless supplies into the back room, John noticed that Moto had become even more feverish and was visibly shivering. He stretched out another blanket over his brother, though John wasn't optimistic that it would make any difference.

"We might have to take some precautions," John said to Brooke. "I don't know how much longer Moto's gonna be able to hold on. I'm starting to admit to myself that it's probably just a matter of time."

"Don't give up on him yet," Brooke said while scratching John's back. "He's too stubborn to give in to whatever this is. He's already lived ten times longer than anyone else we've seen after being infected."

"I don't know what I'll do without him if he can't beat this. I've never had to know life without him. He's always been wherever I've gone. I can't picture a life without that. I don't want to," John said softly before downing what remained of his glass.

"I felt the exact same way about my sister before..." Brooke said. "Now, I doubt that any of my family or friends are alive. It's a hard thing to admit to yourself. I wouldn't wish it on anyone."

"I just wish my mom could've met you," John said. "I know it sounds pretty stupid, but I feel like that would've made it easier to lose her."

254

"It sounds extremely stupid," Brooke laughed. "And I feel exactly the same way. I could not wait until the day I could hand my mom her first grandchild. I never even considered that she might not even be around to meet the man of my life."

"Man of your life, huh?"

"Well, for now, at least. Man of my life unless a better option comes along."

"Unless you don't mind ridiculously bad skin, my chances are getting better by the minute."

Brooke gave an obviously forced smile.

John stopped taking after he'd realized they had just been talking about Moto's condition, and he was already cracking jokes about the virus.

Their small Maglite flashlight, which they'd unscrewed into its candle form, began to grow dim and flicker.

"We're gonna burn through these batteries so fast," John grumbled. "But at the same time, we're gonna go crazy if we have to live in the dark down here. I really need to figure out a way to get us light in both rooms.

"Is there something you could get from the outside?" Brooke asked. "Is there another car battery trick up your sleeve?"

"Maybe something along those lines. Ultimately, I'd love to get one of those generators they use at construction sites or something. But for that to be doable, we'd have to be really protected along the perimeter. Generators are just way too loud. Hopefully Moto's discovery over there is going to pay off, but I just don't think it's very powerful. I don't think we're going to be able to run a heater or anything bigger than a little lamp with it. Speaking of which, I'm gonna go clean the ash off the panels and see if that fire has shifted direction or anything," John said.

"Oh, good thinking," Brooke said. "I'll go with you."

"Well, if we're being honest, my real motivation was just to go use the bathroom," John said in a whisper.

"If we're being honest, I have the same motivation," Brooke whispered back. "And there's no way I'm gonna go out there by myself at night."

After a brief surveillance of the surface revealed nothing more than a cool, calm evening, the two decided to remain outside with the fresh air for a while longer. Though it was cold, the fresh air was more than worth the discomfort. The two remained, enjoying their new, private solace by lying quietly in the open patch of land and staring up through the circular opening in the canopy formed by the surrounding forest. They enjoyed spotting a rare star through the occasional break in the ash with as much excitement as a child spotting their first meteor. Enjoying the air and the quiet grew into enjoying each other's company, which grew into making the most of their first moments of true privacy in far too long.

Though the most comfortable spots had been claimed and no remaining surface in the bunker could provide the level of comfort they had achieved on the leaves above, John and Brooke forced themselves to sleep downstairs. They didn't anticipate that anything would happen but couldn't allow themselves to leave Hillary alone and unsupervised. Though Moto's continually worsening condition was some cause for concern, it didn't seem to John that he was going to be approaching death's doorstep any time soon. Still, guilt set in that they'd allowed themselves to be separated from the two for even the short amount of time that they had. Finally, the cold, hard floor was unable to maintain their consciousness any longer, and sleep overtook them both.

The next morning, Hillary woke Brooke and John with concerns about Moto. John could sense the girl's anxiety but didn't fully comprehend what the young one was really getting at before finally shaking the fog from the previous night's drinking. Once he understood, John jumped up and ran to Moto's room to confirm whether or not Moto was truly gone. Entering the room, John expectantly flipped the light switch with no result. He then felt around on the old desk where he'd left his flashlight and illuminated nothing but a vacant cot. His brother was gone.

"Did he turn you think?" Brooke asked.

"I just don't see that being the case," John said in a worried tone. "He *was* feverish, though. He might've been confused in the dark or something. Fevers can make people do crazy things sometimes."

"Maybe he got stir crazy, or sick, and went outside first," Brooke thought. "Maybe he turned after he was already out there."

"Wow, you might be right," John said. "That makes more sense than anything else. He did admit to me that he's been... well... dehydrating from both ends."

Hillary stood nearby, attempting to eavesdrop on the adults' conversation about Moto. Brooke was wise to the girl, though, and she ended Hillary's chance at listening. Instead, Hillary found herself a pen and sat down to draw next to a fully charged and brightly glowing Maglite candle. It was the hiker's water-damaged notepad; chock-full of mostly ruined notes. She flipped through page after page that had been ruined with gibberish or moisture before finally coming to a blank one near the back with enough room that she could draw. Just before she'd touched pen to paper, John snatched the journal from her.

"This last page. It's from Moto," He observed.

I think we can all see where this is headed. Please do your best to help Hillary understand.
-Much love, Moto

"I can't believe he's giving up," Brooke said, tearing up.

"I've gotta go look for him," John said as he grabbed the pistol, leaving the rifle for Brooke. "I won't be gone too long. I've just gotta try. You'll be ok here, right?"

"Sure, sure. We've got everything we need," Brooke nodded, wiping away at the tears on her cheeks, only for more to immediately replace the previous. "Take Timber with you, too-- just in case."

John kissed Brooke unceremoniously on the lips and left Hillary with a peck on the top of the head before scooping up the dog under one arm and awkwardly making his way up the ladder.

It became obvious that Hillary didn't really understand what had occurred with Moto, and Brooke decided to just leave her in the dark as to the details. Should Moto return, or even if he didn't, she felt that it would make things a lot easier for her to not know everything. After Brooke had spent a long while sitting and worrying about the brothers, it began to feel more and more like a waste of her time.

She distracted herself for a while, reading Moto's note over and over before finally flipping to other pages in the book which they'd yet to explore. She skipped over the sections which bore every gruesome detail as to how the poor man had been separated from his family. Some pages focused on the man's ideas for protecting the bunker, such as a moat-like fire trench, which he'd devised after observing the zombies' reluctance to approach a flame. He went on to share that loud sounds such as a gunshot or even swiping at them with a blade didn't serve as any deterrent at all but had heard that a torch being thrust at them would stop the zombies in their tracks without fail. He planned to test the theories out for himself.

The journal went on to list numerous other observations about the undead sporadically spaced between the man's personal stories. On more than one occasion, he'd seen them dig at the earth or even a brick wall with their bare hands for hours on end. If they had reason to believe someone was still on the other side of an object, they'd claw and claw until their arms were worn down to bloody stubs. If another zombie passerby saw a group fighting to get into a building or through a window, they would instinctively join in on the effort. The only thing that would remove them, according to the journal, was death or the insertion of a different stimulus nearby. He'd found that there was no perfect science as to what would be enough to send them off in a new direction, but different attractions, timed correctly, could result in massive swarms of the undead wandering together in a horde. Individual zombies that had completed a meal or that had reanimated without any nearby stimulus would just stand dormant until some provocation reached them. If there was a larger kill, the zombies would continue to eat until either the victim reanimated or until there was nothing left.

For some reason, the writer of the journal mentioned a time he'd witnessed a zombie eat until its own stomach burst open, spilling out its contents. He apologized that there wasn't much to learn from the story, but it'd made such an impression with him that he couldn't help but put the story to paper. After it had burst, the zombie actually began re-eating its own meal a second time. The man didn't stick around to find out if the zombie had stayed and continued eating its meal for a third round or not. What he did take from the gruesome visual is that whatever the zombies lacked in cognitive ability, the things more than made up for in persistence.

The journal went on to speculate further into the contagion, though much of it wasn't supported by fact or direct observation. In fact, many of the ideas the man presented didn't match up with Brooke's own experiences. She didn't at all agree with the man's assumption that, if a person hadn't turned within a day of being

259

injured or exposed, they were not infected and should no longer be considered a threat.

She skimmed past one part that didn't seem plausible until remembering Steve. She re-read the bit where the hiker described a rumor that almost everyone had been infected and would reanimate upon dying. Perhaps Steve was telling the truth about his injury; maybe he hadn't been bit. No, surely she'd seen someone die and not reanimate. She racked her brain trying to remember a seemingly uninjured person who'd died. She knew that one of the teenagers had waited for his friend to reanimate before shooting him a second time, but perhaps he'd been bitten. Though, there was the elderly man who had been carjacked and had no visible injuries outside of the gunshot wound, but had still reanimated after they'd buried him.

Brooke began to read more carefully, dissecting the words of the naked hiker, but still found nothing that shed light on why she and Moto had endured comparable injuries but had reacted in completely different ways. The more Brooke reflected on their circumstances and outcomes, the less sense she could make of the situation. Finding no answer in the remainder of the journal, Brooke suspected that there very well might not be a person alive who could answer all of her questions. Despite Moto's certainty in his terminality, Brooke still held on to hope that his illness was unrelated to the epidemic. If the hiker was correct, maybe Moto and Steve both suffered from traditional infections, and Moto still stood a chance of making a full recovery.

Just when Brooke began to wonder if it was day or night and began to question whether or not John would return at all, the hinges of the hatch squealed as light spilled down into the bunker. Brooke resisted the urge to call out and ask if John had found Moto just in case it was some unknown person climbing down the ladder. Instead, she readied her rifle and waited silently. The hatch fell closed, and John soon came into view fighting his way down the ladder with Timber wiggling awkwardly under his arm.

"Anything?" Brooke asked as John let the dog jump down.

John mouthed a question silently as to Hillary's whereabouts. When Brooke informed him that'd she'd been sleeping most of the day, he answered casually.

"It was so foggy. I'd catch his tracks here and there, but it's pretty obvious he doesn't want to be found." One corner of John's mouth pulled back into his cheek as happened frequently when he was in deep thought. "I'll check again later, but it's gonna take a lot of luck for me to find him--especially if the ash picks up any more."

"So what's our next step?" Brooke asked.

"We can't do much, other than wait," John shrugged. "If he doesn't get to feeling any worse and his stomach starts growling, I guarantee he'll be back. In the meantime, I'm gonna clean this gun. I tripped on one of Moto's damn creek crossings and dropped the gun into the water like a rookie."

"Wow, so he really doesn't want to be found."

"Yeah, but I take it as a good sign," John said. "If he was really feeling bad, it would've been easy to track down I think."

"You didn't find him?" Hillary asked from the doorway.

"No, sweetie--not yet," Brooke answered honestly. "Are you hungry now?"

John emptied the rounds from the pistol they'd found in the bunker as he pulled out the Hoppe's cleaning kit and took a seat at the lit table. He was overconfident in his abilities from having mostly torn down and assembled the same side arm in training. He wished he could go back to the days of YouTube to find specific techniques for this brand of gun instead of the old trial-and-error method. Finally, the gun was disassembled and John began cleaning out the mud and old powder.

"We're gonna go outside for a bit," Brooke said from just behind John.

"Really? You think that's a good idea?" John asked with a tone that sounded more critical than he'd intended.

"Well how many zombies have we seen inside our little clearing up top since we've been here?" Brooke responded. "Hillary's getting stir crazy, and God knows I could use some sun."

"Ok, but be careful," John said, "I left a little clearing in the brush so I can get back out if things clear up. Let me carry the dog up for you too--for early warning. And make sure the solar panel is cleared off while you're out there, please."

"You hear that, sweetie?" Brooke turned to Hillary. "Let's go play outside!"

261

John worried that Brooke wasn't taking the risk as seriously as she should but couldn't deny that there had been no activity on the surface as the temperatures continued to drop. Once he'd let Timber loose to run with the girls, John stopped himself from closing back the hatch. He could use the fresh air and would also conserve battery by working under the daylight instead of his lamp.

As he set back to cleaning the gun, John realized that he hadn't taken the care he should've to memorize each step in the disassembly process as meticulously as the task required. He had initially intended to finish the job quickly and join in on some much needed fun time with the girls. Instead, John listened to their laughs and a bird's joyous chirping while enduring his frustration with his own stupidity. Each time John thought he'd made a breakthrough in assembling the gun, he'd realize a missed step and have to take apart what he'd just achieved in order to add in the neglected piece.

When he'd nearly finished assembling the pistol, John realized that he hadn't heard anything from the surface for a bit and paused to listen. He thought he could barely make out the sound of Timber growling, but he couldn't be sure. Against his best instincts, John called up to the surface.

"Everything ok up there?"

No response--at least not at first. Shattering the silence, though, echoes of Moto's favorite band filled the hatch.

"Moto, is that you?"

John ducked out of the way just as Moto came tumbling down the hatch, pounding against the ladder's rungs, and slamming into the concrete floor without even an attempt at cushioning the blow. Though his appearance was largely the same, it was obvious to John that this was no longer Moto. His pupils weren't fully white yet, but his eyes had taken on an angry, soulless quality. What had once been Moto pulled itself up from the floor and locked eyes with John. The earbuds were still in Moto's ears, but the cord had come unplugged from the phone, and Moto's song played on for the room, devoid of its usual bass. The creature's eyes squinted with what might have been recognition, but was more likely only an acknowledgment of its next meal. John's first instinct was concern for the girls and confusion as to why Brooke hadn't called out or screamed. Once the zombie started toward him, though, John's focus became self-preservation. He scrambled to piece together the rest of his gun.

"Can I do this?" John asked himself.

John slammed the gun together and paused at the sight of the empty magazine. He looked down to his workspace for a few rounds to put in the gun, but found no bullets there. Moto was working his way around the corner of the desk and John mirrored each of his moves, working to keep the table in between them. John recalled that he had left all of the gun's rounds lying across the bunker on a desk. A desk on the other side of Moto's reanimated corpse.

John considered that he could probably work his way past the zombie, but Moto was so freshly turned that he still moved with more agility than John had become accustomed. Even if he did sprint past it, there was no way he could retrieve the rounds and load them before Moto could reach him. In a moment of clarity, John recalled the "Plan B" bullet that he'd been keeping in his pocket for so long. His escape plan, should he be damned with infection, sat forgotten in the bottom of his tiny pants pocket. After a quick consideration, John confirmed that the bullet was the correct caliber for this gun. He fumbled nervously with the round in his pocket before forcing himself to breathe. He refused to be like the cliché movie characters. He calmly took the bullet and thumbed it into the mag. Once the round was loaded, John slammed the magazine in, and chambered his only shot.

"Hurry, John!" Brooke's voice echoed down into the bunker.

John didn't find it necessary to acknowledge Brooke's advice. He tried to focus his attention on Moto but couldn't help noticing that Brooke had lowered her head down into the hatch. He wanted to yell for her not to watch--to go take care of Hillary just in case more zombies were attracted to the gunshot.

John was finally able to slow his racing mind and focus only on Moto. He calmly raised the gun to point the barrel squarely into Moto's forehead. Before he'd pulled the trigger, the dance across opposite ends of the table continued, and John waited until he felt confident that he'd timed their movements and could anticipate the perfect instant in which to pull the trigger. Just when John had begun to squeeze, Moto's reanimated corpse put an end to the charade by climbing over the top of the table and lurching straight toward John. The gun kicked back and John diverted his eyes. He couldn't watch. Though, he was forced to look again once he heard the form in front of him still moving. John was mortified to find that the bullet had only grazed the zombie's skull, exposing a small section of brain. The wound would've been fatal for any person, but it was not enough to finish off a zombie. Moto continued crawling with surprising speed and was already almost upon him.

John fell back onto the floor with Moto on top of him, sure that this was it. This was how he was going to die. A quick glance up to the hatch revealed that Brooke couldn't bear to watch. She was gone. John didn't blame her for leaving. She had no reason to believe that John couldn't dispose of one lone zombie. John started to call up for her help, but only a strained grunt left his mouth as he fought tooth and nail with his brother. Moto was far heavier than John would've guessed, and he struggled to bench press back up into the zombie's chest. John's elbows being pressed against the floor and the awkward placement of his hands made holding Moto's infectious teeth at bay an almost impossible task. Each time he'd press harder, John's right hand would threaten to slide off into Moto's arm pit. Such a mistake would undoubtedly result in John's demise at the hands of his own brother. John kicked and head-butted at the thing each time it leaned in for the first bite, but the zombie was unflinching at every threat of pain.

Weeks of rationed portions had taken its toll on John's muscular endurance. In no time, his arms began to spasm, and his triceps threatened to give out. With no other options, John found his hand doing what his brain knew was his only remaining hope. John released the awkward placement of his right hand, slid one forearm into the zombie's throat, and thrust his available fingers into the exposed section of brain, furiously grinding at the tissue. At first, there was no visible effect, and so John forced his whole fist into Moto's skull, deeper and deeper until the corpse dropped lifelessly on top of him.

John made no attempt to remove the dead weight and stayed motionless but for his heavy breathing. The ending of Pearl Jam's "Black" played on from Moto's phone in a repeating ditty of guitar, piano, and vocals with equal parts beauty and ferocity. John focused on the music until his breathing became too labored, and he pressed against Moto's head and rolled the lifeless body away. After a long moment to absorb what had just occurred, John's brain was finally able to recognize the pain throbbing all along his arm. A quick glance confirmed that some red blood was pouring out from his wrist and blending with the black. The song grew even more intense. Sharp pieces of Moto's cranium had gashed John open, no doubt exposing him to the infectious blood. The cut went straight along his largest vein, and the brothers' blood spiraled in a growing pool on the floor between them.

John awoke to blackness and nothing but the sound of his own breathing. After some time to process, he realized that he must be on the bunker's cot. He bent his arm to push up to a seated position, but stopped after feeling something like an IV poking him.

"Oh, thank God," Brooke whispered softly. "I wasn't sure if I was saving you or finishing you off."

"You made me an IV?" John forced the words from his dry, raspy throat.

"More or less, given the materials we have."

"We need to bury Moto."

"It's already done."

"You have to tie me up."

"You're gonna be fine."

"His blood was all over my cut."

"It doesn't infect everyone."

The dialogue ended when John's consciousness abruptly left him again. When he re-awakened, he felt even worse despite Brooke's best efforts to nurse him back to health. His limbs felt twice as heavy, and simply summoning the strength to lift his head required his full focus. He was happy to see that Brooke and Hillary were apparently carrying on just as before but feared that his fate might also seal theirs. Despite his constant pleas for Brooke to restrain him, she couldn't bring herself to admit that he was not going to recover from his infection. She was right in that he did gain some strength back once his body was able to replace some of the lost blood, but he had no doubt that his time was drawing to a close.

John continued to sleep for longer spans than he could manage to stay awake. In the times that he was awake, John would try to gain peace from the knowledge that Brooke was making the right decisions for the sake of the girls. Though she wouldn't admit it, John knew that the food supply had to be dwindling, even with only two people's rations. After a vivid dream consisting mostly of childhood memories, John called Brooke to his bedside.

"Listen. After I'm gone or we run out of food or whatever, there's a place you should go," John started.

"John, you're not going anywhere."

"Please, just listen," he continued. "I can't believe I hadn't thought about it before, but this dream just reminded me. As kids, mom used to send Moto and me to this outdoorsy boys' camp nearby. They've got rifles, secure buildings, fences, food, water, everything you could ever need. The gas might even still work. Just get back on the highway, going toward the French Broad, and keep going until you hit exit sixty-six. You can't miss it. There's a huge, white cross built up on the mountain."

"John, we're fine here."

"What's the exit?" John wanted confirmation.

"Sixty-six," Brooke responded.

"You know what's crazy?" John laid his head back to the pillow and stared at the ceiling. "If this outbreak had never happened, I never would've met you. Guarantee it. I never would've seen your face."

"You can't possibly know that for sure," Brooke said. "I'd like to think our paths would've crossed regardless."

"You really believe that?" John asked.

"I just don't want to picture my life without ever having met you," Brooke said. "I wouldn't trade knowing you."

"Even if that life would've been with your family--and no outbreak?" John joked. "That's pretty damn selfish."

"Well, if you include the promise of warm showers; yeah, maybe I could get by without knowing you," Brooke smiled.

John laughed briefly before succumbing to a violent bout of coughing. Blood trickled out from one nostril. Brooke's mouth still showed a smile, but her eyes showed something else. John knew that she knew he wasn't going to make it. Despite that, she still did nothing to protect herself and Hillary from him. John knew that she would stay here with him until the food was gone. Her only chance at survival was to pack up a bag with what was left and find another place with resources. As much as he hated Moto for giving up, John decided in that moment that he too would have to sneak out unannounced.

Once outside, John reflected, for hours on end, on the letter he'd left behind. Given the chance, he'd take out some of the advice and fluff and include more encouragement and love, but that opportunity was gone. John was committed, and he wasn't ever going back. He had chanced a kiss for each of the sleeping girls on his way out. That detail gave him some warmth on his lonely trek through the woods.

John's mind began to betray him, and he'd lose focus and just wander, pacing his steps to the rhythm of Moto's song as it played on in his head. Sometimes, John would almost re-awaken to realize that he had no idea where he was going or what he was doing. His constant tripping on unseen roots and fallen branches became a given. He had brought almost nothing along with him, for fear that any amount he took might prove critical to the girls' survival--though they had more left than they could ever carry.

John stopped to rest against an evergreen, providing a space to sit without being completely overwhelmed by the falling snow. He fumbled the matchbook from his pocket and found that the moisture had already ruined the only item he'd allowed himself to bring. He was startled awake to the sound of a whippoorwill's call and then to the crunch of snow as someone walked by very close to him. He had devoured the one, stale breakfast bar he had allowed himself before sleeping and now realized that he actually felt considerably stronger. Still, he didn't want to chance an encounter. John stayed silent as the zombie walked just past his tree, tripping constantly in the deep snow. The zombie had been hacked with a machete or some sort of blade, the neck cut all the way down to its spine. Each time it tripped in the deep snow, John thought the head might fall off completely. Fortunately, the wanderer never caught his scent or heavy breathing and continued on without incident.

After realizing his condition had improved despite the cold and the lack of rest, John began to think for the first time that perhaps Brooke was right all along. His only pains now were more a result of the stiffness from the cold and the constant aching in his empty stomach. John wondered if he could make it back to the shelter and into bed before the girls had awoken to find his note.

It wasn't long before Timber appeared out of nowhere up ahead. John was anxious to pet the dog, but it stayed several feet ahead of him, impatiently leading John back to the hatch. John laughed to himself when he realized how short of a distance he'd actually covered and was back to the shelter's clearing in no time.

Once there, it was obvious that the girls were preparing to move on. Brooke was climbing out of the hatch, swinging another pack of necessities into their pile on the ground. She continued working for a while, not noticing that John was back. Even after Timber had run up to her anxiously barking and circling, Brooke took no notice. John was able to take several steps forward before Brooke finally looked up to see that he'd returned. Brooke froze upon seeing him, as if she didn't know which emotion to display. She didn't smile, and didn't speak, but just stared.

John felt his chapped lips break apart as he smiled to Brooke who still stood motionless. Was she mad that he'd left her with nothing but a letter? He called out to her, unsure what words would be appropriate, but only a grumble from his strained vocal cords escaped as his greeting.

Without warning, a gun's report echoed through the trees, before being quickly absorbed by the thick blanket of snow. Seeing that Brooke held no gun, John cursed to himself that someone must be close. He soon realized, though, that the shot had been directed at him. Across the clearing stood Hillary, pistol raised. John was relieved to see that she was crying. He thanked God that she'd realized her mistake before taking a more accurate shot. Her aim didn't waver, though. The older looking Hillary instead held the gun firmly pointed at him still. She even raised the barrel slightly as she stepped forward, aiming straight toward his face.

John looked down to find that her first shot had actually not missed its mark. He pressed his palm against his belly and pulled it back to reveal the gaping wound...

And the blood ran black.

- Epilogue -

The last gunshot had left Brooke frozen and numb. It had taken three more shots before one of Hillary's bullets had finally found its target, and the zombie lay motionless in the snow. Brooke was surprised at the deafening silence that followed the echoing blast. No dogs barked, no birds sang, and neither of the girls dared to breathe. She didn't remember bending her knees, but Brooke found herself seated where she'd previously stood. She stared, glossy-eyed, waiting for John to somehow return to her. Timber crept up to the lifeless corpse and lay patiently next to John's deceased form. Hillary cried where she stood, sobbing such that she struggled to catch a breath. She expected Brooke to comfort her, but no comfort was offered. It wasn't until she began to shake from the bitter cold that Brooke finally snapped out of her shock. The relentless rumbling of her stomach seemed like nothing more than a frivolous detail. Hillary's needs were just another strand in all the world's chaotically woven web. The most minute task now seemed insurmountable to Brooke as she pondered her next action. How many more days could her best efforts really buy? Maybe it would be doing Hillary a favor if they both just sat until the cold took them.

It amazed Brooke that the world kept carrying on as if nothing had happened. The snowfall ceased, and the sun even poked out from between clouds during its descent, uncaring and unfazed. She couldn't think of anyone else outside their intimate circle of trees that cared in the least that John was gone forever. She didn't even have a picture to remember him by. She was alone, and she was disgusted by the world's ability to spin on, completely undeterred. Even after the sun had settled into its slumber, the moon appeared and shined more brilliantly than seemed appropriate. How dare Brooke continue to breathe. How dare the moon shine. How dare the snow reflect its light so purely. How dare John leave her.

When nothing remained, Brooke picked up all that she could carry and set out walking for the now infamous *Exit 66*. Hillary followed just behind, and the journey continued on without apology. Timber sensed Brooke's anger and elected to walk alongside Hillary instead, daring not to whine because of his hunger. Just when Brooke began to question whether she could stand the cold any longer, the bite of the winter's winds relented slightly. Eventually, the thought of giving up didn't seem much easier than simply continuing to place one foot in front of the other. Somehow, they carried on and continued East down I-40.

After days of enduring hunger cramps and numb feet, Brooke looked up to find Exit 66 but felt no relief at the sight. The sign had been spray-painted with an extra 6 and looked like anything but a place where they could find solace. Hillary had long ago ceased to talk without provocation, and Brooke knew that they had to find food and shelter if the girl was to maintain some semblance of sanity.

Inside the camp was a sign that read, "God give us hills to climb and the strength to climb them."

"Please, God, no more hills," Brooke thought to herself. Further into the camp she found nothing but the shells of buildings burnt long ago. One shelter had some remaining walls of stone still standing with crude, hand-written poetry next to a broken toilet. After some encouragement from Hillary, they climbed up more winding trails to find one building marked Trailblazer Inn that still stood proudly. Inside was a locked cabinet filled with canned goods, breakfast drinks, and beef jerky.

The girls ate until their stomachs ached with a new type of pain and slept comfortably for the first time in too long. Early the next morning, Brooke awoke to find a neglected, battery operated alarm clock. She put the heavy batteries she'd been carrying to good use and brought the clock to life with a flashing 12:00. She sat patiently turning from channel to channel with the dated radio dial. Even finding a bit of static that sounded slightly different from the rest brought Brooke some hope that there might be music floating through the radio waves, but she reached the dial's end with no luck. She decided to cycle back through the stations once more, slower this time. To her surprise, when the dial reached 105.3, a voice rang out clearly through the brittle, old speakers.

"... in downtown Asheville. We are located in the old BB&T tower, which has survived the airstrikes. Anyone hearing this message is encouraged to join us in our effort to rebuild."

The recording went on to specify what types of professions were especially needed and what actions to take upon reaching the gate in order to be allowed in.

Brooke allowed Hillary to sleep until she awoke on her own. She found some old mountain bikes in a small shed at the base of the hill, and the girls continued down the highway to Asheville. Hillary wasn't able to ride the tall bike but could coast on the downhills by balancing on one pedal.

Torrential rains attacked the girls as they rode but also assisted in the melting of the snow. Brooke was confident that she'd survive the journey but began to worry that Hillary might be approaching her limit. In Swannanoa, she was proven right when Hillary took a hard fall while coasting down a large hill. From there, they abandoned some of their supplies and Hillary's bike. Brooke carried what remained in her pack and pushed Hillary along on the remaining bicycle. As Brooke walked Hillary down another of the unending mountains, a break in the clouds appeared and gave way to a brilliant rainbow. At the base of the mountain range, the windows of Asheville's downtown reflected in the sun's glow.

Brooke stopped at the tower's chain link gate and lowered all of her weapons and baggage. As the radio had instructed, she located the box of road flares and lit one to signal the watchmen. A man came out to inspect her and Hillary for bites and indicated the OK to a sniper in a makeshift tower.

"What about Timber?" Hillary asked.

"Aren't you gonna check the dog?" Brooke asked the man.

"He has to stay out here. You can visit him at the fence later if you'd like," the man answered without eye contact.

Hillary frowned and ducked down to hug Timber around the neck and kissed him for as long as the guard would wait.

The girls were escorted down a winding trail that weaved in and out of torched cars and fallen trees before arriving at the building's luxurious lobby where a whale of a man opened the door.

"Now what in the hell took you two so long?"

Only then did Brooke allow herself to comprehend seeing Sprite's smiling face, tears in his eyes. She noticed him glance past her, she assumed, for John and Moto. She answered him with just a shaking of her head before he could ask. When more tears welled up in the man's eyes, Brooke lost her composure and clung to Sprite with all of her strength. Brooke wasn't confident that she'd be able to keep herself from sobbing until Hillary lunged in to share their hug--her hold around their legs all but toppling them over. Before their embrace had ended, a grossly disfigured man appeared and introduced himself. Brooke knew that Hillary was staring at the man's shriveled skin where an ear should be and prayed that the man didn't take offense. There was a hint of an accent, but the Chinese man's English was surprisingly smooth.

"Welcome, ladies! We're so glad that you found your way to us," the man said. "Sprite here will help you get situated with us, and we'll just save the indoctrination for after you're fed and well-rested."

Sprite lifted Hillary high off the ground after the scarred man had turned to leave. "I'm so glad y'all finally showed up! You're all I've been able to think about."

"You have some explaining to do, jerk!" Brooke slapped Sprite on the shoulder just hard enough to hurt her own hand.

"Well, I know I've got great answers to your questions, but I just can't wait to hear what your stories are like. I can't imagine what kept you."

"Most of the stories aren't something I'll be ready to share for a while, but I do have one bit of news you'll be excited to hear.

Sprite glanced down and smiled at the realization that Brooke was subconsciously rubbing her hand across her barely swollen belly.

-End-

Acknowledgments

My greatest strength is the people that I have been blessed to know. I could not have accomplished this life goal without their help as I have come to rely on them in every facet of my life no matter how big or small. My sincerest gratitude and heartfelt thanks to each of you that played a role in making this book a reality.

First and foremost, to my beautiful wife, Taylor, for her constant patience and encouragement as well as her tremendous influence all while making my interests her own.
In no particular order, as these people's importance could never be weighted. Mom, Dad, Sam and Andrea, Tim and Amanda, Blake, Andrew, Garrett, David, Wayne, Michael, and Jordan.

Also, a special thanks to you, the reader, for purchasing this book from an unknown author and giving me the chance to share my story with you. You are the reason I wrote this book, and I can't express my gratitude enough.

If you enjoyed this novel, please help make this dream of mine a reality and share this book with your friends and keep an eye out in the future for more books from Nathan E. Harvey and Harvey Brothers Publishing.

If you would like to share any comments or questions that you may have, you can find me on Twitter and Facebook.

 @NathanEHarvey   Author Nathan E. Harvey

http://NathanEHarvey.com/
http://HarveyBrothersPublishing.com/

"The road to happiness is never ending. The key is in bringing the destination to wherever you happen to find yourself."

-Nathan E. Harvey